Too Beautiful

and Other Stories

D1553393

Too Beautiful

and Other Stories

MARK PRITCHARD

CLEIS
PRESS

Published in the United States by Cleis Press Inc.,
P.O. Box 14684, San Francisco, California 94114.
Printed in the United States.
Cover design: Scott Idleman
Text design: Karen Quigg
Cleis Press logo art: Juana Alicia
First Edition
10 9 8 7 6 5 4 3 2 1

For S., C., C.,
and especially C.

Acknowledgments

Evening was first published as "Silent Except for Millions of Televisions" in an anthology called *Good to Go* (Seattle: Zero Hour, 1994). *Pretend, Penetration,* and *Too Beautiful* were first published in *Frighten the Horses.* I'm grateful to Katia Noyes, Qiron Adhikary, participants in the Napa Valley Writers Conference, and others whose comments on the manuscript or on individual stories were very helpful. I thank the contributors, staff, subscribers, and friends of *Frighten the Horses,* who supported my vision of a publication that integrated fiction and nonfiction about sex. I'm especially grateful to Sara Miles and Marilyn Jaye Lewis for their advice and encouragement, and to my partner, Cris Gutierrez, for her patience and unending support.

Contents

Pretend

Pretend we're just meeting. After the performance, I'm talking with some people who've come to see my piece, and everybody seems to look at me appreciatively. Among the group I'm standing with is an old lover, and as she touches my wrist fondly and tells me what she liked about the piece, I see you approach.

You're the producer of this show so I smile widely and turn in your direction; you're coming up to me to thank me for appearing. But after I introduce you to my friends and you instantly understand that Solange used to be or maybe still is my lover, I see in your eyes a hint of intrigue, part jealousy, part confusion, underneath the appreciation you express as you talk about my choreography. My friends say goodbye and leave. You finish what you were saying about the piece and I wind up helping you and a few other people clean up the performance space, after which we all go out to a nearby café.

You sit across the table from me and get into a conversation with the guy next to you who was also in the show. I talk with a couple of other guys about their show and then finally someone mentions something besides his or her own art and we start talking about the gay freedom day parade a couple of weeks earlier. The topic drifts over to your end of the table and suddenly you're describing the contingent you marched with, some kind of leather-babe group with lots of SM happening in the middle of Market Street: "She was busting people with this whip and it was all I could do to keep from screaming. I mean it really hurt, because it was so hard to get into it there surrounded by a million people. Not like at home, you know." Then you notice me staring at you, and right before you turn away, blushing, I can see you meant me to hear.

Pretend you don't know anything about me and you're wondering whether I know how to do what you have in mind. I do. In that instant when our eyes met, before you had to look away, I saw in your eyes the mixture of desire and defiance that make up your submission.

The two guys I've been talking with jump in with their SM experiences, and nobody but me seems to have noticed your admission, but that's fine because it was meant just for me. I listen to the rest of the conversation, titillating as it is, with only one ear because I'm watching you as you look down at the table, your long fingers stroking the stem of your wine glass as you compose your face. When you figure it's been long enough and people's attention is no longer on you, you slyly look up and over to your friend, he's listening to the speaker; to the guy who's sitting next to me, he's playing with the label on the beer bottle; and finally to me, and I'm looking right at you, smiling because I know what kind of person you are.

You like someone with strong hands to hold you by the neck, bending your head back for a kiss. You like it when someone takes your long, elegant hands, expressive and useful in real life, and neutralizes them with a scarf tied tightly around your wrists. You get excited at the sight of a prick at eye level, you cream at the thought of kneeling and opening your mouth, the prickhead gigantic as it rolls to the back of your tongue. You like losing the control you exert outside, you desire someone willing to impose his or her will on you, to strive for your submission, to push you toward sensations you don't even know you like until I make you feel them. You like to be made to talk dirty, to beg for something that hurts, to debase yourself. Pretend I don't know any of these things from experience, but from that moment of recognition in the café, from the moment you look up and I'm there.

I stand up and announce I'm leaving. Everyone else prepares to stand up, too. You look directly at me then, not with embarrassment or even pleading, but straight at me to see my intentions. Instead of walking away, I go over to your side, and say, "Walk you home?" then whisper, "Go to the bathroom so the rest of these people can leave."

You say goodbye to the others and go to the toilet. After everyone else goes out, I walk over to the little hallway of the bathrooms and wait for you. You come out smoothing your hands on your skirt made of silk pajama cloth, and start to say something. Instead, my firm hand pushes you against the wall and my tongue penetrates your open mouth, long and hard, bruising your lips and pushing into the intimate spaces under your tongue. I use my tongue to push your teeth and open your mouth wider, and as my hand fastens around your breast and takes possession, the other hand starts opening your belt. I do this so you'll panic. I don't want you to feel any control even from the first, and when your hands reach up to tug mine away, I bite your lip hard and hiss, "Stop it! Put your hands at your side." The tone of my voice frightens and reassures you at the same time, and a moment later, while I'm easing your belt out of the loops, I hear your fingernails scratching on the wall, up up up, as I flatten you against it.

The belt is soft leather, and when I tell you to, you hold your hands out so I can tie them. This is not what you expected; you thought we could go home discreetly, didn't you, you thought you would get safely to your bedroom, teeth brushed and clothes off before we played. You didn't know I was going to tie you with your own belt in the back of the café, forcing you to open your eyes, and lead you out, past everybody sitting there, including several people who were in the audience tonight, and out to the sidewalk.

Pretend I've never been to your house a few blocks away, that I've never shoved you roughly against the door while dumping your purse on the steps so you have to search on your knees for the house keys, your hands still bound and my booted left foot resting on your ass. After you find the keys and manage to get everything back in your purse, I pull you around to face me, and there on your doorstep open my pants and tell you to look at my cock.

Lean forward and smell it without touching it; praise its shape and size and color. Tell me why I shouldn't open your door, shove you inside, and go home, leaving you there alone on your knees with your hands tied. Tell me that if I come in with you instead, you'll suck my cock and let me come in your mouth, that you want me to see your pussy, that you're horny and need to get fucked, that you'll jack off for me and talk dirty and urinate on your clothing, that you love getting fucked in the ass especially, and that you'll beg me to do it to you. Tell me you know that if I come inside, it means I get to do anything I want.

In the hallway past the front door there's a lighted fish aquarium, and in that soft green-gold light, after you've been forced to enter your own house on your knees, I close the door softly with my foot and make you repeat it all, everything you'll do, everything you'll let me do. You say it all again and more, adding everything you can think of, like letting me fuck your boyfriend and letting me tie you to the bed. You volunteer to cut open a small vein in your arm so the blood leaks out slowly enough for me to use it on my prick for lube so I can fuck you while you lose consciousness and possibly die. You talk and talk and beg and since I know you're saying things you've never said to anybody else, I stay.

Begin, then, by opening your mouth. My cock slides in like a bullet into the chamber of a gun, slides to the back of your throat and rests there lightly, not moving. As long as we both relax, you won't gag. Instead of totally degrading you, as you have just volunteered, I tell you how beautiful you are, how noble, how perfect you are, especially when you are on your knees in front of me. Your hands, still bound, reach up, and you cup my testicles with your fingertips. I describe how you look there in the bubbly light of the fish tank, and you answer my voice with soft moans that come from the place in your throat right next to the head of my cock, I can even feel it vibrate with your voice. I tell you to lift your skirt and touch yourself through your panties, and I talk more and more about how beautiful you are and how I desire you—pretend you're hearing it for the first time—and you move your head so that the edge of your palate rubs against my cockhead and your lips purse around the base. I'm careful not to move, because you're in control, so that instead of gagging and pulling your head away, you go up the slide into a jerking, moaning orgasm, stopping only when I yank your head back, pulling you out of your reverie, and demand, "What happened? Tell me!"

"I came. I had an orgasm. I did it with your cock in my mouth and my hands between my legs."

"Very good," I say. "Beg me to please you some more."

"Please me. Do anything you want as long as it makes me feel that way. Even hurt me and slap me and shit on me, do whatever you want, because it's going to turn me on. Let me do all the things I said to please you. Please please me, oh yeah, like I please you."

"Say again about slapping you."

"You can slap my face," you blurt out, an instant before my hand cracks across your cheek, and even though I'd told you it was coming, you squeal in surprise and pain, because it was harder than you expected. Pretend I do everything a little harder than you expect, instead of the truth, which is that I never did anything quite hard enough or long enough, so that instead of feeling a little bored you feel scared and delirious and out of control. I slap you back and forth across the face until, as in that moment in the café, you start to panic. Your hands come up involuntarily to ward off the blows, so I grab them and drag you down the hall. You try to get your footing, but you stumble to the bathroom, where I shove you to the middle of the floor and scream, "Get on your knees!"

You're moaning and crying out incoherently, but instead of collapsing into a little ball and breaking down, you straighten your back and drop your bound hands in front of you. Very clever—instead of fighting, you pretend to submit, hoping you can stay this much in control. But it won't work. I take your hands and undo the belt, snap handcuffs onto one wrist, and drag you over to the sink. In a second the other wrist is cuffed and you're bound to the drainpipe. You groan. I pull your pants open and down over your ass and past your knees. The shoes come off and I put one under each kneecap so that the pain will be less, because you know I always take good care of you.

"Tell me again about how you were going to submit to me," I sneer, as I give your butt a soft blow with your leather belt.

"I am," you insist. "I'll do what you want; I was just scared."

"You're supposed to be scared," I say, swinging harder. You flinch. "Does that hurt?"

"Yes."

"Then you're not turned on enough. Or scared enough. You think you can fight back against me?"

"No."

"Or get away? Or stop me from doing what I want?"

"No."

"Because I don't think you're strong enough to pull the sink out of the wall." Pretend you're not strong enough anyway. I whip harder, the sounds of the whip are changing from a little flap to a low pop. You're starting to jump a little when it hits, not flinching, just reacting, your nerves lighting up every time the belt lands. In order to get a good angle, I have to raise my arm over my head, and as I start whipping you harder and harder, you jump and then cry out every time the belt lands. The marks are getting redder and longer, and the sound it makes is changing to a high-pitched snap. I hit the top of your ass, the sides, the bottom; I skip around and all I really do is listen. I listen to the sound the belt makes and to your breathing. After a while they're in perfect sync.

Then in a low, unearthly voice, you groan, "Oh, do it," and then the whipping really begins. As I raise the belt up over my head and hit you as hard as I can, you vocalize each breath, "Ah! Ah! Ah!" The pace reaches a perfect rhythm, and we go on, I whipping and you taking it, whipping and taking it, and I'm doing it to you as hard as I can, sweating and breathing and watching welts rise on your ass.

When you're perfectly lost in the rhythm and the sensation, I reach forward and grab your hair, dropping the belt and pulling your head back. You scream because you're startled at the change. As I kneel behind you and put my arms around you, reaching down between your legs, you come in a long, wandering spasm that doesn't have any apex or base, it just goes up and over and down and around like a plane with no pilot. I finger your cunt gently but it's not really necessary, you're not coming from there but from someplace within.

After a minute I bring you down simply by letting go of you. You rest for a second and then I unlock the cuffs and pull you to your feet. "You don't need to be on your knees anymore to submit to me, do you?" I say, pulling you down the hall, but you don't answer— you're speechless.

I toss you lightly onto the bed on your belly and relock the cuffs so that your wrists are bound to the wrought iron frame. I take off my pants and tell you you're going to get fucked, first in the cunt and then in the ass. "Knees up to your chest," I order, hauling your ass into the air, and that's how I enter you. Your cunt is soaked from your whipping and you're so turned on that it just turns things up a notch to get fucked. I knead the flesh of your back as I pass in and out of you lightly, then pull all the way out and nuzzle your labia with my cock-head before plunging back in again. I do this repeatedly, and your noises get louder each time. "You like to get penetrated, don't you?" I ask, and you grunt "Yes!"—the first intelligible word you've said in half an hour—again low and uncontrolled. You only sound that way when you're like this.

Pretend I've never fucked your ass before. Pretend I don't know you keep the lube right behind the corner of the bed next to the night table, so that when I reach there and say, "I know where you keep your supplies," it's enormously exciting. That's when you really give up, when I've really stripped you bare, when your privacy is completely breached.

"Fuck my ass," you say, unprompted. "I need you to put your prick in me. I need to be fucked there. I'm your hole." I put my lubricated finger into your asshole, push it in and out a few times, then two go in—you're so relaxed. "Oh Jesus God, in my asshole. I'm empty, I need you to fill me up, please baby, put your prick in my anus. Oh Jesus, I need it, I'm your thing, I'm your slit, I'm your cunt, please fuck me, baby." Three fingers. "Oh shit, you're going to do it in me, you're going to put your cock in and fuck my asshole, please please please it's dirty, oh no, no."

My left hand has been spreading lube on my cock. I take my fingers out and your ass steers the cock to your rectum. Your stream of talk goes on until the moment I enter you, then with a final groan you shut up. My cock slides in steadily, right up to the hilt, and that's where I stay, deep inside your ass and feeling underneath you with my left hand for your clit. You cry out when I touch it. First you orgasm off my fingers. Then you begin moving under my prick and I start thrusting.

A slow in and out. "Bitch," I say. "Cunt!"

You let out a sob. "Oh God yes I need it in my asshole," you screech, every shred of dignity gone. "You can do it in me, you can do it in me. Call me things—debase me."

"Slit, cunt, shit, you hole. You dirty girl." That gets another orgasm, and we go on and on. Calling you names really turns me on; pretend you don't know that. You need to hear the filthy names to come; pretend this is the first time you let yourself get turned on by actually being debased—that until now you've only fantasized about it. Finally I twist my own nipple and squirt into you, choking out profanities, while your orgasm doesn't start and stop, it just goes on and on.

It's the middle of the night. Pretend we're just meeting, that we instantly discover all the things that turn us into perfect lovers, that everything I do goes right to your core. Imagine having me and not giving me up, but keeping me. Picture me with my softening cock inside you as we tell each other how pleased we are. Gradually we talk and laugh about what we went through, and say that we're glad to have found each other—pretend our affair, which actually ended years ago, is just starting. Pretend we frighten and panic each other; pretend we're still obsessed; pretend we don't know how we're going to end up, crying and disgusted and 9,000 miles apart, pretend it was only a dream and now we can start over, having just met and loved each other for the first time, dizzy and dirty and bruised, but happy, finally, for the last time in our lives.

Too Beautiful

There's a phrase in my mind that won't go away. It echoes through my
thoughts as I work, as I shower, as I run my fingers through the hair of
the man who's sucking me, as I walk down the street at dawn—it makes
every experience the same, creates an existential vacuum around everything I do. For days now, ever since I heard it from someone at a
club—a stranger just passing me on the stairs as I made my way up to
the bar, some pretty muscle-boy in his late twenties yammering over his
shoulder at his friend, trying to make himself heard in the clamor of
bass notes and screaming vocals and everyone shouting at the same
time—ever since I heard the asinine phrase spewing out of his mouth,
the line has infected me, following me into my bed and my dreams. I
can't get away—here it comes again—

"—bend the creatives backwards until they break, and then he'll get—"

The beginning and end of the statement were lost in the general din, and only its middle remained, conjuring up a vision of a hellish ad agency, a tyrannical manager, an overworked staff of writers and artists, i.e., the creatives. The term had a desperate sneer to it, seemingly denoting a lower form of life. If you're an accountant or a manager or a librarian, beware entering the art department or copywriting section: The creatives will wig you out with food fights and paper airplanes and sheer insouciance. They can glue plastic dinosaurs and palm trees on their computers, they can burst out singing filthy songs, they can smoke crack in the lounge, whatever turns them on, whatever helps them do their thing. They must be tolerated. But you can engage them in battle, you can run them ragged, you can bend them backwards until they break, and then you'll get—

What? Fired? Your revenge? Your ass in a sling? A promotion? The consequences of driving the copywriters to distraction, whether through overwork or frustration, went unheard. I imagined a room full of devastated twenty-somethings dressed in thrift-store chic, scattered around like dead leaves—or perhaps gibbering and crying like the inmates of an insane asylum, driven out of their minds by deadlines or constant changes or a client who's impossible to please. Or maybe a room full of angry, rebellious youngsters, ready to go out on strike against the firm, they won't bend over backwards anymore, they have demands: No more deadlines, a cappuccino machine, every other Friday off, cable TV in the lounge, and for godsakes *fire* that asshole who's making them bend over backwards.

Unless it's the client who's making them do it. In that case, to hell with the snot-nosed little bastards, plenty more where they came from. He'll get a new set of them, maybe that's it. He'll get a new set of creatives, nice fellows who won't tickle each other in the stairwell; who won't impregnate the girl creatives and make them quit; who won't get sick and die of AIDS like Tommy and Phil and Rick and that extremely nice one, Bob, the sweet one who was bisexual and married and certainly didn't know what he was getting into, certainly more innocent than some. He left a wife we hired as a receptionist, anything to help out, and then when she filed a health insurance claim it turned out they weren't married at all, just living together; and she was a dyke, in fact, which really pissed me off—

The speaker had long passed out of hearing and sight, but I continued to imagine his voice as I struggled up the stairs. The club was chokingly crowded and noisy; it was 12:30 in the morning, the exact hour that everyone orders his third-to-last drink and sucks in his gut and finds someone to seriously cruise in the hopes of going home and having some hard, smeary, honest-to-god fucking.

I went over to the crowd two-deep at the bar and tried to insinuate myself close enough for the bartender—who, like every other bartender in San Francisco, was named Mike—to notice I wanted to order something. Every time I come to this bar I leave Mike a big tip so that the next time he sees me he will serve me immediately, instead of ignoring me as he moves back and forth behind the bar chattering with other customers. They all seem to be engaged in conversations with him, whereas all I want to do is get a drink. Maybe that's it, maybe you have to be his friend and have a conversation with him for him to serve you.

"Gin and tonic!" I finally managed to holler above the cacophony. The upstairs bar was hot with the heat of hundreds of male bodies floating up the stairs and through the floor, with the only windows in the place the little ones in the bathroom, totally useless for ventilation or escape in case of fire—better not start thinking of that.

I stood waiting, my keep-the-change five dollar bill already in my hand, pointing in the general direction of Mike—who looked as if he were completely disregarding my order and drawing mugs of beer, one after the other, for someone else.

I never like to spend time picking out a man. My strategy is to wait until a random moment, then take a look at the person on either side of me and see which one appeals to me more, and try for him. Sometimes I take the one who appeals to me less, for practice, since I hardly ever hit on the first try, in which case I take the other one, the guy I wanted all along. On this particular night I had been developing a superstition about the left side—when confronted with a choice, I had been choosing the left side all night. I follow compulsive little patterns, it doesn't matter, I take the left-hand something, or the red one, or the third one, or the bright one, and try to be satisfied with whatever I end up with.

But my intuition was good that night because on my left I found a lovely, slender, Asian man, androgynous-looking with long black hair; in fact he was the only man with long hair in the bar. As a rule I don't like long hair much, it usually ends up looking like a poodle cut somehow. But this man's hair was different, long and fine and straight and rather girlish, an impression enhanced by the slight bit of makeup he was wearing. To tell you the truth, he was extremely out of place among all the gym clones in the bar, which meant it was my lucky night.

I looked away into the bar mirror, but he had already caught me staring at him, and was facing me. I turned back to him and found him waiting with a cautious expression.

"Hi, I was wondering when you'd show up again," I blurted out without thinking.

He chuckled nervously. "What? You've seen me here before?"

"Sure," I lied, because I would have remembered him if I had. "Wasn't it around Halloween?" I guessed blindly. All sorts of people came out on Halloween; maybe he'd wandered in here.

"Maybe," he said. "I went to a lot of places."

"Weren't you in drag?" I grinned. I couldn't believe my luck, it was as if I were making him up as we went along. This conversation took place at top volume, to be heard over the sound system.

"Yeah, well, sort of…. Look, is that your drink?"

I turned to find Mike standing before me with my gin and tonic. "Thanks, keep the change!" I shouted, reaching over the shoulder of some plastered leather queen who seemed welded to his stool.

I turned back to the man, who looked as if he was about to slip away. "Don't go," I protested. "Let me get you something to drink. Why else be in a bar—"

"No."

"Sure, here, take this. Another one!" I yelled at Mike, who was miraculously in the vicinity. "I'm Mark, what's your name?"

"My name's Mark too," he smiled, taking a gulp of the drink I had handed him.

"I love it!" I yelled. "I always wanted to meet someone with my name."

"Aren't there lots of them?" he asked, cautious again.

"Yeah, it's a baby boom name. Like Paul and Gary and Steve and—" I paused, trying to think of another.

"Yeah," he said vaguely.

"In my grade school class there were three Marks," I yammered on. "I had thought I was the only one."

"Well, I don't know any," he laughed.

"Right, you never meet any in San Francisco. They're all in the suburbs. They're all driving minivans."

He was looking at me patiently, apparently waiting for me to shut up. "Oh," he shouted, and threw one arm around my shoulder and put his lips up to mine. I could taste the drink, cool and tangy, on his tongue. I wanted him suddenly, more than I had wanted anyone or anything in months.

He looked over my shoulder. "Here's your drink again," he said.

Mike was standing there with an evil grin on his face. I took the drink and gave him a twenty. I turned back to Mark and he put his now-empty glass on the counter and grabbed the new one from me and took a gulp. I kissed him again. He let some of the alcohol leak into my mouth, and I managed to take the glass away from him as we pushed our lips together. We broke apart and I knocked back most of the rest of the drink.

Mike was *still* standing there. "Another one?" he prompted.

"This could get expensive," I said to Mark, touching his breastbone. He was wearing a black T-shirt emblazoned with the words HYSTERIC GLAMOUR and a '50s-style drawing of a dominatrix spanking another woman with a hairbrush.

He put his other arm around my neck. "Not for a long time, it won't," he said, his mouth next to my ear. He took little nips on my earlobe. It drove me crazy, but I managed to finish the drink. Now I had to get the alcohol out of my system before I took him home.

"Come on," I screamed, taking him by the hand and pulling him through the crowd and down the stairs to the dance floor. He bounced along behind me as if he were already my boyfriend, and part of my mind was saying *Why is this so easy* while the rest was saying *Shut up and enjoy it.*

We gyrated for a long while. The music was awful but I didn't care. I'm getting too fucking old for this kind of thing, not just because I'm tired of spending my life in the noise and smoke and overcrowding, not just because I'm in my thirties and there are too many younger, prettier men now, but because I can no longer stand the music. It sounds like something that might be the result of bending instruments backwards until they break.

I didn't care because Mark was too beautiful, his long black hair swinging on his shoulders, dancing with his eyes completely closed or maybe slightly open occasionally to watch me, keeping track of me, looking at me speculatively. Something about the way he mechanically brushed his hair back seemed somewhat uninvolved, as if he were going along with the program, perhaps waiting for something, and meanwhile willing to let me amuse him for a while. Despite this I wasn't worried about his running off; I felt in control and happy, really happy, even though I was one of the few people there not on drugs.

Someone beautiful on my left hand had taken a liking to me. I would take him home and wring him out, flatten him. I would do just what I wanted and in the end I would bend him backwards and fuck him and tell him to make me come.

The announcement for last call crackled through the club and you could almost smell the spurt of anxiety as men who hadn't glommed onto someone looked around desperately for that hunk they'd been cruising all night without success, and those who didn't care anymore beat their way to the bar for the limited, but specific, consolation of one for the road.

I pulled Mark against the stream of people to the door and out onto the street, where the sudden dissipation of noise and crowds took my breath away. But the sidewalk was also getting crowded as people from bars and clubs began to spill outside, and I couldn't bear getting involved in one more crowd scene, or, worst of all, running into some of Mark's friends, who might get into a conversation with him and offer him a ride home and take him away from me.

I turned to the left, of course, and we went toward the corner, where I stopped, turned to him, pushed him up against a lamp post and kissed him hard, wanting to break through his detachment, impress myself on him, prove I wasn't just another trick. I found myself gripping his wrist, and he turned it slightly in that way people have of testing your grip, pushing back weakly to show their desire to be taken, to demonstrate they could fight back but won't, that they probably want to give up and let you take them.

With my left hand I reached up and pulled his hair gently, evoking a small sound from his throat that I took for encouragement, and I pulled harder, more suddenly, tilting his head back and opening his mouth wider. He moaned out loud, which was more than I'd heard anybody doing on the street for a long time. It made the Queer Street Patrol look apprehensively toward us as they passed in formation, instantly taking in the scene and realizing they were only seeing two men kissing, performing a consensual act, and that no intervention was required.

He had a long tongue—everything about him was long—and I deliriously felt the tip of his tongue tickle my throat. It made me imagine his long beautiful cock in my mouth. I almost lost it then, almost groaned myself, and that just wouldn't have been right. I let him go and grabbed him by the shoulders. He didn't even have a jacket. I had a slim femmy boy bottom on my hands and I, and nobody else, was going to take him. "You coming home with me?" I suggested.

"I don't know," he said.

I tried to outbutch him, which was curiously difficult considering what a total femme he was. He met my attempt at a hard stare with an equanimity that made me feel foolish. I reached behind his head again and took hold of his hair in an attempt to regain command. "You're coming home with me and you'll do what I want," I sneered.

I didn't get the instant reaction I had hoped for, but after a moment he languidly let his mouth fall open and I could see him submitting. "All right," he said, a little ironically.

I spun away and hailed a cab. I felt victorious, drunk, although I wasn't drunk: I was extremely excited to be bringing this momentous person home with me, a twin with my name, a reflection I could drown in, a wriggling fish to cook. I knew I could safely ride the momentum of this state of mind for hours; I had done it many times and trusted myself in this mood, it was a good mood, a good side of me that liked to control my fucks and take my pleasure from them. At the same time, I knew Mark wasn't just another fuck; he was a miracle. I knew this even without having fucked him yet.

In the cab on the way home we struggled playfully. I've never liked kissing under the gaze of cab drivers, so I just held his wrists until I got a serious "Ow" out of him. Then we sat back happily for the last few blocks.

"I hope my motorcycle doesn't get towed," he said unexpectedly.

"You have a motorcycle? Why didn't you say so?"

"I'm too drunk to ride." He put his hand in mine as it lay in my lap. "And how can I go home with you unless you take me?"

I felt enormously grateful he had said that.

"I want you to stay all night," I said as soon as we got inside the door. I wanted to prevent the hateful phenomenon of people fucking you and then lighting out at three or four A.M., thinking they might do better than that with the guys cruising around the park.

"Mmm," he said noncommittally.

I took that as a challenge, wrapping my arm around his waist and pulling his head back with the other hand. "Don't 'uhn' me, bitch," I threatened. He didn't respond, so I twisted his head a little. "Are you going to do what I want?"

"What do you want?" he asked softly. His gentle patience in the face of my tricks was frustrating, but I wasn't going to let him see that.

"You'll see," I spat. We kissed until he began to whimper again. Then I pushed him down to his knees. While we were dancing I had been thinking about several things to do to him but at the moment they seemed irrelevant; now I just wanted his mouth.

I held his head close to me with my left hand while I opened my pants with the other. I could hear his breath loud in the darkness; I could hear him lick his lips. Then my cock was out, briefly springing in the air until he caught it, holding it with his hands and steering it to his mouth.

Pleasure rang in my head like a drum. I could feel his mouth surrounding me, his hands holding me tight, the warmth of his body close to me. Intense sensations ricocheted inside me and with every new one, I let out a sound; his fingers expertly played my balls and the base of my cock. I could feel my orgasm slowly descending my spine like the glowing ball in Times Square on New Year's Eve, everyone watching and screaming in anticipation: *Ten, nine, eight, seven....*

Too late I gasped that he should stop, too late I pulled his head away. He rubbed my spurting cock across his face, along his jawline, and bowed his head so that some of my come went in his hair. When I finished coming, I reached down and smoothed it deeper into his hair, scooped up the drops that had fallen on his face, and worked them into his hair, too.

"Into the bedroom," I ordered, kicking my pants off and pulling him to his feet, and though my knees were still weak with pleasure, I pushed him ahead of me, down the hall into my room, where I undressed him quickly. Under the black jeans he wore lacy underwear, a garter belt, lacy stockings. If I hadn't just come, the sheer sight of his cock bulging under the panties, poking out from between the garters, would have made me rock hard. I made him kneel on the floor in front of me, then picked up my brush from the dressing table and sat down behind him on the little seat. I brushed my come deep into his hair, worked it in until you couldn't find it anymore, just smell it. "Now leave it there," I said, "leave it there until I go away."

"Don't go away," he mumbled, swaying as the brush dragged through his tresses. I put my hand around his neck and pulled him forward until he was on his hands and knees in front of me. When he realized he was exposing his ass to me and I still had the hairbrush in my hand, I felt him tense.

"I don't know if I'm ready for you to do that," he said.

"All right," I said softly, giving up. I put the brush on the table and laid my hand across the flat of his back. Maybe it was his slenderness, maybe it was just excitement, but even through his back I could feel his heart beating quickly and efficiently, tapping away inside him.

"That feels nice, your hand there," he said quietly.

I was silent, listening to his breath and heartbeat. In the stillness he seemed suddenly close to me, even more so than when he was sucking me. "You're paying attention to me now," he said after a moment. "I like that."

"I've been paying attention to you for a couple of hours."

"Not like this," he said. He arched his back against my hand. He was still on his hands and knees before me, but somehow he had regained control. Suddenly he was like a cat, expecting to be petted and stroked, rather than a dog that was grateful for affection.

I looked at him underneath me, dressed in the garter and stockings, slowly undulating under my hands. His hair hung down to the floor; he was so glamorous. "Did you really go to that bar in drag on Halloween?" I asked.

He grinned, looking up at me through the hair that covered his face. "Yeah, but I bet you didn't see me."

"I think I would have remembered."

"I think you would have, too," he said, and told me what he'd looked like, the leather merry widow and fishnet stockings, the high heels and long black silk gloves that went up past his elbow. He had stolen them from his mother. "We're the same size," he said, "in gloves, anyway. I had a good time knocking everybody dead," he went on. "I felt just like Audrey Hepburn."

I could see him as Audrey, both innocent and sexy, tottering about on the high heels, except that I couldn't remember ever seeing Audrey Hepburn in a merry widow.

"What else did you get from your mother?" I asked idly, reaching down past his butt to stroke his balls.

"Long black cunt hair," he murmured. "So long that if I had a cunt, it would be hidden."

I let my hand stray to the base of his cock, and sure enough, I could feel a luxurious growth, like the soft moss that grows thick on the side of a tree in a dark ravine, his long cunt hair surrounding the base of his prick.

He rocked back on his heels and stood up and turned around, his body suddenly before me as I perched on the low seat in front of the dresser. I reached forward and took hold of his panties and removed them, brought his perfect cock to my mouth and made it wet. It was heavy in my hands, and the drop of come that leaked out of the tip was sweet in my mouth.

He was gentle with me, more gentle than I had been with him, and as he stroked in and out of my mouth, in time with my movements, I felt that perfect openness of mouth and throat I used to practice and seldom attain, the receptivity I insist on from others and seldom feel. When I suck cock I don't become a hole, I become a perfect cunt, a better cunt than a real cunt, one with a tongue inside that massages and rubs, that does the things the cunt can't.

"This is sweet," he said. "It's so good. That's how sweet this is. Baby, you better stop."

But I didn't want to stop, I wanted to go on doing it to his gorgeous cock. One of my hands pulled his butt close to me, the other slid up his leg and into the silky hair at the base of his cock.

"No, this is too good," he protested. "Don't make me come. Don't make me come."

I stopped sucking him long enough to let him stop thrusting into me, if he was really serious about stopping. From the way he shuddered to a halt, I could tell he'd barely held himself in check.

"Oh, man," he whispered, touching my head. I looked up at him, but his face was in shadow and I couldn't see him. "Let me fuck you," he said.

I stood up and took off my T-shirt. "When I brought you home, I thought I was going to be the one doing the fucking," I said sheepishly.

"Isn't life interesting?" he replied in his ironic tone.

I sprawled on my bed, motioning to the bedside table. "All the supplies are there." I pulled a pillow underneath my torso and looked back at his long body. He opened up a condom and peeled it onto his prick. Then I felt cold, lubed fingers prodding me.

"Open," he said. "I'll start you. This is one. This is two. That's the way…. This is three and, hmm, your ass is too beautiful."

"Too beautiful for what?"

"Too beautiful for words." His body shifted, he hovered above me, and I felt his cock slide into me as if I were made for it.

"Now," he said, "make me come."

Evening

This is the kind of story teenagers write when they're sitting in their suburban bedrooms, in the dark of the evening that was beginning when they sat down, a dark that's gotten darker and darker as the headlights come on outside and everything is silent except for millions of televisions. It's the kind of story they put in secret notebooks that are kept on the highest shelf—not the notebooks that are "casually" left out on the desk for Mom to find and read through and scold them over, but the true notebooks that hold everything unspeakable and unreadable. This is the unreadable you made me write for you.

I am a teenager who doesn't belong anywhere, least of all in high school. The high school I go to is a gigantic daily jail that was built ten years ago on river bottom, land miles away from everyplace. It was supposed to be on the outskirts of a "new town" that was never built because the developers went broke. At the same time, a huge fire destroyed the old high school, which was already overcrowded and dingy beyond belief, when some kids trying to refine methedrine in a chemistry lab in the middle of the night caused an explosion.

Now everybody goes to this school that was supposed to be for the upper-middle class kids in the "new town" that was never built. Every morning, huge buses bring the thousands of us here, miles from any habitation, in thick woods by the river levee—even the setting is like a jail. The "new" school looks thirty years old instead of ten because 4,000 kids have been using it though it was designed for 1,800. It's so crowded that everybody has to spend two periods a day warehoused in "study hall" in the gym or the auditorium and even in the swimming pool, built for the rich kids that never came here, and now filled in with dirt and floored over. In the winter it's freezing, though the windows, which have never been cleaned above arm's reach, fog up with our breath.

In the auditorium, kids sneak off to make out in the curtains of the stage; they climb the ladders up onto the catwalks, where they've installed secret nests. I read a news story once about a Soviet factory where no one did any work; the workers furnished little niches with mattresses and lamps and all they did was hang out in them and drink vodka all day. It's like that. There is a storage room up there, forty feet above the stage and hidden from sight behind the grid of lights and catwalks, where no adult has been for years. The furnishings are a bunch of stolen cushions and mattresses that kids brought there and graffiti all over the walls; there's a huge amount of trash and rotten food and cigarette butts and roaches and filth, and no one ever cleans it except the girls once in a while, and then it's just because they're trying to impress somebody.

One Friday I had cut my afternoon classes and gone into the woods with this guy Jimmy, who was supposed to be my boyfriend. We were looking for a place to hang out, but it was too freezing and wet in the woods to even sit down, so we kept trudging around till school let out, and then we sneaked back into the building and into the auditorium. He said, "I'm going to take you someplace we can make out," and took me up the ladder to that room—they called it the Crib. I'd heard about it. Everybody knew about it, in fact, except the adults, and they just weren't paying attention.

When we went in, there were about two dozen people in there, and it was so hazy with smoke from cigs and joints you couldn't see across the room. We started smoking dope. It got later and later. I got so bored because there were all these people there talking about stupid things. What I wanted to do was make out with Jimmy, but he was too timid to do it in front of all those people. Finally some of the people left and I started kissing him. I was horny from the dope, and the more we kissed the hornier I got. I started grinding my crotch up against his. I didn't care if people were watching. Once I realized that people were watching but that I didn't care, I got on top of him and took his cock out and started sucking it. It got quiet in the room.

Then I felt hands come up from behind me and strip my pants off. Some idiot started to poke me. I stopped sucking Jimmy's prick long enough to snap, "At least get it wet, stupid," and everybody laughed, and the guy did get it wet and stuck it in my snatch and came in about five seconds. I didn't even see who it was. When I felt him pull out of me and the sperm drip down out of my pussy, I looked around and said, "Shit, is that it? Isn't there somebody here who knows how to fuck, at least?" Some older kid was there and he came over and put his dick in and fucked me a lot. I grunted on Jimmy's prick and it made him come. When I finally pulled my mouth off Jimmy, I knelt there on my elbows and knees, my face hanging in Jimmy's crotch as his cock deflated, and let the older kid fuck me. When he came he made a sound like somebody throwing up. At least Jimmy was relatively quiet. Then I pulled up my pants and collapsed on a cushion.

When I woke up, there were just two other people there. They were fucking. There was no sign of Jimmy or the other guys; I'd hardly seen them; I didn't even know who they were. I sat up and tried to clear my head, then climbed down the ladder. The stage was pitch dark and it took me three minutes to find an exit. Finally I found a hallway, and walked out to the parking lot and sat in my car. I was so tired.

That's like a high-school caper every kid does. Everybody gets fucked in some tawdry way sooner or later, and that happened to have been my first time. So what? I'm not a Barbie doll, I don't expect everything to be like on TV or something. The whole school was so awful and dirty and cheap anyway that it was really a typical thing for that school.

Some people heard about what had happened. I didn't care. I wondered who that older kid was and if maybe I could lay him again, but he never turned up so he must have been from another school or something. But this guy who was a senior did find me. He came up to me one day while I was sitting in one of the "study halls" and started talking to me as if he knew who I was. We cut for the rest of the day and went out to his car and drove away.

He took me to this apartment that looked weird—sort of super-neat and furnished with furniture and all—and yet it seemed like nobody lived there. "What is this place?" I asked.

"It's a display apartment," he told me.

"You mean people come here to look at a typical apartment for this complex or something?"

"That's right, except they've got a new one now and they never use this one any more. They're just waiting to rent it. Meanwhile I use it."

"How?"

"I work here. My uncle is the manager."

This guy—his name was Matthew—took me into the bedroom and I sat on the bed. It seemed like an enormously long journey to get from that point to fucking, which was all I wanted, and I knew everything would be boring before that. Thankfully he just said, "Strip off all your clothes except for your top," and he got naked. I took everything off except my sleeveless T-shirt that said, IF IT'S TOO LOUD, YOU'RE TOO OLD.

He pushed me down on the bed and put his face between my legs. I held his head there until I came. That felt good. It was the first time I had come with a guy. I was relieved, because I knew I could make myself come if I masturbated, but after that first experience in the Crib, I was afraid sex with guys wouldn't be much fun.

But I came with this guy Matthew and thought, well, all right. I could tell he liked it too because he made me do it again and again. His tongue was on my clit, and the sensations changed as he licked it more and more. First it was really sensitive and he did it light. Then he did it hard, and I thought I was gonna scream. Then it grew less sensitive and he lightened up and I got frantic, I needed more sensation now, not less, and that excited me even more. I was in a secret apartment with some guy licking between my legs, and I was coming in his mouth and begging him, begging him with my voice, "Please. Please. Please."

"Please what?"

"Please do that."

"Do what?"

"Don't stop to talk, motherfucker!" I caught the first thing that came to hand, his ear, and twisted it. "Just do it. Talk later, for chrissake."

We still hadn't fucked but I wasn't bored. It hadn't even occurred to me that anything besides fucking would happen; I hadn't thought he'd be interested, so getting my pussy eaten was a plus. In fact, I was starting to wonder if we could just do this instead of fuck. That might definitely be pushing my luck too far, but I wanted to delay doing it as long as possible.

"Please eat my cunt, please do that, I'll talk dirty to you if you just keep doing it."

"Mm-hmm," he grunted affirmatively, not stopping.

"You're eating my pussy, you're sucking out my cherry.... You evil motherfucker, you bitch, you've got your face in my cunt, it feels good, it feels good, it feels good...."

Then my clit got less sensitive and he was doing it hard, I could feel the suction on my clit, the little nub getting swollen and red as I envisioned it. He was moving his face in and out in fuck motions. I suddenly got a weird cartoon vision that my cunt was a rocket engine all set to blast him in the face, and then I felt his teeth on the soft tissue of my clit, gently scraping and biting, and I exploded, bucking up into his frantic mouth, and somehow he stayed on, he stayed with it, biting that hard target, holding on like a little animal. The thought of vermin put the finishing touch on my orgasm; it felt like the back of my head blew off, my fists were pounding the bed and hitting him wherever I could, and I was yelling, "No! No! God!" Then I crashed.

He let me lie there for a second, then I vaguely heard him rip open a condom and put it on. He touched my cunt with his prick before I was ready, and I yelled again, startled. He ignored me and pushed it in; I was soaked. I knew I wouldn't be able to stand it if he fucked me, because I was too sensitive, but he hit bottom and stayed right there like a catfish, waiting while I caught up to myself. "You evil motherfucker," I said again, finally opening my eyes.

He was grinning. He couldn't stop grinning and he couldn't think of anything to say, either. I closed my eyes again and let him fuck me. It was different than in the Crib. When he had gone down on me, it was as if his mouth had opened me; now he was pumping into my body like the oil derricks I had seen in Texas, sloonging back and forth, up and down. The motion, when it was steady, was interesting. But it wasn't nearly as good as getting sucked; I knew I wasn't going to come. I was wondering if I should fake an orgasm to make him feel good, but I didn't have the energy. He fucked on and on, and then to make him finish I started talking again. I told him it felt good, that I loved his cock, that I wanted him to do it to me, et cetera. Finally he came with a gasp.

I went into the bathroom and tried with a brush to get the knots out of my hair. I looked at myself in the mirror, an ordinary suburban troublemaker. I didn't think I looked like anything special, but then I realized what he saw when he looked at me: fresh pussy, jutting tits, an open mouth. I made "erotic" faces at myself in the mirror; I put the brush handle between my legs and worked it back and forth salaciously. He came into the bathroom suddenly and grinned at me. Picking the rubber off his shrunken prick, he said, "You're beautiful," and threw it in the toilet.

"No, I'm not," I said, though the trip through his eyes had been educational. I looked really funny to myself that way—but still not beautiful.

"You are," he said, and named all the points—tits, ass, pussy— that I had just run though. Boys, God. So predictable. *Nota bene:* They are so fucking predictable. Of course, it hadn't been predictable when he ate my cunt. That's the part I liked.

While he was running through the menu of my delectables, I started thinking about getting out of there and going home. "What time is it?" I asked while he was still talking.

"Five," he said promptly.

"I have to go."

That night he called me for no reason. I mean that literally. He said, "Hi" and then couldn't think of a thing to say. "I liked it today," he blurted finally.

"Me too," I said, "but I can't talk here." He wanted me to say something dirty to him. I wouldn't.

The next time we screwed was a few days later on a Friday. We cut school at about 11:30 and went to the weird apartment. I asked him if there was any real food in there or if it was fake too like everything else. He said, "I know where some food is" and buried his face in my cunt again. Well, all right. This guy, he wasn't such a conversationalist, but he knew how to have sex, and he made me come. He actually *liked* to eat pussy. That's something.

Amateur

Late in the afternoon the wind blows hard down the streets of the seedy neighborhood. In the summer, as the fog comes in off the ocean, it shoves cold wind before it, sea air rushing in under the hot air twenty miles inland. To stand outside on California Street at four in the afternoon is to squint against the dirt and the bits of trash flying, zip up your jacket as the sun is covered, and think of a place of refuge from the wind.

Tammy always tries to be inside when the fog roars in. To venture out in the cool gray mornings is pleasant, but after noon when the glare hits and the wind begins, she feels like shriveling. She prefers to sit inside and watch the tourists stagger against the wind as they clutch their shopping bags and head doggedly toward the cable car terminal at Van Ness Avenue. Tammy is safe in her apartment, four floors above the street, sitting on her floor in the front room, trying to rest.

It feels like resting, because she feels tired each afternoon when the fog comes in, though she has spent the day doing nothing but a couple of desultory errands, grocery shopping at the Cala on Hyde Street, or walking up Polk toward the richer neighborhood to check the sales at boutiques. These days Tammy isn't getting much done. Since getting laid off, she's been living on unemployment, which for this cheap apartment and her completely dull lifestyle is plenty, plus the occasional bucks from dealing dope when some comes her way.

From her room on the fourth floor, Tammy can see people walking up and down California. Lately she's been playing with the idea of getting into the sex industry, as her friend Sapphire calls it. Sapphire is a call girl who mostly works in a house in San Rafael, across the bridge in Marin County, though she lives a few blocks away in the Tenderloin where hookers are on the street all night. Sapphire used to work the street and finally worked her way into the brothel in San Rafael, and has offered to get Tammy in there too. Tammy is a sure thing, according to Sapphire, because she's pretty and has long hair and good tits. Tammy can write her own ticket, says Sapphire.

Tammy looks down on a man, tall in jeans and a white T-shirt, his black jacket flaring out behind him in the wind, his black hair flying. She imagines the man is a client on his way to her apartment. In a moment he'll ring the buzzer, she'll let him in, and he'll pay her to fuck him.

The man continues past her building and down the street.

Tammy can imagine, can see, the men approaching. That one called me and is coming in to fuck me. That one, no; I wouldn't touch that one. That one is all right. She can imagine them ringing her buzzer, her reply as she buzzes them in from above. After that, the next thing she can imagine is them putting on their jackets and leaving. That she can't imagine any part of the encounter with these men is a sign to her that maybe she isn't ready yet to become a prostitute.

"I like the idea, though," she tells her friend Jackie in Boston. "I like the idea of being a whore, being outside society, being an outlaw."

"What does that mean?" Jackie asks. "What do you mean, being outside society."

"I can't stand working in offices, I can't stand dressing up and going to work. I can't stand reporting to a boss. I want to be the boss, I want men to pay me just because I've got something they want."

"I'm sorry," Jackie said. "Did I hear you right? You think that when men are paying you for sex, it means you're in charge? Honey, I have the feeling that they're gonna think that paying entitles them to do whatever the fuck they want."

"Mark's not like that."

"Well, your relationship with Mark may not be completely free of financial considerations, but it's not the same as having an appointment and having sex with some john. I mean, he doesn't actually give you money, does he?"

"A couple of times he did. He paid for a class I was taking. Then after the class ended he gave me money anyway once, he said it was just a present."

"Mmm. Well, having a sugar daddy isn't quite the same thing, all theory aside."

"He's only ten years older than I am."

"Well, why are you with him?"

"He's nice and he doesn't make many demands. He just lets me run my trip."

"Exactly, he's a sugar daddy. What *is* your trip, by the way?"

"I'm trying to learn how to ejaculate." She told Jackie about a video she'd seen of women masturbating, having big G-spot orgasms, and shooting out long streams of clear liquid.

"I'm sure that'll be very popular with your clients."

After she hung up with Jackie, she wondered if Jackie, who was a dyke, had been offended by the idea of her becoming a prostitute, or if Jackie, who was also an AIDS activist, merely thought she was silly and trivial. They had been friends for a long time and had even had a sexual thing for a while in college back east. After that was over and Tammy had moved out to California, they were still good friends, but sometimes she had the feeling Jackie was waiting for her to just grow up.

Tammy felt it was easy to be Jackie, who was queer and therefore had a community and a cause and something to yell about. Everybody these days seemed to be part of an oppressed group that had some chip on its shoulder, even Jackie who was really just like her, a white suburban kid, except that Jackie had the fortune to turn out queer. Tammy had tried, but finally accepted Jackie's dismissive evaluation—"You're straight as a nail"—even though Jackie had said that in anger when Tammy tried to get her back, after they'd broken up.

Queers were rebels, they were outside society. Where did Jackie get off, asking her what she meant by that? Did Tammy have to say, "I want to be like you, driven and angry and with three girlfriends, always fashionable, getting quoted on the news; I want to have a sense of my place in the world"?

"I want to have a sense of my place in the world," she told Mark after they fucked, when night finally came and the wind died down.

"Lots of people feel disconnected when they get laid off from their jobs," he said. He held her in his arms; tenderness came naturally to him after sex.

"Jackie says you're my sugar daddy."

"You told her about the Corvette? Darn, I thought that was our little secret."

"That's what most straight girls do, they define themselves by their husbands and boyfriends. Like I'm your property."

"You are? I didn't know that. I need to take more advantage of my status. Move so I can lie on your shoulder."

"But I told her it's not like that." Tammy didn't move.

"We don't talk much about our relationship. We don't even say that word."

"Have you ever paid someone for sex?"

"No…do peep shows count? I went to a peep show once, but we weren't allowed to give the dancers tips. They were on hourly. Actually I knew one of them and went—"

"If you were going to pay someone for sex, how much would you pay?"

"Why don't you ask your pal Sapphire how much she gets paid?"

"If I were a prostitute, would that excite you?"

"Not enough to pay you for it."

"Even if I ejaculated?"

The phone rang and they both jumped a little. He pulled the blanket over her as she simultaneously dove for the phone. He let her up reluctantly.

"Tammy, this is Saph. I know you haven't really made up your mind yet but I've got a proposition for you. I have a client who wants two girls, and the girl I usually do this kind of thing with is on a meditation retreat. You wouldn't have to do that much, I'd make sure he got his rocks off with me. Mostly you'd just be playing with me. You'd probably have to spread your legs for him and act sexy, you know. You don't even have to touch him if you don't want to. He's an old client and he can be trusted not to overstep his bounds. What do you think?"

"How much?"

"It'll be two hundred for each of us per hour. If we play our cards right, we can get him for two hours. That's four hundred bucks for each of us."

"Where?"

"In the Marina—can you take a cab?"

"I'll get Mark to take me."

"I'll tell him your name is Ruby."

Tammy took the address, hung up, and went into the bathroom. "I need you to take me to a job."

Half an hour later they were walking into the garage at the Holiday Inn where Mark had stashed his car.

"I'm impressed," he said. "A minute ago you were wondering about your place in the world."

"I think I just want to be a prostitute."

"You know, you're right. I am excited, not by the fact that you're about to get paid to do some rich guy, but that I'm driving you to have sex. We're going to get there early. Let's fool around in the car outside his house."

"That probably wouldn't be professional." They got into the car. "Suck my cock?"

"Fuck you, just drive," she laughed.

They turned north onto Van Ness and into the traffic of people heading to the bridge. The lights from cars and signs dazzled her; she felt like she was on mushrooms. After six blocks, Mark's car ran out of gas.

"Give me money to take a cab with."

"Fuck you, you're about to make two hundred bucks. How about coming back here and going out to dinner with me after?"

"No, I'll call you tomorrow or something."

She climbed out of the car and started running, more from excitement than from being late, since she was still really early, and because she wanted to leave Mark behind. She realized she didn't want him involved even to the degree of dropping her off. She wondered if she should begin to cultivate a more professional distance.

After three blocks she got a cab and told the driver the trick's address. When they got there she was still twenty minutes early. Sapphire had given her a set time to arrive. She wanted time to soften the dude up and lay out some ground rules. Saph was going to represent Tammy as her girlfriend and tell the guy that Tammy was a lesbian who didn't want to fuck him and would only play with her. "I'll chill him out for you," she'd said.

Tammy told the cabby to take her up the street to a bar. She paid him and went inside. Since it was Friday night and the first of the month, the place was full of yuppies trying to score with each other. The music was several years old, it was what was popular when she'd been in college, and she realized that she was the same age as the yuppies in the bar. She even blended in, having worn what she expected a trick would regard as a sexy outfit: a black cocktail dress, stockings, high heels. It was what she'd worn to the Christmas party at a law firm one year. The drunken lawyers had predictably swarmed all over her, which just increased her contempt for them and made her wish she was a lesbian. Probably the trick was a lawyer too, if he was so rich.

Waiting for her drink, she got out a cigarette. An ex-frat boy hurried to light it for her, and then she felt obligated to make conversation. He told her he was a professional athlete.

"Do you play for the Giants?"

"Yeah, that's right."

"Then why aren't you playing tonight?" She followed the schedule.

"I'm injured."

"What happened, a groin injury?" she asked.

"Not even close," he said, moving six inches nearer. She had meant it as a nasty comment and he took it as a come-on, she realized with disgust.

"Oh, then you must have gotten hit in the head with a pitch."

"Not that either."

"Well, it has to be something that would make you so stupid that you wouldn't realize I don't want to talk to you," she said loudly over the music.

"You fucking bitch, fuck you," he cried, moving away.

I *am* a fucking bitch, I'm a fucking whore, she thought with satisfaction, smirking at herself in the mirror, drinking her martini. These people think I'm one of them but I'm a spy, I'm here to subvert their merry fun. I'm a whore, I'm outside society. I'm doing it.

Being a bitch was so much fun she wanted to do it again, but she didn't have time. She finished her drink and headed out the door.

The frat boy caught up to her a few doors down the street.

"You're a fucking bitch, you know that?"

"Let me go, you asshole. I'll start screaming."

"You're nothing! I'll slap you from here to sundown...."

Her first scream was choked off when his hand connected with her mouth. He let go of her and she staggered across the sidewalk, falling onto the hood of a parked car. She drew another breath and let out another scream. That made him hesitate, and gave her time for another. Finally a couple of guys came out of the bar.

"Help me!" she screamed. "This asshole hit me!"

"She's my girlfriend," the frat boy explained. "We're just having an argument."

"Get me out of here," Tammy cried, running between the two other guys, both of whom looked confused.

She ran back into the bar and looked around feverishly for a telephone. When she found it, she realized she didn't know whom to call. Everybody in the bar was looking at her with astonishment. She wiped her face and saw blood on her hand. Her mouth was bloody.

"Oh, shit."

She left the phone and went up to a guy at the bar who looked as if he was by himself. "Excuse me, sorry to bother you, but I'm having kind of an emergency."

He stared at her, wide-eyed. "Are you okay?"

"I tripped, that's all. I hit my head on the edge of the phone thing. I just need a ride home—it's a couple of blocks away."

"Are you sure you don't want to go to the emergency room?"

"No, no—can you just take me home?"

They walked a block and a half to his car. He kept asking her if she was sure she was okay.

"Yes, yes, just get me home."

He gave her a handkerchief. They pulled up in front of the trick's address. The bleeding seemed to have stopped. "Thanks."

"Let me come up with you." He turned off the car in the driveway and started to get out.

"No! Don't—" she hissed, so the trick wouldn't hear. "This isn't my driveway.... Look, thank you, but I'll be fine."

"Just let me make sure you get inside."

"I'll be fine, really," she pleaded. She made little shooing motions.

"Thank you, really. Maybe I'll see you again."

"Let me give you my number."

"I—oh, all right." She stood there while he extracted his business card from his wallet. He worked at the Men's Wearhouse, she saw in the streetlight. "Fine…Scott. Fine. I'll call you. Here's your handkerchief…."

"Keep it—that's okay."

She didn't want him to see her ring the doorbell. But she realized he would wait until she went inside, so she had no choice. She rang it and turned back to see him watching, still standing next to his car. "It's actually my sister's house," she whispered.

The gate buzzed and she went inside and closed it with a clang. A few feet farther was the front door of the house; it buzzed and she entered.

There were steps leading upstairs; they were shadowy. A man was at the top. "Ruby?" he asked.

"Hi," she said, as cheerfully as possible. She got to the top, she saw Saph behind him.

"Hi, honey," Saph said.

"Can I just use the powder room for a moment?" Tammy asked.

The guy led them to the bathroom. "Come on in with me for a minute, honey," Tammy said to Saph. She made sure the door was closed before the light clicked on.

"Holy shit! What happened to you?" Saph whispered.

"Some fucking asshole in a bar tried to rape me. I don't look that bad, do I?"

"Well, you have to wash your mouth…. Shit, what happened?"

"I just told you…. I'll be okay, go out there and keep the man happy. I'll be out in a minute."

She looked at herself in the mirror after Sapphire left. Her hair was completely messed up, and her mouth was bloody. She washed her face but that just made the cut on her lip start again. It was already swelling. Maybe she could just tell them to turn off the light.

After ten minutes, when she had gotten the bleeding to stop again and had brushed her hair, she emerged from the bathroom.

The hallway was dark. She went toward the lit room where she could hear noises. At the doorway she paused. Saph was on the floor, straddling the guy's cock, fucking him. She looked up at Tammy and shook her head furiously and waved her away.

Tammy went back to the bathroom and sat on the toilet lid without turning on the light. She had fucked up. She wouldn't get paid; Sapphire probably wouldn't invite her to do this again. Her lip was swelling and she'd look like shit and she'd just spent twenty dollars on cab rides and a drink for nothing.

The window was open a little and the night air, smelling of jasmine and fog, came into the quiet bathroom. Outside Tammy could hear the foghorns on the bay and, from the other room, the cries, real and faked, of pleasure and fulfillment.

Trina

The last time she got together with Daniel, Jain almost didn't leave the house. She was ready to tell him she didn't want to see him anymore; she was prepared for his arguments, and resigned to having sex anyway—he would treat her roughly, keeping her up as late as possible, knowing it really was the last time. She brought rubbers and lube and gloves, since it never occurred to him to buy any. She was prepared, in a way, even for the unexpected, though she supposed he would never do anything really violent. His violence wasn't real, it was just realistic.

Still, when it came time to pick up her bag and leave her apartment, she found herself weary. The late-afternoon sun coming through the windows made her drowsy; the apartment seemed like a very comfortable place to be, the couch heaped with laundry that needed to be folded. How easy it would be to collapse there and sleep. Finally, she made a move, locked the door, found the car, and bulled her way across town through late-afternoon traffic. At Potrero, just a few blocks from his studio, some neighborhood kids in pickup trucks with deafening bass speakers stopped right in the middle of the intersection to talk to each other, and she started screaming, "You stupid motherfucking assholes, get out of the street to have your fucking conversation!" Wrapped in their bubble of booming noise, they never heard her, but moved on eventually.

Daniel failed to notice her mood, as usual. He showed her his newest two-day masterpiece, a huge rendering of the city's skyline for which some corporation was paying thousands. Wiping his hands excitedly on a rag stinking of mineral spirits, he shifted from one foot to the other and waited for her to say something.

"No cars on the Embarcadero Freeway," Jain said finally.

"That's right," he said, with something approaching glee.

"I get it, it's after the earthquake," she said. "The flagpole on the Ferry Building is crooked, the clock says 5:04. Very cute. Who's the client, an insurance company?"

"A heavy equipment manufacturer. They make the Jaws of Life."

The telephone rang and Daniel tossed the rag onto the big workbench he used to build the frames for his canvasses. While he talked on the phone from the kitchen she looked at the rag and thought about wiping it across the canvas in long, smeary strokes, but he worked so fast it would take him only a few hours to repair the damage. She searched the painting for an unobtrusive spot to vandalize, something he wouldn't notice. There were small figures on a ferry in the foreground; with embarrassment she recognized Daniel and herself. Since they had become lovers, he always painted them into his works, saying it was a charm that would keep them together. Mentally she replaced the male figure of Daniel with that of the small, muscular woman who worked at the coffee bar in the lobby of Jain's office building: Deanna. Jain had accidentally-on-purpose run into Deanna the day before as the coffee bar closed at three P.M. and, following up on weeks of indecision, asked her out. To Jain's amazement, Deanna had looked right into her eyes and said yes. They were to meet for a drink tomorrow, Saturday.

Daniel came back from the phone and asked her what she was looking at. "You and me," she said defensively.

He took her in her arms and bent to kiss her neck. Out of the corner of her eye, she managed to maintain the illusion in the painting of her and Deanna, riding the ferry over the bay, and became aroused. Moving her hips, Jain put her crotch against his thigh and pressed gently. This was a fragile time. Daniel always seduced her according to schedule, and by his reckoning, she wouldn't be aroused enough yet to push her crotch against him, so he didn't even notice. In a minute, when it was time for her to be excited, he would push too hard.

Until that happened, she rocked against his leg muscles, which were hard from standing and painting, and thought only of Deanna's soft chestnut hair and wide mouth, what her body must look like naked, whether her cunt hair was lighter or darker than the hair on her head, and the thickness of her tongue on Jain's clit. Trembling, she came against Daniel's leg, and a moment later he put his hand on her tit and said, "Turns me on."

She took a couple of breaths, coming back to him, and finally mumbled, "What?"

"Turns me on that you're looking at us in my painting."

She felt him getting hard against her. She turned to face him and they kissed. She didn't mind his body, even if he didn't have a clue about what she liked. The fact that he did some things that made her come was complete coincidence; she supposed he probably made love to every woman exactly the same way.

With her left hand she unzipped his jeans. Reaching inside, she scraped lightly with her fingernails against the cloth of the silk briefs she'd given him early in their affair. Since then he'd worn them every time they saw one another. Or maybe he'd gone out and bought a dozen, all the same blue.

Daniel wasn't utterly predictable. The third time they'd fucked, just when Jain was wondering when this guy would tip his hand, he'd tied her to a chair and slapped her face over and over. He did it well (almost too well, as if he'd practiced), whacking the soft places just hard enough, never endangering the eyes, calling her *bitch* and *cunt*. It didn't make her come at the time, but later, at home, when she masturbated.

Since then he'd spiced straight fucking with a little SM every so often. She never knew when he would go into this mode, but it happened often enough, though for no discernible reason, that she'd once asked sarcastically, "Do you have a schedule set up, or what?" He thought she was talking about his painting, and happily explained his work schedule to her as she relaxed in her ropes and thought about doing her bills.

Sinking to her knees on a small stool—he was so tall this was the only way she could reach—she took out his cock. This stool, a small padded stand that looked like a kneeler from an Episcopal church, was the one piece of erotic furniture in his house. The first time she saw the stool it already had two permanent depressions embedded in the cushion, so she knew she wasn't the first one to kneel there and suck Daniel's cock; she knew he had gotten it just for this purpose. The transparent nature of the stool almost took away its erotic charge, but at least he knew what he liked.

Fortunately, she liked sucking his cock as much as he liked having it sucked. Not wanting to be as predictable as him, however, she gripped the base and rammed her face down on his cock. She'd never dispensed with his accustomed teasing, light licks before, and had never taken it this deeply. She struggled with the way his cock filled the back of her mouth, found a way to breathe while still throating him, and never panicked. She was holding him too tightly to become afraid.

Up above somewhere, Daniel was trying to express surprise and pleasure, which for him were conflicting emotions. Jain's other hand was covertly reaching underneath her skirt, touching her wet slit, because one of the preparations she'd made before leaving the house was to remove her underpants. She rotated her fingers around the clit as the other hand pushed his cockhead around her throat the way she would clean out a saucepan. She considered fantasizing about Deanna, knowing it would make her come, and decided rather to pay attention to the task of getting Daniel off. Then maybe he would take her out for a drink. Since getting this crush on Deanna, she liked to look covertly at other women, and just last week when they went out for dinner there was a woman who seemed to stare back. She was convinced this voyeurism was good for getting back into practice with women.

But right now she was sucking off her boyfriend. She brought up her free hand, sticky with her juice, and wiped it on the shaft of his dick. The slippery jizz helped her pump his cock back and forth; he needed this in-and-out movement to come. He responded by thrusting into her throat, only the first shove tentative, and after that he finally forgot himself and let out a groan. She held tight as he fucked her mouth; she sucked him as hard as she could, and as an added impetus she set up a low rhythmic groaning that excited her, too. The finger on her left hand had a life of its own, frantically wiping at her clitoris as if trying to erase it. She broke out into a sweat. *Fucking me, fucking me, fucking me,* she said to herself over and over, and remembered him slapping her that time and saying, *Filthy bitch, I'll fuck your mouth.* Now he was doing it, really fucking, making her face into a cunt, *a hole,* as he said: *You've got so many holes for me to fuck.* Now she disappeared into the rhythm, thinking no more about her knees aching despite the cushion, or the smell of paint and solvent, or how much she disliked him, or even of her own orgasm, but really became a hole, his hole, a glorious nothing hole for him to fuck. The only reason she noticed his come shooting out was that he changed the rhythm and let out a loud groan.

Heedlessly pumping his stuff into her, he almost knocked her off the stool, but she held on. His thrusts came slower then, but harder, and she had a momentary vision of him sweeping her up in an arc on the end of his prick. With a final thrust and deep grunt, he stopped. They were both breathing hard.

She hadn't had an orgasm. Doing herself while she sucked him was just a way to keep herself interested, and she'd had to stop when he came because she needed the other hand to hold on. Now she reached down and began casually diddling herself again, trying to stay in the vacant frame of arousal she'd been able to reach. Some of his come was deep in her throat and she swallowed; some was behind her teeth, so like a porn actress she let it drip out the side of her mouth, knowing he couldn't see, just relishing the dirty feeling it gave her. Reaching up, she took some from her face and put it between her legs to make herself slicker. *Filthy bitch.*

Above her, Daniel slowly got his breath back. He groaned again. Now he'd be solicitous, she knew. Instead of staying in the brutal persona, which came close to exciting her, he would regain control and be nice and waste it all. *Schmuck*, she thought, letting her hand drop away, giving up on having an orgasm for a while.

She was still sucking gently when she felt his hand on the side of her face; he gently pushed her off his prick and reached out to steady her. She hung her head—couldn't he see she wanted to submit to the brute and not the nice boy, that she hadn't even come yet, that she despised him for his shallowness? She wiped her mouth with the back of her hand.

He stepped back. "How you doin'?" he asked, friendly.

She exhaled impatiently. "Fine," she said, raising her head to look at him. He was smiling contentedly. *He looks so pleased,* she thought, *he might not even get me off.* She had forgotten about going out for a drink.

"Want to get on the bed?"

Imagine that's an order, she thought sarcastically. Rising, she walked on stiff legs across the cold concrete floor to the small stairway leading into his bedroom. This smaller room had been built inside the large studio space, and there were no windows; inside it was dark. She collapsed on the bed and stretched painfully to rid her neck and legs of kinks. He turned on the bedside lamp and sat down next to her.

She lay still. *Do it, do something,* she thought. *Don't give me time to rest, don't wait for me to tell you I'm okay. Don't ask me what I want.* He laid a hand on her, sexlessly, a gesture meant to comfort.

They stayed that way for a while. Finally Jain said, as gently as possible, "I'm fine, if you're waiting for me to recover or something. Just have your way with me; it's what I want."

Daniel stood up and went over to the dresser. *He does seem to have a plan,* she thought. *Good thing I said something, we'd have sat here indefinitely.* Taking advantage of his absence, she stretched one more time, shut her eyes, and tried to get interested in whatever he had in mind. When she felt the leather cuffs close around her wrists, she purred and arched her back, urging him on. Just let him run his program and maybe it would be worth the wait.

More cuffs closed around her ankles, and she heard him clip the ropes to the eye bolts on the bed frame. Now she was spread-eagled in the center of the bed, completely exposed and comfortable. She pulled against the ropes. *At least I can't get loose,* she thought. *Now let him make me want to.*

"Look at me."

She opened her eyes to see him standing naked. It was a bit of a surprise, for she hadn't heard him taking off his clothes. He stood by the side of the bed, bending over her like a willow. Even when he climbed between her legs, he was tall and long, and almost alarmingly attenuated, like a piece of taffy. She sometimes pictured him splitting in half at the stomach, his arms and torso going one direction, ass and legs loping off in another.

"Tell me you want me."

"I want you, I want your cock," she said calmly. "I had it in my mouth and now I want it in my cunt. That's why I'm here. I come here for you to fuck my cunt and fuck my mouth."

"I fucked you in the mouth really hard."

"You fucked me in the mouth really hard, like nobody ever did before. I never took anybody that deeply, but I took you. Because I wanted it." She thought, *He'll never know how much is truth and how much is bullshit.*

"Because you had to," he suggested, ignoring or forgetting the fact it had been her idea.

"I had to—you forced your cock between my lips, I had to suck it and take your jizz in my throat."

"Was it good?" he smiled.

"It was good," she confirmed, as if in church.

"Gonna fuck you now for a minute."

She let her eyes roll back. *Deanna*, she thought, *now I call upon you. Get in between my legs and help this poor schmuck out. Make me come, make me come, make me come. Baby, your hair. If only you knew how every morning I wanted to touch your beautiful long hair, feel it in between my breasts, scissor your cunt up against mine, and rub our parts together. Soon, baby. Just look into my eyes tomorrow night and tell me you like girls just like me, tell me you want me, tell me you'll lick my pussy, baby. Make me come, make me come.*

Daniel was sliding two fingers in and out of her cunt; she felt it from a distance. The pressure on her wrists as she pulled gently on the restraints was more exciting than what he was doing, but she couldn't come that way either, not till somebody played with her clit. She thought she heard a noise out in the studio. Daniel continued his fingering, showing no sign, so she assumed it was nothing. Then Jain heard a definite footfall on the steps and jerked her head up.

A young woman in a motorcycle jacket stood in the doorway, smiling at her. She had thick black hair and red lipstick and looked for all the world like one of the neighborhood girls—she had even teased her hair in front—but the leather jacket and the gold ring through her nostril gave her away as something more. The Mission District girls hadn't caught up to that combination quite yet.

"Hi, it's me," the woman said. She came nearer. Daniel withdrew his fingers from Jain's vagina and stood up next to the bed; the woman came up to his chest. He put his arm over her shoulder.

"I'm Trina," the woman said, not moving, just smiling at Jain. "So. You're really beautiful. Daniel's told me about you, and I've wanted to meet you for a long time."

Jain cleared her throat but found nothing to say. Trina reached down and removed her boots, leaning on Daniel for balance. Then she took off her skirt and panties. Head raised, Jain was still staring at her, truly surprised with Daniel for the first time in months.

Trina reached into a pocket in the jacket and brought out a knife; the blade sprang out faster than any prick she had ever seen. Jain felt her cunt throb at the sight of it, the noise it made opening, the reflection of the light off the blade and into Trina's eyes. Jain murmured, then groaned loudly as Trina put the blade against her white undershirt, the only thing she had on now except for the jacket, and caught the fabric with the point of the blade.

Jain stared at Trina's hand as it made the blade slice upward into the fabric between her breasts; one long, slow movement upward and the shirt was peeled back halfway down. She walked away from Daniel and toward the bed, locking Jain's eyes with her own and holding the knife straight up before her. Jain groaned again and then again; the groans became her breath. She was almost coming—if only Trina's eyes would slice between her legs, she could die and never stop coming again.

Trina's jacket creaked as she squatted over Jain's belly. She held the knife in front of Jain's eyes and moved it slowly, the moans that floated steadily through the air becoming background, a heartbeat.

"You want it?" Trina asked quietly, completely unlike the way Daniel would ask. This wasn't a request for permission, it was an invitation to confess.

"Yes, God," Jain sang in place of one of the moans. She knew Trina would do what Trina intended whether she consented or not; it was sheer graciousness to let Jain express willingness.

"All right. This is your sister, baby," Trina said. "Kiss her." Trina brought the silver blade to Jain's lips. It was cold, maybe from a ride on a motorcycle, but when Trina made a small movement and slightly cut Jain's upper lip, the blade felt suddenly warm.

"Oh, no," Jain said, and started to come. "Again, give it to me again," she pleaded, and the blade returned to her reaching lips and cut her in exactly the same place on the other side. Jain groaned and cried and thrashed her body, sometimes touching Trina's warm skin as she squatted over her, but keeping her head absolutely still and submissive to the knife, her sister.

When she finished coming, she saw Trina point the knife toward her own heart again and this time rip down, cutting her undershirt all the way open, letting her breasts fall out. Holding the blade flat against Jain's throat, Trina knelt down and Jain suckled on her brown nipples. "Um," Trina said, her voice near Jain's ear, the black hair falling over her shoulders. Jain had no thought for who this woman might be, what Daniel was doing, or what day it was. She thought about the cold blade and the stone-like nipples in her mouth and Trina's knee up against her cunt. She wondered if she were going to die, and if so, whether she would come at the same time.

She felt Trina's body tense and begin rocking against her. Trina sat up and Jain's mouth fell away. She looked up flatly at Trina, and her mouth opened slightly, willing to take. Her head shook back and forth in answer to an unasked question: No, I will not resist.

Trina lifted the blade and dragged the point across Jain's collarbone and the top of her breast toward her left armpit. It made a long scratch, not breaking the skin. She raised the knife in the air again where Jain could see it, where her eyes could beg. She brought it down deftly and shaved off some armpit hair. "Mmm, beautiful," Trina said. She never whispered, never cooed, just spoke quietly. "Too pretty to cut it all off. Not tonight, anyway. I like it too much."

Jain swallowed heavily. "I want to taste my blood," she begged.

Trina caught her breath and moved her leg so she could strad-dle Jain's. "Yes," she nodded. She rocked back and forth. She raised the knife in the air again. *It would be easy to kill me,* Jain thought. *I'm not afraid.* She stared hungrily at Trina's eyes.

Trina brought the knife down slowly until it was resting on a fleshy place on Jain's forearm, and took several quick, deep breaths. As the breaths stopped Jain felt a flash of warmth. She looked and saw blood run from a cut, and seconds later felt a sharp pain.

Then the blade was before her mouth, wet. "Do not cut your tongue," Trina said, deadly serious, and Jain obeyed, licking the salty, ob-scene jizz off the knife. Then Trina was coming, the knife thrust away from them, her body heavily pushing and thrusting on top of Jain. Jain's arm hurt like hell, and it made her come. Trina's ragged breathing and grunting sounded male. "Ugh, ugh, ugh." The confusion excited Jain even more.

Jain strained against the ropes to embrace her but it was impos-sible. Trina tossed her head and cried out, and when she was finished she laid a hand on Jain's chest, resting, holding herself up. They looked at each other.

After a minute, Trina crawled forward and slowly lowered her cunt onto Jain's mouth. Jain was lost in heavy wetness, the smell and the mixture of scratchy hair and butter-soft tissue. Trina's clit was small and hard and she began to suck it. She felt Trina holding down her tied-up arms, felt lost in this girl's body.

Jain felt Daniel climb up on the bed and push his cock into her. Now full. The motion of the two people together, thrusting, tearing at her, using her.

Jain concentrated on sucking Trina's clit, promising herself in a lucid moment never to forget what it felt like, if she never saw this woman again, this little clit, this wide cunt. She couldn't even reach inside the vagina with her tongue. Trina didn't let her; she was coming. Trina's body shook; she was probably yelling but Jain couldn't hear. Jain's lower body was far away but Daniel was coming too.

Gradually her senses were given back to her. Jain felt Trina raise up, and her legs released Jain's head. She could hear the others breathing. The ropes were taken off. Jain opened her eyes. Trina was still wearing the jacket and Jain took a good look at her. She was small and round and strong, her hair now really messed up.

Trina handed something to Daniel and stepped onto the floor. She got on her knees next to the bed like a kid ready to say her prayers and held Jain while Daniel pushed the dildo into her from behind. This time Trina's breath was hot in Jain's face; she panted like an animal. Once in a while she opened her eyes and looked at Jain wildly. Finally she looked panicked and said, "Oh, God" and came. They kissed, tongues wrapping.

"Please let me have it," Jain whispered. "Just like it is. With your stuff on it."

Trina climbed up onto the bed and pushed her over onto her hands and knees. She held out her hand for the dildo, looking only at Jain, and said, "Now you get it like me. Here it is. Feel it, baby. My stuff's inside you now, like you said. In your mouth and in your cunt. Take it." Jain cradled her own head in her arms and looked underneath to see the dildo going in and out.

With her free hand, Trina drew her nails across Jain's back, first softly, then harder and deeper. "Ah!" Jain yelled. "Aw, God, baby." Her nails went deeper. "Ah! Ah! Ah! Do it. Make it bleed!" Trina dug as deeply as she could. Finally she thrust wet fingers into Jain's mouth. Jain felt her cunt clamp down on the dildo. Spasms began shaking her body and she wailed with pleasure and excitement because the dildo wouldn't stop moving no matter how hard she gripped it. Now the fingers were fucking her mouth too and Trina snuck a finger down and just by touching her clit made her come. She envisioned a large bomb going off inside a small room. Her body jerked and bucked uncontrollably, and sounds she didn't recognize came out of her mouth. Only at the end of the orgasm was she able to groan, "God oh God oh God oh God oh...."

After a while Trina made her get up. They went to the bathroom and Trina applied stinging medicine to Jain's cuts. "You have to submit to this, too," Trina said matter-of-factly. Jain wasn't paying attention, she let the stranger tend to her. Trina was still wearing the leather jacket, and Jain longed to put it on, feel its weight, take on Trina's body and heart. In the bathroom the sound of their breathing, once the water was turned off, was deafening. It was hot in the little room and smelled like girl sex. After the first aid was finished Jain leaned against the sink and rested her head on Trina's shoulder. They were alone.

Daniel was stripping the bed when they came out. "How do I get this fucking blood off my sheets?" he demanded.

"You don't, you hang them on the line," Trina countered. "That's what you do on the wedding night. Hang the bloody sheet on the line so everybody can see she was a virgin. Thus honor is maintained."

"Just put them in cold water," Jain translated, arm in Trina's arm. While Daniel went into the bathroom and plunged the sheets into the tub, Jain sat on the edge of the bed, rubbing her muscles, which had grown stiff while tied up. She watched Trina, breasts bobbing free, comb her hair.

"Can I really have the knife?" she asked boldly.

Trina smiled wickedly. "After I teach you how to handle it. Lesson one is cleaning. When he gets done."

Jain shook her head to clear the cobwebs. "Trina," she said, "who *are* you?"

"Friend of his. Just what you see," the woman said. She began putting on her clothes.

"You're not going home?" Jain said, then mentally kicked herself.

"I have to pick up my kid, it's late."

Jain stifled the urge to beg Trina to let her come along. "Can I have your phone number?"

Trina snorted. "Girl wants the knife, she wants the phone number. Demanding girl." Jain blushed.

Then Trina came over and stood in front of Jain where she sat. "You get the knife, you get the phone number, and you get me, okay?" Jain wrapped her arms around Trina's hips and held her until Daniel came out of the bathroom, and then they went in and Trina taught her how to clean the knife.

While Daniel was letting Trina out of the studio, Jain pulled on her T-shirt and jacket and put the knife into the pocket. She heard a motorcycle start up outside. When he came back, Daniel grinned and held out his arms to Jain. She let him hold her, hardly paying any attention.

"Isn't she something?" Daniel asked.

She disengaged herself gently. She went over to the bottle of wine that sat on the dresser, carried it into the bathroom, took a paper cup out of the dispenser there, and poured herself some. Daniel followed her to the doorway and stood watching her.

She took a drink and said, "So who is she?"

"She's a mechanic. She works at the garage where I bring the van. When I went to pick it up a few weeks ago she signed me out and then came with me to the van. When I got in, she reached over and took that picture of you that's on the dashboard and said, 'Who is this?' She said she'd seen you once at the DMV and wanted to meet you and wasn't going to let the chance go by again. She was very specific about wanting to meet you and flirted with me until I agreed to invite her over. But first she had to get another look at you, so I told her to come to the Rancheria when we had dinner there last week."

"She was there while we were eating?" Jain asked, remembering being stared at.

"Yeah, she wanted to look at you."

Jain drank some wine. "So that's why you insisted on going there."

"After that she called me and asked me out and plied me with liquor until I told her what we do in bed. Then she said to invite her over here tonight. I wouldn't have done it, except I thought you'd like it."

"You thought I'd like it," Jain echoed flatly. Her skin flushed, from anger and embarrassment, and the memory of how much she had liked it. "You're an asshole, you know that?"

He looked confused. "Whattaya mean?"

She shook her head, deciding she didn't have the energy to break up with him tonight. But would in the morning. She stood turned three-quarters away from him, weary in the late hour. For comfort, she fingered the knife in her pocket and imagined the sound his key would make on the concrete floor of the studio when she dropped it through the mail slot from outside and walked away.

Caller Number One

"Oh God…. Suck my cock, you bitch, you fucking bitch, you fucking cunt…."

She's really good at it. Of all his lovers, she has become the best at giving blowjobs. It used to take seemingly forever; she's got it down to four-and-a-half minutes of head rush that feels like an airliner is landing in his brain. He always wants to hear her talk while she's sucking him, which is impossible, so he does the talking.

"You're doing it to me…. Your mouth is full of my cock… Soon I'll do it in your mouth, you bitch, fucking slut…. It's perfect…."

The best thing about her blowjobs is that she never does the same thing twice. He's been wondering for a while how she does that, but never manages to follow closely enough to care.

"Go ahead, slut, suck my cock. Cover it with your spit and fill your mouth with it. Give me pleasure, you cunt."

He can't remember what she does, not even enough to be able to reproduce it on another boy when he goes to sex clubs, and sometimes he wishes he could take her along just to show him how.

"Oh shit, I can't believe it…. It feels so fucking good. Do it, do it all over my dick. Oh fuck…."

She knows he's getting close when he stops calling her names.

"You're doing it…. Oh God, I'm fucking your mouth. Oh shit, it's so good. Oh God…."

Just when she thinks she's going to hear him start coming, which he does with a gasp of air, followed by a low growl, followed by a whine that starts out low and goes higher and higher, just when she thinks he's going to start spilling come in her mouth, he pulls back and slaps her hard.

"Ughhh!" She tumbles from her knees, catching herself with her hands on the floor. Then she feels his hand on her hair, and she scrambles across the floor of the apartment to keep from being dragged.

"I came so close. Fuck, you're good. Kneel down by the bed."

He throws her down in approximately the right place and kicks her legs apart. She gasps, startled, every time he does something she doesn't expect. Even if she doesn't say any words, the gasps turn him on.

"Brace yourself on one hand and stick the other between your legs. Masturbate. I want to watch you."

She jams on her clit and hears him take out a rubber and put it on. She never comes this way, only from his going down on her, and she knows he knows it. Therefore he's making her do this not just to provide a visual accompaniment while he covers his dick, but also to prevent her from coming tonight, since the sensation she's giving herself will make her too numb to come later, by any means.

Still, it feels good. She lets her head rest on the arm that's bracing her, and tries to concentrate on the sensation, and on the idea that she's about to get fucked. She expects to feel him approach her, but instead he takes the phone off the hook.

"Don't stop what you're doing. Give me a nice little show. Come on, do it for the boys in the back row. That's the way."

He is dialing; she can hear him punch in the numbers. Then there are a few long pauses, each punctuated by a single button push. She wonders what he's doing. It's like he's going through some voice mail system.

"Ever called one of those party lines? The ones where there's a bunch of guys all listening to each other breathe and hoping a chick comes on the line and says something? Well, tonight, you're the featured guest."

"Wha—?"

"It's your chance to make their dreams come true. Tonight, they're going to talk to a real live girl, and not just one who's pretending to get fucked."

He drops the phone on the bed next to her, and she feels his cock in between her legs.

"Stop touching yourself. Take my cock in your hand and stick it in. There!" He pushes up inside her.

"Ohhh," she says loudly. She doesn't notice him picking up the phone again. He punches one more button, listens a moment, then sticks it in front of her mouth.

"Hold it," he whispers. "Use one hand to hold it and the other to hold yourself up."

He thrusts deeply inside her and she gasps.

"That's it. Hear anything?"

There's a busy silence on the line. She hears a hopeful voice:

"Hello, anyone there?"

"Hello?" she answers.

"Hi," the voice replies.

"Now start talking. Tell all the guys on that line what's happening to you." He pushes into her hard.

"Oh, oh, oh," she gasps, in reaction to his thrusts.

"Hello? Is somebody there?" asks a male voice on the line.

"What was that?" someone else asks.

He stops for a moment; she feels his cock trembling inside her. "Tell them what you're doing. Say 'I'm getting fucked right now.'"

She looks at the phone.

"Say it."

She licks her lips. "I'm getting fucked right now."

"What do you look like?" asks a whisper.

"Ughhhff!" she grunts as he pushes inside her again. "Unnnkkhhh!"

"Oh man," another voice says.

"It's a real chick," says a third.

"Tell them you're getting fucked. Describe what's happening."

"Oh shit. Listen. I'm getting fucked right now." She steadies herself on the bed and he moves with her, joined at the groin. "Uhhn. My boyfriend is doing it to me and I'm talking on the phone while he's fucking me."

"No shit!"

"Yeah, take it, baby."

"What are they saying?" he asks.

"They're saying, 'Take it.'"

"Keep talking. Tell them how good it feels."

"Who is that?"

"It must be her boyfriend. Keep talking, baby."

"Oh God…" she sighs in frustration. She's never talked dirty as much as he's wanted her to, now she has to perform for who-knows-how many people in addition to him.

The guys on the line start saying, "Hey, are you still there? Keep talking, baby!"

"I don't know what to say!" she hisses at him.

"Just tell them what's going on."

"You're the one who knows what they want to hear, not me."

"Then repeat: 'His cock's in my cunt.'"

She sighs. "His cock's in my cunt."

"'I can feel it deep inside me.'"

"I can feel it deep ighhhhhh inside me," she grunts as he pushes into her hard.

"'It feels so good I can't stand it.'"

"Aw yeah, aw yeah," someone says.

"It feels so good I can't stand it."

"'It makes me want to come.'"

"It makes me want to come," she repeats.

"Do it, baby!"

"Come, baby, squeeze it out."

He's pushing into her slowly and steadily; if he pushes too hard or too fast, she gasps and loses track of what she's supposed to say.

"You think you can take it from here on in?" he asks her.

"Yeah, just take it…. Ohhgg…take it a little easy."

"Naw, do it hard, man!" some guy cries.

"Fuck her, man," someone else echoes.

"He's fucking me," she says quickly. "He's giving it to me good."

"Oh yeah…" sighs a man.

"Tell 'em how you like it," he urges.

"I love it—it feels good. It feels good. And he's pushing it into me. He's fucking my hole. A minute ago I sucked his cock and now he's fucking me."

Various sighs of admiration. Her lover holds her tightly by the hips and thrusts steadily into her; her head feels light.

"I love getting fucked. I love it when he fucks me. Oh, it feels so fucking good!"

"Yeah, it feels good!" laughs a participant.

"Now come, baby," someone urges.

"Yeah, do it."

"Come!"

"Do it, baby!"

She realizes what they're all used to—not on this line, probably, where women seldom go, but when they call sex lines and pay a woman to talk dirty to them, someone who fakes an orgasm with each one to make them come. Now they want the same from her.

"Ohh," she breathes, "ohh, he's doing it to me so good! Ohh, I'm getting so excited. Ohh, it makes me want to come."

"Yeah, do it, baby!"

"Come on, bitch! Come!"

"Do it, baby!"

"Take it!"

"Squeeze his dick, baby, push back at him and fuck him!"

It's nice to hear somebody say more than two words.

"Oh yeah, you guys just keep talking like that," she says. "Tell me what to do. Tell me what to do to his dick to make him come."

"Squeeze it!"

"Fuck it!"

"No, I want to hear you guys talk dirty too! Understand?

Don't just keep saying 'do it,' let's have a little imagination here." Behind her, snickers.

"Squeeze his dick, baby," the same guy ventures.

"Yeah, I'll squeeze his dick. What else?"

"Say, 'fuck me,'" someone else suggests.

"Ohh, fuck me. And?"

"Talk about your cunt."

"Talk about your prick!" she retorts. "What kind of obscene callers are you guys?"

"Baby, my dick is waiting to fill you up," someone avows. She's starting to distinguish the voices. This guy is the most voluble one.

"Oh, yeah, tell me about it. Make me hot," she urges. "If you tell me about it, you'll make me come."

"If I put my dick inside you, you'd start coming from the moment I started fucking you."

"Mmm, that would make my cunt really hot," she answers.

"I'd fuck you really good, I'd fuck you slow at first and then I'd get faster and faster."

"I'll bet your cock is nice and big. I love to have a nice hard cock in my cunt, it makes me feel so hot."

Her lover is thrusting with more urgency now.

"Your cunt would get hot and red and juicy, you'd start wiggling around, you'd love my cock."

"Mmm, keep talking like that," she says. "You're really turning me on."

"You'd feel so good fucking me that you'd beg for more."

"Oh, please do it to me. Please keep fucking me," she says, taking his suggestion. "I'd beg for you to fuck me."

"Yeah, beg, bitch," comes a voice.

"Ughh, ughh," she grunts, pushing hard against her lover. "Oh Jesus."

"Do it, baby, beg for it," urges the first guy.

"Please, please do it. I'll do anything. Just fuck me, just fuck me."

"Ohhhhh…."

She thinks she hears someone coming. "Please, please fuck me, I need it, I need your prick."

"Oh shit!" someone else exclaims.

"Do it, do it, come in me, do it in me," she breathes. "Uhh, uhh, uhh—"

"Oh fuck," her lover mutters.

"Do it now!" she says. "Come on, do it! Please! I want to feel it."

"Arrrgghhhhh…."

"You're squirming under my prick," says the talkative one. "I'm fucking you harder and harder."

"Yes, do it! Fuck me hard."

"Ohh!" her lover exclaims.

"Fuck me, fuck me, fuck me, come on, do it in me."

Her lover is pounding her now, and she knows he's just about to come. He's going faster and faster. She can't say any more, only grunt.

"Feel my prick, baby,"

"Beg for it, bitch."

"Fuck him good, baby."

"Ugh ugh ugh ugh."

"Fuck your fucking cunt," her lover grunts, his voice strangled. "You fucking bitch, you fucking slut, oh shit, oh shit, oh shit."

"Oh oh oh oh," she says.

"Take it, honey. He's doing it in you, isn't he? Feel his prick. You can't get away from it."

"Oh shit, he's doing it!" she yells.

"Oh God!"

"Unnhhh!"

"Fuck...."

Her lover whines like a dog. She feels him stop fucking; when he's coming, he's thinking so hard about his pleasure that he can't even remember to push. Everything freezes for an instant and then she feels his fist lightly strike her back. He gasps a long breath in, and she realizes he's been holding it.

"Oh God," she says. "He's coming now. He's coming right this instant. His stuff's getting all over my cunt. Oh Jesus. Oh do it, do it," she says. "That's the way. Come on. Do it for me. Do it for me." She can hear all the guys grunting as they come. Then there's silence on the line. Then she hears a voice.

"Wow, baby, that was really something else."

"Thank you."

"Call again sometime, okay?"

"Uh, okay...."

"Really."

"Yeah, baby, do it."

"Yeah, tomorrow night!"

"Um, excuse me for a second." She covers the mouthpiece. "They want me to call again tomorrow night."

He snickers. "Okay."

"All right, I'll call at the same time tomorrow night."

She hangs up. They collapse on the bed and lie there giggling. After a minute she jabs a finger in his chest. "What time *is* it?"

჻

The next night, before she begins the call, he gives her a further assignment. It's not enough for eight or ten guys to listen to them fuck. He wants to exhibit her more intimately. They agree on the details, she sucks his cock to make him hard, he enters her, and she dials. Soon:

"I want to tell you guys about how much I like to suck cock. I suck my lover's dick every chance I get, and I make sure it's better for him every time."

"Yeah, baby."

"Tell it, baby."

"My tongue licks the underside of his prick, nnngh, it's soft and sweet, nnngh, and he's telling me to suck his cock, nnngh, and he's calling me all kinds of dirty names...."

"Yeahhhh...."

"Like bitch and slut and cunt and shit, nnngh, and every time he calls me a dirty name, nnngh, it makes me hotter, nnngh."

"What are you doing right now?"

"I'm getting fucked."

"Tell 'em you like it."

"I'm getting fucked and I like it, nnngh."

"Fuck yeah she does."

"Shut up, man. Keep talking, baby."

"I slide my tongue up his prick, nnngh, and brush my fingers against his balls, nnngh, and when he calls me bitch and slut and cunt, nnngh, I know he's getting really turned on."

"Are you turned on now, bitch?"

"Fuck yes I'm turned on."

"Bitch."

"Oh God."

"You like that?"

"Oh yes, call me trash, call me dirty names."

"You fucking slut."

"That's right, everyone join in, go ahead, abuse me while I get fucked."

"Shit."

"Cunt."

"Whore."

"Oh yes, call me your dirty whore."

"Dirty whore, you like to get fucked, don't you?"

"I'm getting fucked right now, nnngh, and I love it. I love to get fucked, nnngh, by a hard wet prick, nnngh, while the motherfucker puts his hands around my neck, nnngh, and squeezes."

"You like it, don't you bitch?"

"I love it. I wish you could see my cunt while it's getting fucked, nnngh. I wish you guys were here right now to fuck me."

"Oh baby."

She notices that whenever she really touches or impresses them, they call her baby.

"Hey bitch," a guy says suddenly. "Answer me this. Does it really turn you on? Or are you just shittin' us?"

"What do you think?"

A pause.

"Hey come on, man, don't interrupt."

"Yeah baby, just get back to that cocksucking story."

"Okay, but first a word from our sponsor," she said, keeping her sexy voice going while she fulfilled her boyfriend's latest request. "I know you guys love it when I tell you how much I like to get fucked, how much I like sucking cock, and you like it especially because I'm actually getting fucked right now. Unnngcchh!" she exclaimed, as her lover gave her a hard one. "Right now."

"Yeah, baby."

"I bet you never thought you'd hear a girl really say this shit, not for free."

"Yeah, if they love you," one guy put in.

"Oh man, my old lady never talked dirty."

"Well, I can make it so you guys keep getting it for free, and not with everybody else listening, but just you and me, one on one. Interested?"

"Yeah...."

"All you have to do is send me your phone number. You think you can deal with that?"

"How about if you just say *your* phone number."

"No, I want your number. Now this is not a commercial operation and I'm not going to do anything with your number. This is not Friends and Family. All I want to do is be able to do these phone scenes with you guys and not have to pay this dollar ninety-nine a minute. And I bet you guys would like to keep from paying too, right?"

"Yeah, baby, so what's your number?"

"No, you guys send me your numbers. Now if you happen to live with other people, you better make sure you really want me to have that number, because you never know when I'll call, okay? I might end up talking to your girlfriend or your brother instead of you. But anyway I'll call you and we'll have a little one-on-one. You can talk dirty to me and say anything you want to. You won't even have to worry about other people hearing it, like you might on this line. Like if you want me to talk about something that's a little embarrassing. Maybe you like to talk about pee, or about sucking dick, or about fucking dogs. I'll talk about anything you want to."

"Whoa, man." One of the guys is already embarrassed.

"So you're gonna mail me your phone number. Again, you better make sure it's a number you want me to call. Now I'm going to give my address. It's a post office box, and somebody else picks up the mail there, okay, so don't think you're gonna track me down. Here's the address." She gave it. "Care of Baby. That's my name, Baby."

"What's that address again, Baby?"

She repeated it. "Now I'll repeat that once more at the end of our show. For now, back to our story."

Her lover resumed moving his prick back in and out. She grunted on his dick and told them all about how she sucked his cock, how he held her by the hair when he fucked her mouth, how soft his balls were in her hands, how she worshipped his prick, and how she loved it when he talked dirty to her. She told them she wanted them all to watch her get fucked in the mouth, because then they could be next, they could spray their come all over her face, they could choke out filthy names, they could treat her like a hole. Her own lover fucked faster and faster, and as the guys on the phone started coming and her monologue reached a climax, he came too.

Afterward they all were still, breathing heavily.

"Now, I'll give that address one more time in a minute. You all wipe off your fingers and find a pen. I'll give you thirty seconds. While some of you are looking for a pen, I'll tell you a little about myself. I'm thirty-seven, I go to the gym four times a week, and I can out-fuck any twenty-one-year-old in town. I'm dirtier and better-looking, and I know things that will make you weak in the knees. I'll be the best you ever had, even if we never meet. Now that address is coming up." She repeated it twice. "I hope you got that. Care of Baby. This is Baby, now, wishing you all a good night."

"Hey baby, tomorrow?"

She smiles. "I might come back here sometime, but I think we'll try the one-on-ones for a while. So you better send me your phone numbers if you want to hear me anytime soon. This is Baby signing off." She puts the phone down.

~

A week later, her lover comes over, and after they've been making out for a few minutes, he takes a small pile of mail out of his pack. There are ten envelopes. As they'd speculated, they contain more than just notes with phone numbers. There are photographs, stories, love poems, complete names and addresses, invitations to perform feats outside the scope of phone sex, and even an attempt at a dried flower, although the flower hasn't had much time to dry in the four days it's been in the envelope.

They kiss and he pulls her pants off and moves downward to go down on her. Licking his lips, he pushes his mouth forward to her pussy. She sighs and adjusts herself on the bed. He mouths and licks her cunt, searching for a place that will get her off, and when he finds it, he pulls a random envelope from the pile, digs through the memorabilia for the phone number, dials, and holds the phone up to her. She takes it.

A man answers. "Hello?"

"Hello, Caller Number One. This is Baby."

An intake of breath. "Hello—oh, I'm glad you called." He sounds delighted enough, she says to herself.

"You know what we're gonna do, don't you?"

"Yeah." The voice is staticky; he must be using a portable phone.

"Ohh!" she says involuntarily as her lover touches a good spot. "Oh, that feels good. Guess what I'm doing."

"You're fucking."

"No, guess again."

"You're doing yourself."

"No, you get one more guess."

"You're taking a piss."

She chuckles. "Is that what you'd like? You'd like me to take a piss for you?"

There's an embarrassed pause.

"That must be it, huh? You want me to talk about peeing. I don't hear you contradicting me. Well, unfortunately that's not what I'm doing right now, although it can be arranged. Right now I'm lying down getting my pussy eaten, and I thought I'd tell you all about it. Would you like that? Would you like to hear about me getting my pussy eaten?"

"Mmm, sure." He sounds more relaxed.

"Tell me. Tell me you want to hear about it—and don't use the word 'it.' Mmm," she added, reacting to her lover's labors.

"I want to hear all about your pussy, Baby."

"I want to tell you all about it. First tell me some more. Did you hear me on the phone last week?"

"Yeah, twice in a row."

"Ah, a fan. Did you come?"

"I sure did."

"And are you doing yourself now?"

"Mmm-hmm, I am."

"Well, tell me what you're doing. Then I'll tell you all about my pussy. I hope you think that's fair."

"Fair enough. I'm lying on the couch. My pants are down around my ankles because I didn't want to take the time to take off my shoes. I've got my cock in my hand and it's already hard."

"Mmm, tell me just a little more about it. It makes me wet to hear you talk about your dick. Mmm, I'm getting done, it feels so good."

"Gee—I don't know what to say about it. It's just a dick."

"Well, is it cut or uncut?"

"Huh?"

"Circumcised or not?" My, he *is* a straight boy.

"Oh. Circumcised. I guess you want me to tell you how big it is."

"Please, and don't feel you have to exaggerate. I'd much rather get to know you as you are, it'll just make it easier to turn you on later."

"I never measured—I guess it's about six inches. Hard, that is."

"Never measured, well, bless you. Now I'll tell you about my pussy. I have one of those cunts with big pussy lips, very external, and I've never shaved my cunt hair in my life. That's because I love to feel it brush against my lover's mouth. Now, I'm not even going to tell you who's doing me right now, could be a man or woman, I'll let you imagine."

"A man."

"Okay, if you like. And oh boy, do I ever like what he's doing. A couple nights ago I talked about getting fucked and how much I liked it—but if you noticed I didn't come. That's because I never come from getting fucked. But I do come from getting my cunt eaten, and that means you're gonna hear a real orgasm tonight. It probably ain't gonna be like some fake-out phone sex orgasm, so be prepared."

"I'd love to listen to you come, whatever you do."

"You're sweet. Ohhh. God, he's really doing me good. His tongue is licking up and down my pussy, he's getting my cunt hair all wet. I love it when it gets all wet with his spit and my pussy juice, and by the way, my pussy juice tastes great. Doesn't it?" she added, stroking her lover's head. "Oh, now he's pushing his tongue between my cunt lips. He's looking for my clit. If he starts doing my clit I don't know how long I'm going to be able to keep talking.... Oh shit...."

"Oh God, keep talking. I love your voice. Every time you say the word 'pussy' I think I'm gonna go crazy."

"Well, don't come before me, I know I'm gonna come, just wait for me.... You should always wait for her to come, you know. Oh shit, he's licking my clit now. Oh shit, that feels so good. His mouth is all over my pussy. Oh yeah, suck on me. I'm creaming his mouth."

"Oh Baby...."

"Listen. Listen to me. I'm getting so fucking turned on. I'm getting eaten and I want to get fucked. Oh please. Oh it feels so good. Oh oh oh oh...."

She loses the ability to speak, barely managing to remember to hang onto the phone. She can feel her orgasm coming down the track, although she rarely thinks about it so literally. Sex is not a metaphor to her but an experience, and she doesn't even fantasize or think about anything but what's actually happening. Her orgasm approaching is more like looking up at the night sky for a meteor, waiting for something that you expect but can never predict.

"Nnn. Nnn. Nnn...."

Her lover's tongue is quick on her clit, stroking soft but better than she can do with her hand, relentlessly moving against her, creating a perfect friction. Her muscles are tensing.

"Baby, my hand is on my prick. I can see you lying there and imagine your beautiful face.... I want to watch you so badly."

"Oh, oh, oh, oh," she whines, her moans becoming more urgent. "Oh shit. Oh fuck. Oh do me. Nnnnnnnnnnnnn—"

It thunders down upon her and her moans turn loud. She is mechanically holding the phone, having forgotten about her caller. With her other hand she pulls her lover's head hard between her legs and pushes, smothering him.

The voice on the phone is loud, too. "Oh Jesus, oh God, oh Baby, I'm doing it. Ohhhhhh fuck! Oh God!"

"Nnnnngghhhhhhh, uuuunnghhh!" Her body quakes with spasm after spasm. "Oh fuck!" And finally she relaxes.

"Oh Baby. Oh Baby," the voice trails off.

"Oh man." She collects herself, pants for a second. "Mmmm. Are you still there."

"Yeah." A little ragged.

"I hope you liked that, Caller Number One." Her lover rolls off and rests next to her.

"Am I Caller Number One?"

"Well, you're the first one I called back. And don't be too proud, because it was a random selection. But I liked listening to you. Now don't move. Tell me exactly where your come landed."

"Heh. Hmm, let's see, all over my fingers and my belly."

"I love to eat come, Number One. Whenever I do my lover, I love licking it off my fingers. Would you like to try it?"

"Mmm. Okay, why not?"

"How do you like it?"

"Hmm. I dunno."

"Well, someday you might just get used to it. Don't tell me that's the first time you ever tasted your own come?"

"Well, yeah."

"Well, let me tell you, honey. You don't have to be afraid of it. Now, after that nice big orgasm, I kind of have to pee."

"Ah."

"I bet you'd like to hear that."

"Well."

"Or at least hear me talk about it. Mmm, I feel really full. I kind of have to do it."

"Oh Baby...."

"I just have to. But I need to lie here for a second. Maybe I'll wait just a minute. How long should I wait."

"Er, well...."

"I mean for you to get hard again. So you can jack off while I piss all over your hard dick."

"Oh wow. I guess about two minutes, if you put it that way."

"Mmm, well you know how it is. When you get excited your muscles all kind of draw up tight. And they get really tight when you come. And then when you're done they relax, and among the muscles that relax are the ones that control your bladder, and suddenly you realize just how bad you have to do it. You start to feel that weight inside you and feel really full, and you know there's a big reservoir of hot, yellow piss all waiting inside, ready to stream out, and when it does it feels really good, such a relief, and for certain people, there's nothing better than to let it out all over someone's big hard dick. Because that way it feels good to them, too."

Her lover, lying next to her, is touching himself. His prick is hard and he's holding it loosely while touching one of his nipples with the other hand. Getting off on her talking about peeing. She feels like such a center of attention.

"Have you ever had someone do that? Or maybe you've just watched someone do it."

"No." His voice is more ragged than it was after he'd come.

"Tell me if your cock is hard yet."

"Gettin' there."

"Then tell me, wouldn't you like to watch me do it? Maybe we're driving in the car, and I need to pee, and we're looking for a place for me to do it, and we just can't find one. We drive and drive and the urge to do it is getting stronger and stronger. I tell you, 'I don't know if I can hold it any longer.' And you tell me you have to hold it."

"You have to hold it."

"And while we're driving and I'm telling you all about how I have to pee, I can see your cock getting hard. And I realize that the situation excites you. You like it that I need to pee and can't do it. You like it that I've got this urge that I can barely restrain. And if I hold it too long, I'll have to do it all over myself. And although I'd like for you to watch me do it, I'd much rather do it all over your hard prick.

"So you pull the car over," she continues, "and come around to my side. I get out and you sit down in my seat with your legs out the door, and I kneel down and open your pants. Your cock is already hard so I don't have to put it in my mouth to get it hard, but I do it anyway, because I love the taste of prick. And then I take my underpants off and pull up my little white dress. It almost hurts to move because I have to do it so bad."

"Oh Baby…. Oh shit…."

"And I climb on top of you while you sit there, and put my arms around your neck, and say, 'I have to do it so bad, I don't know what to do, please, I can't find any place to do it, just let me do it on your prick. I want to make your prick feel good. Please let me get your prick all hot and wet with my pee.'"

"Oh Baby—do it! Do it on my cock!"

"Oh shit—I have to do it. Almost. I'm gonna squeeze it out now...."

"Oh shit! Oh shit! Oh fuck!!"

"There, I'm peeing. I'm doing it. I'm doing it all over you. It's rolling down your cock. It's getting all over your cock and balls. Oh, your prick is getting all covered in my pee."

"Oh no no no! Oh shit, I'm coming, Baby, fuck me, God, oh shit."

"It's still coming out, so hot and yellow and smelly. I've got a lot of it. Oh, it feels good to let it come out all over you. I'm so glad you got it."

Next to her, her lover is gasping and coming, she watches him squirt, but the guy on the phone is the one she's talking to.

"Oh baby, your cock is all wet now. It's messy. I did it all over you. I'd better lick it off...."

"Oh no...."

"Mmm, honey, the taste of your piss-covered cock in my mouth is so good. Mmm, I lick up all I can.... Oh baby, let's do this again sometime."

"Jesus Christ." The guy is clearly astonished.

"Caller Number One, I hope you liked that."

"Jesus, Baby.... That was the best come I ever had in my life. Motherfucker, I can't believe I did that."

"Mmm, honey, it's just because you turn me on real good that I can do you like that. I think I'm gonna call you again."

"Oh baby. Please do."

"Don't hold your breath, though, because there are others, and I'm not the monogamous type. Anyway, you may have enough to go on for a while."

"Baby—thank you."

"It was my pleasure. This is Baby, saying she loves you. Good night."
She rolls over and licks up her lover's come.

჻

Caller Number Two, whom she talked to three days later, wanted her to pretend to be twelve years old. She said she wouldn't do twelve but she'd do fifteen, and the guy settled for that. He said he had surprised her in a video store, catching her looking through the adult section, and led her into the back room where she had to fuck him in exchange for his not calling her parents. He called her "thieving little bitch" and while building up to his orgasm kept referring to some incident in which she had stolen money from him, or cheated him out of something. Then after he came he felt like continuing to insult her, so she hung up.

Number Three seemed really young. He said he was nineteen, so she figured he was sixteen or so. He wanted to talk about her tits and pushing his cock in between them. While they were doing this fantasy, she suggested that his cock was "accidentally touching my lips" and that turned out to be what he really wanted to hear, of course.

Number Four was kind of an uptight guy who wouldn't reveal what his fantasy was. She went through a fairly straight sucking/fucking rap with him, all the while trying to get him to open up. She could barely tell when he came.

By this time, her boyfriend was getting a little tired of her always being on the phone while they fucked. He fucked her without the phone fantasy for a while; once he actually gagged her. She found that a little insulting, since he didn't do it in the context of a kidnapping fantasy or anything; he just said, "I'm tired of hearing you yapping," and stuffed part of a T-shirt in her mouth and fucked her hard from behind. It felt good, but she couldn't get his words out of her mind; even when he was done, and took the gag out, she no longer felt much like talking.

The next time they had sex, a tone of gloom pervaded the date. Nothing seemed to go right; nothing felt right. Finally he reached into a drawer and pulled out the envelopes and handed one to her, a guy she hadn't called yet (he had marked the envelopes of the previous men with numbers). But as soon as she identified herself, the guy said, "No thanks, I'm not interested. No, I have all the credit cards I need," and hung up. Bad timing there, too. Finally she went down on her boyfriend and made him come, but all the talking he'd done before, when he'd started this whole telephone thing, didn't work, and he soon shut up and just let her work. Which is what it felt like.

When he went into the bathroom, she lay on his bed and stared at the dirty white ceiling and listened to the noises coming in the window from the Tenderloin street. After a few minutes she heard the shower start, and when she could hear that he had stepped inside, she quickly gathered her things, swept the envelopes into her bag, and left.

She headed down Geary toward the bus stop. She hadn't had a chance to take a piss and now she needed to. It made her think of Caller Number One; in fact, she thought of him almost every time she took a piss now. *He* wouldn't get tired of hearing her talk. He had probably waited by the phone ever since he'd heard from her last, now a month ago.

She went into a the first big hotel she came to and found a bank of pay telephones at the end of a cavernous hallway outside an empty ballroom. It was after 11 P.M. and there was no one around. She dug through her bag and found the envelope marked "1" and dialed the number. "Hello, Caller Number One," she said. "This is Baby."

He was very glad to hear her voice.

Exploitation

The bordello was in a five-story concrete building covered by a rusting piece of gold-painted grillwork. An assortment of signs hung on the façade; written in a mixture of Japanese and English, they advertised the Nice Billiard Club, Twin Bar, and Bar Bobby (which featured a giant photo of Bobby Darin at its entrance). On top of the building, a giant animated neon sign, visible from the train station nearby, spelled out the name of a brand of sake popular with salarymen.

On the third floor rear of the building, an unmarked black-painted door led to a tiny lobby. There was a one-way mirror in which you could study your face while listening to a slow, booming sound from the karaoke system in Bar Bobby. A doorman on the other side of the glass buzzed you in, and then it was just like every bordello in the world.

The name of the establishment, at least the name on the match-books, was Diamond Land, but "bordello" fit the red velvet on the walls and the dark wood furniture in the waiting room and the flamenco guitar music on the sound system. The doorman, a heavy thug wearing a polyester gray suit, welcomed Dean curtly and turned back to a comic book he was reading. Dean turned as one of the other doors to the waiting room opened and a younger man, his hair coiffed in a '50s ducktail, came in.

"Welcome, sir, ah, you have been here before, I think," the manager said in English. He presented Dean with a business card. Dean reciprocated and they politely studied each other's cards for a moment, even though they had indeed been through the same routine a week before. He wondered how many other foreigners came to the bordello, and if the manager really recognized him.

After going through a few polite phrases and receiving the standard compliment on his rudimentary Japanese, Dean said in English, "I would like to meet a young lady."

"Of course." The manager motioned Dean to a couch.

A girl instantly appeared with a tray containing a whiskey-and-water setup. She approached Dean and served his drink nervously, as if she were not used to being near a foreigner. She was wearing a see-through blouse, not badly cut, and looked young. Dean wondered if the girls took turns being waitresses, and if the girls preferred it to having sex with the guests. He watched her straight, jet-black hair sway as she labored over the cocktail. He guessed she was Chinese, perhaps from Malaysia.

After serving him, the girl stood up swiftly, her round breasts hardly bobbing at all, and bowed backwards out of the room. The manager had disappeared and Dean was alone with the doorman. He took a sip of the drink.

Four young women entered the room, followed by a middle-aged woman. Dean resisted the urge to stand. Three of them sat down on another couch set at a right angle to Dean, the fourth in a ridiculous '60s-style armchair across from him. The mama-san remained standing. "Please," she said, smiling broadly and nodding.

The women wore varied, cheap-looking outfits. The one on the couch nearest Dean was dressed the most attractively—a simple beige skirt, a white blouse that was open only one more button than a girl would wear it on the street. She was slender and had a casual, almost defiant air; perhaps she was the only one who was Japanese. Few hookers in Japan were Japanese; like most dirty jobs, whoring was done by imported workers.

The other women, dressed in a collection of mini-dresses that resembled uniforms, all looked like Filipinas. They projected an air of desperation and eagerness. Such girls were lured to Japan by mobsters who advertised for clerical workers, then consigned them to work as whores until their air tickets had been paid off and they had turned a healthy profit.

Their anxiety depressed Dean, but he smiled at them, and said, "Hello, girls. How are you tonight?"

The Japanese woman piped up, "Fine, thank you," and the others echoed her.

"Oh, you all speak good English," Dean declared, mirroring the treatment he got when he tried to speak Japanese.

The women smiled and giggled. One blurted out, "I am majoring in English."

Dean looked at her in surprise. She was the middle one on the couch. "Are you a student?"

"Yes, in the Philippines," she said, as the others looked on jealously. She pressed her knees together and took out a religious medal hanging on a chain around her neck. "My father was American," she added.

Dean took a sip of the whiskey and glanced downward, feeling vaguely responsible for her plight. It seemed one thing to go to a bordello where he knew the women were exploited in the crudest ways; it seemed too much, though, to carry on the exploitation to the second generation, even though he recognized that if he really had any moral pretensions he wouldn't be here at all. Or maybe people with moral pretensions were precisely the ones who went to bordellos.

He didn't want to sit there and consume his drink, for fear the waitress would appear and freshen it, and he would be charged even more. He set his glass down and extended his hand to the self-possessed, Japanese-looking girl. She stood up with an air of victory. The mama-san led the two of them to another doorway, not the one the women had entered from. He automatically paused at the door for the girl and the mama-san to go first, and they automatically waited for him. Dean looked back and saw the English major swallow heavily; then he went through.

There was a sort of cashier's window, smoked so neither Dean nor the person on the other side could identify each other as they conducted their transaction. Fingertips pushed out a piece of paper with an amount written on it, and Dean pushed the money, equal to three days' pay, into the little trough, where it disappeared. This money was just for the house; he would pay his companion separately, and the house, he supposed, would get most of that, too. They turned down a dimly lit hallway, leaving the mama-san behind.

The woman led him past doors through which Japanese pop music could be heard. Pairs of shoes were lined up outside some of them. They stopped at a door that opened without a key, and the woman said softly, "Please…remove your shoes." He kicked them off. As Dean went inside, she slipped off her high heels, then crouched, lined up their shoes, and entered.

The room, lit only by a tiny, bedside lamp, looked like a small motel room, with a large bed that filled most of the space. There was a table on either side of the bed, and one straight-backed chair. The room smelled of cleaning products.

The woman locked the door and bolted it and walked past Dean to stand by the bed. Turning and facing him, she said in English, "Please. Make yourself at home."

Dean chuckled. "Are you an English student, too?"

"I study English in school."

"Now? You're in school now?"

"No, high school," she said, confirming his suspicion that she'd used the present tense accidentally. She was surely older than high school age.

"I teach English," he said, "in the U.S. Star school, across from the station. Right next to that little park."

"Mm, I know it. I ask them once. Expensive."

"What's your name?"

"Cam Tranh. And yours?"

"Dean Burnett."

"How do you do?" she said automatically.

Dean sighed. She was being polite. Since coming to Japan six weeks before, he kept getting stuck in currents of politeness that swept him through situations before anybody had really said anything. "Listen, Cam—is that right?"

"Please call me Camille."

"Okay, listen, Camille," he smiled, sitting on the bed and removing his socks. "Please don't be polite with me."

"No?" she asked dubiously.

Dean pointed vaguely in the general direction of the street. "Outside," he said, "everyone is polite. Very good manners."

"Yes."

"In here," he said, laying his hand on the bed, "not polite. Very bad manners." He smiled up at her.

"Yes," she nodded, then said delicately, "you may abuse me."

He almost laughed out loud in surprise, but at the same time, the words shot to his crotch. He took a deep breath. "Take your clothes off," he ordered, a tremor in his voice.

She unbuttoned her blouse in a studied way, slowly but not too slowly, looking at him flirtatiously. Her tongue licked her lips, and she began rocking her hips to an inaudible beat. He stifled a feeling of annoyance, not wanting her standard routine.

"Say that again," he ordered.

"Eh?" she asked, looking up.

"Tell me again to abuse you."

She paused quizzically, then said, "Abuse me."

"Do you know how to use that kind of English, Camille?" he asked intently.

"Yes, a little," she said, removing the blouse and hanging it on the straight-backed chair. Her bra was white and lacy, as he expected it would be. She reached behind her back to remove it.

"Go on," Dean urged.

"Fuck me," she essayed, removing the bra. Her breasts popped free.

"Yes?"

She shrugged. "That is all." She reached behind her to unbutton her skirt.

He leaned back on his elbows to allow his hard-on a little more space. It was pretty hard. "Repeat after me," Dean said. "'Fuck my cunt.'"

"Fuck my cunt. Cunt is here?" she asked, motioning.

"Yes, that's your cunt. Say it again."

"Fuck my cunt," she said conscientiously. "Fuck me, fuck my cunt."

"'Fuck my dirty cunt.'"

She frowned, standing before him in panties and stockings. "This cunt is not dirty, it's clean."

"Yes, of course, but we call it dirty," Dean laughed.

She arched her eyebrows, and said grudgingly, "Fuck my dirty cunt." She reached to remove her stockings.

"No, leave them. Just the panties."

She slid the panties slowly past her delta of hair and then raised one leg up and out in an odd, birdlike way. She slipped the panties off the other leg, then stood passively, her hands at her sides. She waited a moment, then said uncertainly, "Fuck my mouth?"

Dean applauded, and she smiled shyly.

"Fuck my dirty mouth," she said ingenuously. It made him laugh. She walked toward him tentatively. Still fully clothed, he reached out for her and buried his face in her cunt hair. She seemed surprised, but let him, stroking his hair gently.

Then she bent down and kissed him and began unbuttoning his shirt. He let her undress him, feeling dizzy with arousal. The first time at the bordello, he had selected a woman who was perhaps from Singapore, whose breath smelled of cigarettes and whose repertoire was limited to thrusting back up at him so hard he was almost thrown off. She had gamely learned the filthy words that Dean taught her, but spoke them in such a mechanical way that they lost all meaning. Dean had returned to the bordello to try to erase that experience; he had been very glad, this time, that she had not been one of the choices.

Camille unzipped his trousers and pulled them off, leaving him wearing shorts, an obvious hard-on standing under the fabric. She removed his socks and then knelt in front of the bed as he sat up. She ran her hands over his thighs, seemingly intrigued by the amount of hair on his body.

"Camille, I would like you to talk while we have sex."

"Okay."

"The words I just told you."

"Yes, okay. Fuck my cunt, my mouth." She looked into his face as she spoke. "Do you want to fuck?"

"Yes, and I want to do other things. Can I do anything I want?"

"Please ask now," she said calmly. "Even if we supposed to have bad manners."

He touched her face. "Your English is better than I thought, isn't it?"

"What do you think?"

"I think it's pretty good."

"Thank you. My father was American. Like you." She smiled sardonically. "He married to my mother in Republic of South Vietnam."

"Oh…." Dean looked away. He had a momentary vision of a round-robin of hearty American men ringing Southeast Asia, firing sperm and bullets carelessly—then wiped it from his mind. "Did he take her out of the country?"

"Yes, to Philippines."

"And now?"

She shook her head slightly as if to dismiss the subject. They were silent for a moment, then got on the bed. He knelt next to her and watched her part her legs and cunt hair in a manner that seemed both businesslike and bawdy. She had a long, slender body and sallow skin that seemed different from most Japanese. He stared as she fluffed her cunt hair and parted her labia. "What do you want to do?" she asked, her head turned toward him.

"Watch you," he said.

"You can watch me. What else?"

"I want to touch you and put my fingers in you. From behind."

"Yes," she nodded.

"When I put my fingers in you, start talking—I'll teach you some more things to say. Then we'll fuck."

He taught her more words that aroused him, watching her lips as she spoke. Her mouth, alternately erotic and cold, fascinated him. He tried to forget how artificial the situation was, tried to pretend it was just another English class and he was giving a lesson in specialized vocabulary. An absurd thought came to mind of actually coming to the bordello to teach English once a week, the same way he visited various companies, banks, and factories and taught English to their employees.

The lesson over, she closed her eyes and began stroking her body with one hand and his cock, which had softened somewhat, with the other. She pinched her nipple and arched her back, her eyes still closed. He wondered what was going through her mind, what thoughts she used to arouse herself.

She opened her eyes. "You must pay me."

He started. "Of course."

She continued to play with her breasts. "Please pay me now."

He went over to his jacket and opened his wallet. "How much?" he asked.

"How much do you have?"

He looked. "Twenty thousand yen."

She nodded. "That's all right, but no fuck."

"How about thirty thousand?"

"You have it?"

"Yes."

She sighed. "For forty thousand, you can do everything. You can fuck my mouth."

He looked at her. "Tell me."

She caught his cue. "You can touch me every place. You can fuck me. You can fuck my dirty mouth. You can do it in my dirty asshole. I'm your whore. Fuck your dirty whore, please fuck me."

He was hard again.

"Please put the money on the table."

It was three weeks before Dean had enough cash to return to the bordello again.

Inside, the young Chinese girl who had served him his drink during his previous visit had joined the Filipino girls on the couch, but Camille was not present. "Excuse me," he said to the girl who was the English major. "The girl I went with before? Her name is Camille? Is she here?"

The girl glanced at the mama-san and turned back with a big nervous smile. "Not here," she said simply.

Dean stared at her, then extended his hand. "I'll take you," he said. As they disappeared into the doorway leading to the rooms, he heard one of rejected girls mutter something about how they'd better learn English if they wanted to go with a gaijin.

Dean followed the girl to one of the rooms and sat down on the bed. The girl stood before him and started stripping. He caught one of her hands gently. "What's your name?"

"Wanda," she said, startled.

"Wanda, I want to find Camille."

"I'm sorry?" the girl said.

"Camille—Cam Tranh. The woman from Vietnam. The one I took when I came here a few weeks ago."

"Please, I am not understanding," she said. "Please speak more slowly."

He took out forty thousand yen and put it on the table; her eyes widened.

"Too much. Too much for here."

"Too much? That's what I paid last time—never mind, just tell me about Camille. She still works here, doesn't she?"

"Please speak more slowly," she said, embarrassed for him.

"Look. Do you remember me? I was here three weeks ago."

"Yes, I remember."

"I took another woman. Do you remember her?"

"Yes, I remember."

"Where is she?"

Wanda looked off to the side. Her eyes focused for a moment on the wall of the room next door, then back to Dean.

He slowly understood. "She's busy? Is that it? She's with another client?"

She approached him with her blouse unbuttoned. "Please take me," she said, putting her arms around him as he sat on the bed.

"No," he said.

"Please," she repeated. "Or boss is angry with me. I must please you."

He guiltily removed his clothes.

The next day, Dean was walking past the park next to his office when he saw Camille sitting on a bench. She stood up and came over to him, smiling.

"I'm so glad to see you," Dean said, dumbfounded.

"You were there last night," she said. She motioned for them to start walking. It was a warm, sunny day in mid-spring; the cherry blossoms were beginning to bloom.

"Yes, I wanted to see you. The girl—Wanda—did she tell you I was looking for you?"

"No, another girl told me. She remember you. Did you like Wanda?"

"Oh—fine. I wasn't really into it."

She snorted. "Why not? She's cute."

"I guess I only wanted to see you."

"Nn," Camille grunted.

Dean was learning to understand the various levels of grunts in Japanese, and this was the most noncommittal. "Have you been well?" he asked.

She snorted again. "Jean-san," she said mockingly, "'please don't be polite with me.'"

He flushed.

"Are you occupied today?" she asked. She reached out her hand and brushed her fingertips along his upper arm.

"No, it's Sunday. I'm off."

"Off to where?"

"Off work. The school is closed."

"Mm. I must work at six. Meanwhile I am free."

"Well, would you like to get a cup of coffee?"

Camille glanced at him archly. "Of course," she said. Dean suddenly guessed she had been expecting him to propose something more intimate, but it was only a guess. Anyway, now he was committed to having coffee.

He led her into a dark coffee shop. As in the bordello, there was flamenco guitar music playing; it was a fad. The proprietor waited on them, glancing curiously at Dean and even more curiously at Camille. Their silence continued until the proprietor brought their order. Camille turned her head to watch him go.

She looked candidly at Dean. "He knows."

"What?"

"He knows I am a whore."

"Really? You mean, he can guess?"

She shrugged, lifting her glass to her lips. "First ice-coffee of summer," she said, sipping the sugary drink.

Dean sat back, grateful for the air conditioning. "It's nice to see you," he said. "Really. In fact, I'm glad we're seeing each other here instead of at the bordello."

"At what?"

"At Diamond Land."

"Mm," she nodded briefly.

"This way we can talk," he explained.

She regarded him patiently. "Is that what you want?" she asked. "You want to talk with me?"

"Of course I do."

"Perhaps you want to sell me an English lesson," she said sarcastically.

"No, I want to get to know you," he protested.

"That's nice."

Some housewives came into the café and looked around for a place to sit. When they spotted Dean and Camille, they whispered to each other, then chose a table as far away as possible.

"Do you ever meet men outside the club?" Dean asked.

"You mean like this? No, they would not like to be with me," she said, sweeping her hair back. "I am a gaijin, a foreigner. It is clear I am a whore."

"No, it isn't. You look like a regular person," Dean protested.

"To Japanese it is clear. A foreign girl, dressed like a foreigner, sitting with Japanese man, must be a whore. Anyway, they would not be seen with gaijin. Maybe if she is American, but not with a whore."

Dean smiled. "I am glad to be seen with you."

"Thank you," she said, looking at the table of housewives.

"I would like to see you some more."

"At Diamond Land?"

"Outside Diamond Land, actually," he said.

"At Diamond Land is simple," she said evenly.

"But expensive for me," he said, smiling more broadly.

"Not so expensive," she said, as if she didn't care whether he came. "But I understand. You want me as your girlfriend."

He felt embarrassed, afraid she would think he was trying to get in her pants for free. "Well…. What I'd really like— I mean—"

She looked at him directly, waiting for him to explain. The guitar music was replaced by Japanese pop.

He ran his hand through his hair. "Camille…the other night… I liked being with you." He paused. "I would like to be with you again."

"Mm," she said. "Why don't you want me as your girlfriend?"

He smiled nervously. "Is that what you want, to be my girlfriend?"

She shrugged, poking at her empty glass with her finger.

"It could be nice, actually," Dean said, more decisively. "We could see each other all the time. We would go out to eat and you would come home and sleep with me. We could go to the mountains together on vacation."

She nodded patiently.

He looked into her eyes boldly. "But in bed, you'll have to do anything I want. You'll have to fuck me any time I want and any way I want. You'll have to say anything I want you to say. In fact, you won't be my girlfriend in bed; you'll be my whore."

"*Évidemment,*" she said.

He reached across and touched her hand.

Her fingers were cold from the glass. Looking into his eyes, she brought his hand forward to her mouth and licked his palm. Then she gave him back his hand, glancing disdainfully at the table of housewives.

His blood pounded. "Let's go somewhere now."

"Yes," she said.

They paid their bill and went out through the heavy wooden door into the street, where the warm air washed up around them in waves. She led him a few blocks through the bar district and down a side street lined with garages and vacant lots. They came to an incongruous, three-story building decorated on the outside like a French Quarter house and called the Cajun Hotel. *At least it won't have flamenco guitar playing,* Dean thought.

He paid through a chink in a smoked-glass window. Their room closely resembled the one in the bordello, and Dean wondered if her boss owned this place, too. It was decorated in pastel colors. The hues suffered from artificial lighting; shutters hanging on the wall gave the illusion of windows, but in fact there were none. The room felt enclosed, safe, private.

Camille went over to a small refrigerator, inserted money, and took out two orange drinks for them. She served one in a glass for him and sank into a chair, picking her long hair off her neck and pressing the cold, wet bottle there. She sighed and looked up at him, smiling slightly. "It's nice here. Dark and cool."

He had broken into a sweat during their five-minute walk; now he felt the chill on his damp skin where his shirt clung to him. He removed his clothing; she watched, amused. When he was naked except for his underpants, he stood before her with one hand on his hip.

She swept her hair over her shoulders again with a toss of her head and leaned back in the chair, dropping her unopened soda bottle on the floor. She unbuttoned her blouse; he trembled to see she wore no bra. She saw him staring and said, "See, it is clear I am a whore." She stood up briefly, leaving the shirt hanging open, and removed her blue jeans; she wore no underpants.

She sat down again as he approached her. She glanced up at him briefly, then violently stripped off his underpants, took his cock deep in her mouth, and hugged him close to her. He gathered her hair off her neck as she sucked him, and held on, sometimes pulling her head up or back to control her movements.

After a few minutes, he came. She took his come in her mouth, then sank back, spitting it into a hankie. Both of them were sweating again. He wanted to embrace her but she was sitting too far back, so he knelt and laid his head in her lap. She ran her fingers through his hair gently.

After a minute he stood up and led her to the bed, then knelt in front of her again. Parting her legs, he pressed forward with his mouth, nuzzling her cunt hair. Her hands on his head lay still, more disbelieving than unwilling. He started licking and kissing her cunt lips. She began to respond, moving her hips in slow, vague curves, but after a minute she raised herself on her elbow, fingers pressed against his collarbone to gently fend him off. "Let's fuck."

"Okay," Dean said. "Do you want to?"

"Mm," she said positively.

"Do you really want to? Isn't it too much like work?"

She sighed. "I thought you like to fuck me."

"I do, I just thought…. Well, this is your time off, right? So why work when you're off?"

She laughed sarcastically. "Ha. I'm off. Yes."

He touched her belly, soft and flat. "If you're going to be my girlfriend, it means I give you pleasure, too."

"That's nice," she said skeptically. She lay back on her elbows, shaking her hair off her shoulders.

"In America, women expect men to please them. If I didn't give you pleasure, you'd think I was a bad lover."

"Well, we are not in America."

"Come on. What makes you feel good?"

"Mm," she said. "You want to know?"

"Yeah, I want to know. What gives you pleasure? Tell me."

She was silent for a minute. "I don't feel so much pleasure. I am acting sometimes. I make noise. Some like it so." She poked his thigh with her finger. "You like it."

"Yes, but I like it better when you are not acting."

"If I am not acting, you will not like it."

"Hmm. Maybe so." He suddenly reached down and pulled her legs around so she faced him. "I'm going to go down on you. Because it gives me pleasure. Act all you want."

He lowered his mouth to her cunt and began kissing her gently. Her hands came up and gently held his head, sometimes ranging into his hair to stroke or pull it. She seemed to be wet, at least. After a few minutes, he backed away a little, brought his hand up, and firmly pushed two fingers into her. That made her shudder and groan a little, and he thought it was a genuine reaction, but couldn't be sure.

"Are you acting?" he asked.

She merely grunted.

He took his fingers out and pushed three into her. She drew her breath in sharply. "Still acting?"

She exhaled. "It was surprising."

"Okay, here's a rule. You can't make any noise, okay? Not even real noise. I'm going to fuck you with my hand and you're going to take it. Don't make a sound."

He began pushing and pulling his hand in and out of her. She shut her eyes and started moving with his thrusts. She began playing with her nipples, and after a moment opened her eyes and turned her head to look at him. "Shhh," he grinned.

Her mouth opened, she shut her eyes for a moment, then opened them again, scanning the ceiling blindly. Her cunt tightened on his hand, then loosened, and after another minute he pulled out his hand and pursed all four fingers together and thrust them inside her.

"Ahhh!" she yelled.

"Quiet," he said.

She dropped her hands from her breasts and lay passive on the bed, his hand pushing up inside her. Her wetness made her flesh feel like velvet. Finally she began moving her hips again, and she reached down and touched him, asking him to move more slowly, too. He did, trying to follow her pleasure. Her breathing deepened as his hand pushed into her, and her head began lolling from side to side.

She suddenly reached down and held his hand still in a tight grip, pushing her pelvis forward against him. She held him tightly there, not moving for more than a minute. She took several tight breaths, and he thought he heard a strangled sound in her throat. Finally she released his hand and fell back, rolling away from him.

He let her lie there for a little while, then bent down and swept away the hair around her ear. "Hey," he said, kissing her shoulder. "What happened?"

She was silent, her body heavy. She reached up to touch his hand on her shoulder.

"Are you okay?" he asked.

She sighed and didn't answer.

"Was that okay? Did it feel good? Did it hurt? Did you come?"

Silence, then she licked her lips. "It was better," she murmured, "for a while. Then too much." She sat up.

"Does that mean you came?"

She put her hand to her forehead. "Excuse me," she said, getting up and going into the bathroom. She shut the door and Dean heard water running. He sat on the bed uncertainly, the air conditioning chill on his skin.

She came out of the bathroom and sat next to him. "Please fuck me if you wish," she said. "I must be going soon."

He sighed. "Okay. Lie down."

Penetrating her had excited him, but now he had grown soft again. She sucked him for a minute, then lay down and pressed him against her cunt, whispering the words she knew made him hard. Soon he was inside her. She began moving and urging him on, dragging her nails gently across his thighs and touching his nipples. He knew she was just doing it to get him to come, but it worked.

After lying beside him for a few moments, she went into the bathroom again and he got dressed. When she came out, he was just putting on his shirt. She walked up to him and kissed him deeply. He kissed her back, surprised and pleased. Her tongue pushed aggressively inside his mouth, more intimately than fucking. He felt his cock stir again and thought, *She is wonderful. She makes me feel good. I love this.*

The kiss broke and she glanced down for a moment, then into his face. "Are you going to pay me?" she asked, holding him around the waist.

He looked into her eyes, searching for the intimacy he had just felt in her kiss. "Yes," he said finally.

"Good," she said, genuinely relieved. "Thank you."

"That's what really gives you pleasure, isn't it?" he asked, suddenly angry.

"Eh?"

"Money."

"It's not money that gives me pleasure." She went over to her clothes.

"You seem to mention it at crucial moments," he said pointedly.

"Many of Diamond Land's girls live in boss's apartment building," she explained. "I don't like to. I live in my apartment. It's small and dark but I pay and I have a little freedom. That gives me pleasure."

"Camille, why don't you come live with me?" he blurted.

She smiled wryly. "Then I am really your girlfriend, yes?"

"Yeah, I guess so," Dean said, then realized he still sounded indecisive. "Yes," he said emphatically. "You'd be my girlfriend. You'd sleep with me and we'd go places together. You'd meet my friends. I'd be proud of you."

"Or maybe I am your wife, too, aren't I?" She buttoned her blouse with brusque motions, looking off into space.

"If you like," he said defiantly.

"'If I like' doesn't matter," she retorted. "I still must continue in Diamond Land."

"Well," he said tentatively, "I guess you want the money."

"Yes," she said, "I need money."

"How much do you make at Diamond Land?" he asked.

"It is not how much I make," she said. "It is how much I must pay to boss. I owe him."

"Why do you owe him?" Dean asked.

"He is..." she said in a low voice, then extended a crooked little finger. He had never seen this gesture before but guessed it signified a *yakuza*. The gangsters supposedly had their little fingers cut off as punishment for misdeeds.

Dean nodded. "How much a week?"

Her eyes wandered across the ceiling. "About thirty man yen." Three hundred thousand yen.

He stared at her; the amount was more than two thousand dollars. "Camille, I make thirty man yen in a month."

She looked back at him, expressionless.

"Are you saying I would have to pay your boss thirty man yen a week?"

"I am not saying this. I am saying I must work or have money." She was annoyed. "So I will continue as a whore," she concluded.

"I see—look, I'm sorry."

She picked up her shoes and came to sit next to him. "Jean-san," she said, "I am sorry, not you."

He kissed her again. She responded somewhat less enthusiastically than before. In a moment she broke away and said, "I surely must go."

She put on her shoes.

"Come live with me anyway," he said suddenly.

"I don't know," she said tightly. "Probably it is not allowed."

"Not allowed by whom?"

"By boss."

"What does he care? How does he know?"

"He will know." She stood up.

He shrugged helplessly, searching for something to say. "Well, can you at least meet me again next week?" he asked.

"Mmm," she said ambiguously, looking at him for the first time in several minutes. She plunged her hands into her jacket pockets. They stared at each other for a moment, then he took out his wallet and gave her twenty thousand. She took it with a quiet "Thank you."

It was after five, and the late afternoon sun burned bright orange through the smog. At the end of the side street lay the main boulevard that led to the train station. Taxis and buses swept past, and crowds of shoppers were heading toward the train.

She shook his hand neutrally as if they were business acquaintances. "Thank you for meeting me. It's nice to be your girlfriend."

Daddy's Play Party

"Are you sure this is the right address?" asks Spike. The chain that leads from her nose piercing to her nipple sways wildly as she brakes her '71 Plymouth Road Runner to a stop in front of the Metropolitan Community Church.

I reach for my bag before I remember it isn't there. My purple bag, in which for years I'd carried everything I needed, I'd left at home.

I'd tried to convince Spike that I had to have something in which to carry the lube, condoms, gloves, and dildo I thought I needed, but she'd just growled, "They'll have all that stuff—except the cock, and if you need to penetrate someone, just use your own. Gawd, I can't believe I have to tell a man to use his own dick."

Instead of the bag, I'm loaded down with an unfamiliar leather jacket from one of Spike's pals, a dyke whose figure is as boyish as mine—5'6", and 130 pounds. I begin searching the various pockets of the jacket for the address, unzipping them and digging around. I've brought a lot of supplies anyway; a girl can't be too sure.

I mean, a man. I have to have the right attitude. Until a month ago I was a nellie faggot; I carried a purple bag, I wore matching earrings, I swished like a broom, I called myself Celestia.

Then I lost a bet. I had told Spike if she stayed sober two years, I'd turn butch. Today is my coming out.

I wear a leather jacket and chaps (bought for this occasion, only $180, practically a steal) and a leather motorcycle cap; I've invested four scratchy weeks raising a mustache; I've been taking butch lessons from Spike, the toughest dyke in town; and my new name is…Burt.

It sounds like *burp*, I know. But it's butcher—I mean, more butch—than Leonard.

Four pockets full of condoms, handi-wipes, and little lube tubes later, I pull out the flier. It's decorated with Pooh bears, which I guess is supposed to symbolize the "bear" community—macho daddies with beards and beer guts. This tongue-in-cheek use of the teddy bear as a symbol of sexiness and power has always struck me as ridiculous. Shouldn't they pick something a little scarier? Like a rattlesnake, maybe, or the tarantula that Spike has tattooed on her bicep. In big letters the flier says, DADDY'S PLAY PARTY. And beneath that, BRING YOUR BOY FOR FUN AND GAMES!

"The address is right," I say.

Spike leans down across the gear shift and looks out my window. "Hmm, guess so. Must be some weird shit at the M.C.C. these days." While she's over on my side, she sniffs me. "I smell something—are you wearing baby powder? I can't believe this!"

"Well, how's a gir— I mean, how's a man supposed to stay cool and dry?"

"You're not supposed to be cool and dry. You're supposed to be a hot, sweaty, hairy, big hunk o' man who's got massive balls of sperm. You're supposed to smell like a hard-drivin' trucker who's been up all night and has a piss hard-on he needs to get rid of. Real men don't care about being cool and dry. They don't use deodorant, they use attitude, and if people don't like your natural male animal smell, you tell 'em where to go!" Her platinum spikes, the silver chain, the rings in her eyebrows, all quiver in indignation.

"Oh," I reply.

"And stop blushing," she groans. "Look, smear something on you when you get in there. Some lube or Crisco or whatever. Just don't go in smelling like a rose. God, in the old days you could count on there being enough dope smoke so nobody would notice, but everybody's cleaned up."

"Like you," I smiled.

"Yeah, well…somethin' had to give."

"Spike, I really wish you could go in there with me."

"Don't whine—*Burt,*" she adds grudgingly. "You've been to plenty of sex parties."

"The Faerie Queen Temple Whore Sacred Pleasure Space is not the same thing as Daddy's Play Party," I point out.

"Yeah, tell me about it," she guffaws.

"You've been to things like this," I plead. "You're so tough that fags let you into their parties. You're one of the guys. Come on."

"Don't wheedle—Burt," she commands. "Stop complaining. Get an attitude. Now!" she barks, and I jump a little.

"Well, I'm sweating now," I say quietly.

"Good, maybe it'll overwhelm some of that flowery shit."

"Perhaps this is a good time for some affirmations," I suggest.

"Oh, all right," she says wearily. "If they help you." She gives the throbbing motor some gas, causing it to go *vroom!*

"I'm a man!" I exclaim.

She hits the accelerator again, *vroom!*

"I'm a masculine hunk o' guy!" My voice gets lower.

Vroom!

"I eat steak for breakfast, fried chicken for lunch, and ribs for dinner!"

Vroom!

"I'm loud, noisy, gross, sweaty, violent! I can drink my weight! I meet, compete, and vanquish!"

Vroom, vroom, vroom!

"Outta my way, wimps! I'm a world o' hurt! A fightin', stinkin', manly man! Here comes trouble! Here comes *Burt!*" The engine roars to jetliner decibels, then trails off in a series of sputters and pops.

"Excellent," Spike says, as enthusiastically as she can. "Now, go get 'em, mister!"

I open the door, step out, and slam it as hard as I can. Then I realize I'm still clutching the flier. "Oh, here," I say, reaching down to hand it to her. "Take this."

"Burt!" she scolds. "What would a tough guy do?"

I hesitate for a minute, then crumple up the paper and throw it on the ground.

"Attaway!" Spike exclaims. "And don't forget: There's no such thing as *too tough*." She pops the clutch and burns rubber in one place, the car heaving and bucking like a wild bronco. "Aaaaughh!" she screams, peeling out and disappearing around the corner. As the roar dies away and my hearing returns, I can hear that Spike has set off every car alarm on the block.

I take a deep breath and turn on the heel of my spit-shined motorcycle boot, almost colliding with a yuppie dad pushing twins in a baby carriage. "Rrrrghhhf!" I growl, pushing past him.

"Well, excuse me!" he huffs.

I heave open the door of the church and find myself in a lobby. There's a man in a T-shirt that says DADDY. He doesn't look so tough, but you know, the really tough ones don't have to.

"Are you here for the party?" he asks me.

"Right," I say sarcastically.

"In there," he says, pointing to a door. "But where's your boy?"

"Didn't bring my 'boy' today," I say gruffly, "but if he's good, the little fucker can come next time."

The man opens his mouth and closes it, unable to respond. Hmph, I guess he wasn't so tough after all.

From inside the room I hear high-pitched shouting. Sounds like somebody's having a good time in there. Sweat is rolling off me like butter off a roll, and my leather creaks as I stride over to the door of the play party and rip it open.

Inside there are about two dozen men playing. They're surrounded by blocks, board games, stuffed animals, and two dozen small boys orbiting the space like Indy racers, ignoring their daddies, screaming and vrooming, imitating the roar of Spike's car.

As the door shuts behind me, they all look up, all the boys and daddies, and they all stop and stare at me in my black leather outfit as if I'm Darth Vader.

There is dead silence for a moment, and then one of the kids asks, "Hey, mister. Was that your car?"

I shift, and the leather creaks. "Yeah," I growl. "That was my car."

All the kids run over to me and bounce up and down frantically, screaming, "Gimme a ride! Gimme a ride! Please please please please please!"

I am a big hit at Daddy's Play Party.

Sunset

I met Lee at the birthday party of an old boyfriend. His house, an ugly squat thing where he's lived for thirteen years, is out toward the ocean, in the Sunset District. To get there I take the N streetcar, which instantly feels so nostalgic I want to run screaming out of the car, but I don't, I can handle this, it's just a birthday party. The streetcar is modern and electronic now; it whines and hisses around the bend at the end of the Sunset Tunnel and past the huge parking garage at the university medical center. We fucked once in that garage in his car in the middle of the afternoon, the gloomy parking shadows hiding us from the passersby as I rested my head on my arms on the back shelf. He entered me while balancing on either side of the gearshift of the V.W. bug. It turned out to be worth it—although I got a terrific cramp in my thigh—because that was the last time we had unprotected sex. Right after that I got involved with a woman and we had unprotected sex and Tommy got mad and wouldn't do it with me for three days. Then he became enormously mature all of a sudden and announced that from now on we were only going to have safe sex, if I was going to be such a bastard and fuck that fish whose cunt has been God-knows-where.

Safe sex was not what Tommy and I had come together to do, however, and that affair lasted only another nineteen months before we finally decided it just wasn't worth it. That was six years ago and I'm still going to his annual birthday party. I'm a loyal boyfriend, but Tommy inspires loyalty, or maybe he just needs help.

On the walk from the streetcar line to Tommy's house I look up at the clouds, which for once are not the fearsome roaring fog that usually wipes across this neighborhood like a freezing sponge, but high fluffy thunderheads full of rain, pink from the sunset, dark on the land sides, and peaceful. While I'm walking down the street admiring the sky and considering walking around the block or maybe all the way to the beach so I won't have to go into the party, a car roars by me. It's Tommy's current lover, a baritone in the symphony chorus. His name is Edward and Tommy insists on calling him Ed, Eddie, Edie, Ward, anything but his given name. Edward's been running an errand in his little orange B.M.W. The party has probably run out of garlic chicken wings, Tommy's favorite food: He actually has a running tab at a restaurant on Irving. They make them by the dozen, just for him.

I walk up in front of the house in time to see Edward mounting the stairs with the drooling paper bag; the door opens and "Bali Hai" drifts out into the quiet naked street. There aren't any trees in the Sunset District; it all used to be sand dunes. The lack of trees and the sameness of the little houses make the district look like a boring suburb. I don't know how I stood it.

Inside I kiss Tommy and hand him his present, shake Edward's hand as he takes my coat, and go to the kitchen to mix myself a drink. A woman is using the vodka and I wait, smiling patiently. She looks at me and says, "Let me," sloshing an extra-large amount into my glass. "Oops, well, that ought to get you started."

She's blond and brown-eyed, her hair almost straight to her shoulders. "You're the architect, aren't you?" she asks. I nod.

"There's a real problem with this kitchen," she goes on. "The light's not doing any good. It comes in the window and just sits there. It doesn't help a thing."

I look at the window, wondering whether she actually thinks I'm the architect of this house, which is at least as old as I am, and wondering whether it would be less trouble to straighten out the confusion or more fun not to. She's gesturing wildly with her drink, pivoting around the kitchen because you can't take more than one step in any direction, and enumerating the faults of the design. Well, she's right. I watch her go on, entertained, sipping my drink, trying to taste the void in the taste made by the enormous shot of vodka, and wondering whose she is.

"I can't stand it anymore!" she finally cries, and takes me by the arm and leads me to the living room. This is a small vault with an arched ceiling, just right for a picture-window burial. There are three guys propped up on the couch, apparently Tommy's coworkers at the med center, regarding each other with something like fear and talking about drug "cocktails."

The woman sits on the arm of an empty chair, a sort of green one with padding of thick dead felt, and pulls me down into the seat. "I'm working on a movie about light," she announces. "Look at this window. You can see the house across the street, isn't that charming?

If they had their drapes open they could see us. It's a real community, you know what I mean?"

I'm starting to like this woman more all the time. "My name's George," I say, offering my hand. "Lee," she says shortly, taking my hand and kissing me hard on the mouth.

Tommy comes bombing into the room, followed closely by Edward and six other guests from God-knows-where. "Everybody!" he shouts. "You must hear this. George here has gotten me a marvelous present, that great collection of crypto-homosexual love songs on CD. We're all going to listen to it right now." He gestures to Edward, who stops "You've Got to Be Taught" in the middle—if that song has a middle—and puts on my present. "The Man I Love" fills the air.

Tommy wants to dance but he can't get to me as long as Lee is perched between us on the arm of the chair, so he says, "My dear" and picks her up and dances with her for a few moments. She's still carrying her drink and spills it on Tommy's shoe deliberately. Shooting her an evil glance he lets her go, albeit gracefully, and lifts me up and into his arms. We dance together, my face burning, because "The Man I Love" used to be on an album that we used to listen to all the time when I lived here with Tommy, and we would dance, not just to this song, but to the whole album, right here in the living room, but with the drapes closed. I'm embarrassed not only because he's forcing me to dance and we obviously dance well together, but because he saw Lee kiss me, because I liked it, because she's watching now with the rest of them, but especially because I got this sappy present for Tommy without thinking he'd involve me in a performance like this and I should have gotten him some binoculars or something.

The song ends after a few years and we all laugh and I say, "Happy birthday" and kiss Tommy again. He's been smoking dope, and I wonder if he's still growing it in the back yard behind the pampas grass in the special soil we laid down there among the sand, joking that's where we'd bury each other's boyfriends, before the time when dead boyfriends became very unfunny. Through some miracle the dope we grew there was pretty good, despite the foggy weather, the sand, the raccoons, and our paranoia that made us harvest it too soon. After Tommy became so mature, he mowed it down but I later heard he was growing it again.

Now another song starts and I make eye contact with Edward; he gets the hint and cuts in. I watch them for what I judge is long enough, and then go into the kitchen.

Edward has laid out the garlic chicken wings in a delicate pattern, which Lee is determinedly destroying. I pick one up and eat it and say, "Well."

"So you're an old boyfriend," she says.

"I'm *the* old boyfriend," I correct her. "We danced to our song, we're now eating our food, we're standing at our kitchen table. Gives me the creeps."

She yawns and picks up another piece of chicken. I take it out of her hands and eat it, looking into her eyes. She grows quiet. "You're the only new thing here," I say.

"If you could just give me your mouth again," she says. We look at each other, my nerves thrilling, and I hear Edward's weird deep voice singing along with "Can't Help Lovin' That Man of Mine." I take Lee to the hallway, guiding her along with a touch on the arm, and right before we reach the empty main bedroom I veer instead into the small spare bedroom, the one where all the coats are piled, and bring her inside and shut the door not quite all the way.

We bring our mouths together and both draw in our breath sharply. I put one hand behind her neck and, realizing she's a little taller than I am, draw her head down to mine, with a delicious feeling of being surrounded. I remember I've never had sex with Tommy (or anyone else) in this room and feel a guilty stab of excitement. She puts an arm around my neck and holds me. I've still got her other wrist in my hand, so I squeeze it tight until it hurts and she breaks off the kiss with a gasp.

She shakes her head like a nervous mare and then looks into my eyes. I undo her pants quickly; she tries to reciprocate but I brush her hands aside: later. She steps out of her shoes as the pants fall, and I do something I've never done before. Still looking into her eyes, I open a drawer of the desk, the only other piece of furniture besides the bed and a chair, and take out the scissors that I know are there and slide one of the blades under her panties. She shivers violently at the touch of the cold steel; her mouth opens in shock. I close my hand, snipping the panties apart across the crotch panel. Another snip and they disappear. I drop the scissors to the floor and she clutches me, rubbing her whole body against mine, her voice coming out in a soft moan as she comes.

Pummeling her body against mine, she nips at my ear and neck, sinks her teeth in deeply and makes me cry out, drags her finger-nails across the seat of my pants and into the crack of my ass. Finally, when her orgasm wanes, she falls to her knees and pulls my pants open. She grabs the scissors and grins up at me, then cuts my under-pants to shreds; the cold steel fills me with terror. My cock leaps into her mouth and she sighs and sucks it, pressing the flat of the scissors blades between my buttocks; the cold metal makes my asshole contract violently.

The doorbell rings and a moment later, while my mind is somewhere in another universe, Edward, holding a couple of coats, opens the door to the room. I turn my head and look at him as he sees us, steps in the room, out, in, out, and finally holds out the coats to me. I smile and take them and he goes away. I put the coats on the bed.

Lee has never stopped, and it's starting to feel pretty good. I take the scissors out of her hand and put them aside so I can concentrate on what's happening to my cock: her fingernails light on my balls, exploring, the sensation making me tremble; a rich feeling of being taken in, surrounded; the realization that if she doesn't stop, I won't be able to, so I say, "Wait a minute."

She looks up at me impatiently. "I want you to come in my mouth," she says. "Is there a problem?"

"No, I've been tested," I say. "I'm fine."

"I know," she says, and starts in again, stopping only briefly to grunt, "Fuck my mouth, do it in my mouth, and do it now," so I take her head and thrust into her and then explode, starting at the top of my head and going down my spine through my asshole out my prick, a big *wham* of an orgasm that feels like the ceiling fell on me. Spots float in front of my eyes; they turn white, and I feel her hands gripping my butt, forcing me as deeply in her as I can get.

Finally, I stop coming and she jerks her head away violently, gasping for breath, coughing; my sperm is propelled from her throat and lands on my bare knee. "God!" she barks. "Sorry…just a second." She takes my cock in her hand and sucks lovingly on it again for a moment.

She stands up and bends over the coats, scooping them under her. "Quick," she says, "put it in. Put it in my cunt, I want to feel it." I obey her, thrusting inside, although I'm oversensitive now after coming and it makes my flesh crawl. She bucks back against me, grinding her pussy around my cock, which is still half-hard, and just as she starts coming, in a different way this time with a different moan, low and long, the door opens and I put my hand out for another coat.

It's not Edward, though, it's Tommy. Lee is orgasming and she looks around and then away again, shutting her eyes. I hold her tight against me and let her ride, realizing she doesn't care about Tommy and supposing I don't either. When she stops, there's silence in the room except for her breathing; Tommy has come in and shut the door.

"You were right, Tommy," she finally says in a throaty voice. "He really does have a beautiful cock."

"You two know each other?" I ask.

"Lee's my girlfriend," Tommy says with undisguised glee. "I followed your example, as you see." I must have still had a vacant look, so he said impatiently, "Fucking a *girl*."

"Oh," I respond.

"Woman," Lee corrects him. "You don't fuck girls, you don't fuck boys, you fuck women and men, asshole."

Tommy grins. He starts taking off his pants. "She's political, too," he says in an old Firesign Theater cartoon voice. We used to talk that way to each other all the time—it was a dope thing you did when people still smoked dope, you put on records and ended up memorizing them because they'd play on the turntable again and again: Everybody was too stoned to get up and change them. Reagan hadn't been elected yet, we were professing "Gay Liberation," and you could smoke dope and still be a nursing student, as Tommy was, without worrying about passing a drug test.

Tommy's gained a little weight over the years and he sucks it in as, naked, he comes over to me. I wonder briefly what about the party but then I think, *It's his house, it's his birthday, it's his girlfriend, so the hell with the party.* I shiver as his hand strokes my shoulder; his touch evokes the old desire and pain that kept me hanging around for nineteen months while we screamed at each other.

Then he touches my nipples and the old pain disappears. My cock, which is still inside Lee, starts to get hard again; it's too soon but it's happening anyway. Lee takes a few deep breaths as she feels my restored prick, and says, "How do you like your birthday present, Tommy?"

She pulls off me then and watches as Tommy turns me around and puts his mouth on mine. Right away I love it again, his particular smell and taste, the little noises he makes in his throat when he's aroused. I can feel his fingers on my dick, wiping back and forth, using the wetness that's already there, and then he breaks off the kiss and licks his fingers—she's his girlfriend, after all. As I sink to my knees and start nuzzling his cock, I catch sight of her grinning; then my view is blocked by Tommy's body, my mouth is blocked by Tommy's dick, and I forget about everything, except in the other room somebody has restarted the CD, and as "The Man I Love" begins, it's like we're dancing all over again.

Booth Girl

People coming down the hallway can see her better than she can see them, because the hallway is fairly dark and she is in the illuminated booth. But the lights are mostly behind her, and their brilliance illuminates the hallway a little too. She is not nude at the moment, but wearing a bra and panties, with an unbuttoned chiffon blouse over her shoulders. Her job is to coax men into the narrow black space the other window looks on. There a customer pays a minimum of ten dollars for the pleasure of speaking with her for a few minutes. More money buys more time, full nudity, and a variety of solo sexual acts. The customer, sitting on the other side of the glass, can respond in any way he pleases. She gets half of the money, plus a small hourly minimum.

Shauna sits slumped on the pillows, on display. Although earning any significant money depends on her ability to lure men into the booth—that is, into their side of the booth, on the other side of the glass—she doesn't feel very alluring today. There is a black hole at the pit of her stomach absorbing every bit of energy. Her body, which is supposed to be so sexy that men will feed money into a slot for the privilege of seeing it for a few moments, and which is in fact curvy and lush to a degree that entrances most people, feels fat and dull. Her eyes, which are supposed to be bright and flirtatious, are red-rimmed. She struggles to keep her face composed, at least. She's alone. Her Japanese girlfriend is leaving her.

Men wander into the hallway. It's easy to tell the regulars from the tourists and first-timers. The regulars glance in her direction, then either come right into the booth because it's what they came for, or more often, go into one of the video booths, or head past her window and go off to the left, where the hallway continues at an angle. That's where the bathroom is, and more video booths.

First-timers see her, stop in their tracks, and, when she makes eye contact, usually retreat. They're startled that someone can see them there in the theater, that a living person, even if it's just a stripper, can look them in the face. They aren't expecting to be seen or looked at by anybody. They're self-conscious, a little embarrassed, about coming in here at all. They don't want anyone to know they're there. They're there to look, not to be looked at. So when she looks at them, it scares them a little.

Except when they're young and drunk. A drunken frat boy, after stopping dead in his tracks, will aggressively approach the window and gawk. She will smile and invite him inside, into the private area that's his side of the booth. He'll try to get her to do something for free while he stands in the hall, and she'll try to get him to come in and pay. Often he refuses, and sometimes there's a group of them, and they persist in badgering her and demanding a free show and block the hall for others. Then she has to call the desk and get one of the boys who work there to disperse them. This happens all the time on the night shift. There is even a little sign in the corner of the window, cribbed from the zoo, reading:

PLEASE DO NOT TAP ON THE WINDOW
OR OTHERWISE ANNOY THE PERFORMERS

But in the afternoon, it's slow. No one's drunk, which is just as well. The drunks are sloppy; they can't put together a coherent fantasy; they can't manage to put the money in the slot. They have no sense of time and when their time is up, they argue that they've been cheated. Sometimes they can't even get a hard-on. A general waste of time for everyone.

The afternoon custom tends toward the single, lonely, horny male. Small groups sometimes come in, and not just white guys. North Beach is right next to Chinatown and she sees a lot of Asian men—locals or tourists. The younger they are, the more likely they're in a group.

A single white guy wearing a faded dark green T-shirt and khakis comes down the hallway and ducks into a video booth without looking at her. Another man, wearing a dark jacket and jeans, stands in the distance, at the intersection of this hallway with the main one, seemingly at loose ends. Someone else comes up the hallway from the bathroom, passes her without a glance.

To occupy and distract herself, she has brought some home-work. She's getting a Master's at the Conservatory of Music, and she's brought a score to study: *The Love for Three Oranges*. It's a goofy comic opera about a man who, under a spell, develops a romantic obsession for, well, three oranges. Silly, funny, uncommonly beautiful.

Her Japanese girlfriend Naoko was a summer pianist. They come in droves from Japan every summer, part of a special program that brings "promising students" from the upper middle class. The program is more of a Fun Summer in California than a serious study program, the girls spending more time on tourism than music. The only Japanese summer pianist who bothered to practice late, Naoko had run into Shauna on the way out of the school one evening. Shauna had offered her a ride to her apartment, they'd had dinner together, and by the next week Naoko had become Shauna's lover. Naoko had silky black hair, perfect hands, Hello Kitty music folders, an enthusiasm for car-chase movies, a round ass, big feet and good English. She was beautiful, and Shauna had fallen for her.

Shauna raises her eyes from the Prokofiev to the hallway and lowers them again. She follows the bass line, observes how it dances with the sung melody, supports it, provides a secure ground, yet also offers a subtle commentary. It's as if the bass line were a well-trained but slightly sarcastic male partner for a ballerina.

A man is approaching. She sizes him up: early thirties, scuffed sneakers, jeans. He's returning her gaze and smiling, and he nods as he steps into his side of the booth.

She closes a curtain on the hallway window and opens the curtain that covers the customer window. The guy is shutting and locking the door. "Hi," he says, smiling amiably.

"Hi," Shauna says. "My name's Trixie, what's yours?"

He looks a little confused because he can hardly hear her. That's because the microphone isn't on; she won't switch it on until he puts some money in. She smiles and points to the slot and shouts, "You have to start with ten dollars." This shout can be heard through the thick glass. She goes through this drill with every first-timer.

But the guy already has a twenty out and is putting it into the slot. The bill reader mechanism hums and clicks, and a little counter goes clickety-click up to 20.

"Hi, there," Shauna says. "Can you hear me now?"

"Yeah," the guy says.

"What's your name?"

"Don."

"My name's Trixie."

"Oh. Is it really?"

"It really is. My mom was a character." Another standard exchange.

The guy smiles like he doesn't believe her, but grasps that she has to use some kind of fake name. In fact, it's a house rule. The dancers at the theater all have stage names like Cassandra, Annabella, Misty, Cassidy. Flower names are popular—Honeysuckle, Violet, Ivy—as are pomo handles like Amnesia, Poison, Vixen. Shauna is one of those girls who has sort of a stripper name already. In fact, someone who works there is actually named Brandy, and when she came along some girl named Kathy was already using Brandy. So Brandy became Kahlua.

"What do you want to do today, Don?" she asks, sizing him up. He seems to be without any distinguishing characteristics. "What are you feeling like?"

"Well, geez, I dunno," he says. Seemingly unsure, but actually, it's just that he can't bring himself to say. Even though this is a strip joint that exists for the primary purpose of giving men a place to masturbate in front of women, most guys seem to have trouble admitting, or even understanding, that that's what they came for. They have to be given permission, sometimes many times over, to take out their dicks and jack off.

"You just make yourself comfortable. I will too, okay?" She takes off the chiffon blouse and her bra, and runs her hands over her breasts.

"Okay," he chuckles.

"Is there anything in particular you'd like?" she asks. "Do you have anything to show me?" She looks pointedly at his crotch. The counter is already down to 17.

He moves his hands to his belt buckle and unfastens it, still a little uncertain.

"I'd like to see it," she says. "Would you like to see me, too?"

"Sure."

She kneels facing him in the spot where the little spotlight in front of the window illuminates her crotch. She hooks her thumbs into the waistline of her panties and slowly peels them down her thighs until he can see her snatch, indistinctly at least. Meanwhile he has managed to open his pants. He has been perching on the bench, but now he stands and pulls down his boxer shorts to reveal his dick. It's a normal size, half-hard, uncut. He props it upward a little with his thumb.

"That's so nice," she says, trying to sound enthusiastic. "I'd like to see what you do with that."

In response he runs his fingers over it, stroking a little, exposing the head.

"Is there anything you'd like me to do?" she asks again.

"Well, I don't know."

Most men say they don't know. There's a long explanation on the door of the booth that leads to the hallway that explains that, inside, customers can have "a one-on-one erotic fantasy experience of your dreams." In truth, most of the interactions take place along a pretty narrow range. For one thing, the girl and the customer are on opposite sides of a thick plate of glass; the "experience" is pretty much limited to masturbation. Secondly, the dreams don't get very wild, or at least the guys aren't very articulate about them. Drawing guys out of their shells is one of the most challenging parts of the job.

"Show it to me," she says. "I like dicks, especially when they're hard."

"Really?"

"Yeah! I wouldn't work here if I didn't like sex!"

How many times has she said that line? Shauna's been working the booth for five months now, two or three times a week. Though the booth is promoted as their chance to "talk to a live nude girl," in fact she always does most of the talking. She knows, now, what men want to hear. A great deal of the time she is stroking their egos, assuring them they're beautiful, that their dicks are beautiful and she really likes them, likes seeing dicks stand up, harden, spurt. At first she found it remarkable, that men's egos were so in need of, yes, pumping up. Then she found it poignant and a little sad. Now she doesn't even think about it, it's just a fact of life in the booth.

Shauna coaxes Don until he finally is jacking off proudly in front of her. She smiles and masturbates along with him, or makes the motions of doing so. In fact, with Naoko leaving, she feels like she will never get turned on again, will never have sex again. But a job's a job.

"Oh, yeah, that looks real good," Shauna says. The counter is clicking down. It's now at three. Don's time is almost up.

Many of them barely get to the point of openly masturbating before their time runs out, and they have to put in more money to continue. This is where you lose some of them, because even though the secondary purpose of the booth is obvious—that is, to get men to pay as much money as possible for the privilege of jacking off alone in front of a pretty girl—the men seem surprised when their money runs out and they have to pay more. They want it to go on longer, now that they're finally hard and halfway to orgasm, and usually they want it for free.

It's hard to blame them. The girl must create and establish a fantasy, namely that she truly enjoys, is even aroused by, the sight of men masturbating in front of her. The more a performer can build this fantasy, the better experience the man has. And yet if the money runs out in the middle, the fantasy she's encouraged dictates that, if she's really enjoying it that much, she'll let them continue for free. But the whole point of the system, the real point, is that it costs money.

This built-in contradiction is something almost all the men have trouble with.

A buzzer goes off. Don's rhythm falters. "What—is my time up?"

"Yeah, sorry," she says, then reminds herself not to say that. Never say you're sorry for not doing something you don't want to do. It was a habit she's trying to get out of.

"I'd like to finish with you," she says. In the middle of her statement her microphone goes dead.

He says something and she pantomimes that she can't hear and he needs to put more money in. Don looks a little miffed but digs a five out of his pants—his cock bobbing hard in the air—and manages to put it in the slot. The mechanism clicks up to five.

"There we go," Shauna says, sounding as pleased as she can muster.

"How much time does that give me?"

"A minute and a half."

"Okay," he says, looking slightly pissed, but he seizes his cock again and starts jacking off furiously, determined to finish in a minute. She knows he's thinking, *Fuck, I spent $25 to jack off.* Realizing he's decided not to spend any more, Shauna decides to encourage his orgasm.

"Oh yeah," she says, falling into her orgasm patter. "Come on, show me what happens. Oh, yeah, it's turning me on. Oh, I have to do it too. Oh, come on, baby, that's it, yeah." She waits for a sign that he's starting to come, and then she raises the volume and pace, pretending real arousal. "Oh yeah, that's it, oh it feels good, it feels good to me too, come on, come on." Squeezing his eyes closed, his mouth distorted, Don comes with a grunt.

"Oh yeah," she cheers. His face looks like that of a dog straining at a leash. She doesn't look at his cock or at the come jumping out, just at his face flushing. After a few seconds he takes a gasping breath and grunts again, seeming to squeeze out a little more. Then his body relaxes and he sits back on the bench with a thump.

She has been kneeling, leaning forward, and now sits back on the cushions, removing her hand from her pussy where it's been hovering over her clit like a hummingbird. Don sighs, plucks a tissue from the dispenser on the wall, cleans off his fingers. Then he gets more tissue and wipes up the mess he made on the floor.

"Nice of you to do that," she observes. "Most guys just leave it."

"No problem," he says. He tosses the tissues in the trash can, and without another glance at her, puts his dick away, tucks in his shirt, and leaves. She shuts the curtain to the customer side as the clock runs out on his last five bucks.

She looks at the little clock tucked into the corner of the booth out of view of the customers. Two hours and twenty-one minutes left. She straightens up her abode, puts her costume back on, and opens up the curtain to the hallway again.

There are a couple of men standing several feet away, looking very startled that a curtain has just opened to reveal a half-naked girl. They look like construction workers or housepainters, who often come in late in the afternoon at the end of their shift; these guys are a little early.

She smiles and tries to meet their eyes, receives a dead stare in return. Macho types always look at her with contempt, or what looks like it. Shitheads, she thinks. It would kill them to show a little honest feeling. They're looking at her with the same tough-guy expressions you see on mobsters in bad Mafia movies. It's hard to resist making faces back and sticking her tongue out at them, just to get a rise out of them, but she keeps smiling. Pissing off some guy who thinks he's a Real Man just makes it more likely he'll take it out on some other woman down the line.

One of them approaches the window and the other follows. They start talking to her through the window and the first one makes a jacking-off motion. She nods and points to the door where he should go in. But they both want to come in.

There's a microphone she can use that's connected to a loud-speaker in the hall. It's there for the dancers to use to coax the customers. She picks it up and says, "Just one customer at a time." This seems to make them offended. They give her the finger. She manages not to reciprocate.

They retreat out of sight. A guy has been standing a few feet away watching the scene with amusement. She's still holding the microphone. "Wanna see the show?" she asks, humor in her voice. He smiles and shrugs. "Come on in," she says. She lowers her voice, putting on the ironic-seductive voice she reserves for twenty-some-things. "Come on. You know you want it. It's a show just for you. It's your love show. Come on, sailor." He laughs, shrugs again, slouches away. The hallway is empty except for the guy in the jeans standing at the other end. She puts the microphone down. The management forbids using the microphone to joke or perform; it's there strictly to coax. She's heard of the girl who, crazy with boredom one day, starting singing country-western songs into the microphone. Seems harmless enough, but she was fired, they say.

A few minutes later several Asian men in their thirties and forties appear. They're dressed in cheap suits and are being herded by a younger man with a name tag, evidently a tour guide. She sits passively while the tour guide speaks to them, gesticulating, no doubt explaining the various offerings at the theater, the video booths, and the peep show. He mimes the act of putting money in the slot. Several of the men sneak glances at her during the talk, and then all their heads swivel to her as the guide gestures in her direction. After a moment the group drifts apart. One by one they go nervously into the peep show booths.

A couple of preppy-looking guys come around the corner and size her up. She smiles at them but leaves the microphone alone. One of them comes in. She closes the hallway curtain, opens the ones on his side. "Hi, there."

"Hey," he says.

"It's ten dollars to start."

"Start what?"

"I can't hear you talking because the mike won't come on till you put money in."

"Oh, *man*," the guy whines. He leaves. She quickly closes the curtain and reopens the ones to the hallway. There the guy is talking to his friend, who looks at her hatefully. What did they expect, anyway?

The biggest surprise about this job was that so many men found it so difficult to be straightforward about booth reality—that they're there to jack off, and that it's going to cost them. Clearly they *understand* that that's the case; they just didn't seem to be able to translate that into easy dealings with the performer. Negotiate if you want, but don't act surprised that you have to pay at all. I mean, come *on*.

When Shauna and Naoko started having sex, she could tell Naoko was pretty inexperienced. She could kiss pretty well, but the first time she took a good look at Shauna's pussy, Shauna had the feeling it was the first time she'd seen one up close. She touched Shauna hesitantly, shy at first. Shauna tried to encourage her gently, telling her what felt good. She showed her on Naoko's own body. "Like this. That feel good? Yeah?" She would laugh at Naoko's flushed responses. Naoko was an easy comer, and her responses utterly girlish. Even right after she came, she'd act flustered, as if she'd accidentally knocked something over, all the while holding Shauna's wrist tightly so her hand stayed against her pussy.

Afterward Naoko would claim not to understand when Shauna asked her if she'd had an orgasm. There was something taboo, at least to Naoko, about having an orgasm, or maybe just having an orgasm with a girl. Maybe she didn't understand what an orgasm was. She was only twenty. Who knows what girls learn over there.

One of the construction workers appears from the bathroom side and comes into the booth. Shauna hurriedly shuts the curtain on the college boys and turns to the man, who grumpily puts a ten-dollar bill in the slot. The counter clicks up to 10. She decides to nip any misunderstandings in the bud. "What's your name?"

"Ramon."

"Ramon, it's two and a half minutes for your ten dollars."

He curses under his breath and says, "Get naked, bitch."

She strips, thinking she may as well give him his money's worth. "Yes, Ramon, you want me to be your bitch? Look at me, look at how nasty I am. Look how scary my pussy is. I'll be your scary-pussy bitch."

Someone's knocking on the hallway glass, behind the curtain—one of those college guys, no doubt.

She ignores the knocking and masturbates for Ramon, who sits stroking his dick, eyes fixed on her pussy, saying nothing. She keeps talking to him. "Come on, Ramon, keep jacking off your dirty prick, yes, baby. You're so dirty, mama's boy is so dirty. Come on, come for mama." Where did that come from? It's because he looks like a three-year-old sitting there—still trying to act macho, he has a toddler's imperious expression. "Come on, Ramon. Let me see you come."

The timer runs out. She stops, smiles, points in the direction of the slot. "That's it."

"Keep going, bitch," he says, and continues jacking off, a little faster.

She shrugs and smiles. "The time's up on ten dollars. Can you spend a little while longer? I like doing this for you."

He sits there unmoving except for his hand on his dick.

"Because otherwise I need to shut these curtains."

He grunts something in Spanish, probably *fuck you,* and comes. Staggering forward, he sprays his come on the glass between them, and when he finishes, spits there as well. Then zips up and leaves.

She shuts the curtain and sits there for a moment. Well, that's what happens sometimes, she thinks.

She picks up a telephone receiver that's connected to the front desk. "Hi. This is Trixie in the booth. Can someone come here and do a little cleanup on the glass? Please? The last guy made a mess. I would really appreciate it. Thanks." The dancers have to be extra friendly and nice with the guys who work there. The guys, pierced and tattooed punk rockers who hang out at the front counter, are supposed to clean up regularly. They go from booth to booth—the tiny video booths and the ones that look out onto the stage—with a mop and bucket. And they were supposed to come in and mop up the Live Nude Girl booth when asked. But sometimes they just didn't. No explanation, no acknowledgment that they didn't do their job. And it was no use getting mad at them and bitching them out. Exposure over time to dozens of cute young chicks hardened them against feminine manipulation. The only thing you could do was ask nicely and hope they felt like raising a finger.

This is what causes her to wonder why she feels obliged to give the customers a good show for their ten bucks. If the guys who work there can be sullen and lazy about their work, if the kid at the coffee shop and the bus driver and especially the customers can be monosyllabic and slack-jawed, why does she have to be such a good little trouper, like Shirley Temple in the clutches of white slavers? She imagines doing a dance there in the booth with a little hat and cane, singing "On the Good Ship Lollipop" as if it were the dirtiest song imaginable.

Actually it is kind of a dirty song, if you think about it that way.

She knows it might be five or ten minutes before someone comes to clean the glass, so she opens the hallway curtain.

It's not easy to follow Prokofiev in the booth, because the jukebox is always cranked up loud. It's called the "jukebox" but is really an in-house digital music system programmed to repeat every two hours, and it's blasted on the stage and throughout the house on loudspeakers. Lots of modern pop and rock. The music is ostensibly for the girls on the stage to dance to, even though they don't do much dancing. It's more like swaying than dancing. Anybody who gets it into her head that she's going to rock out on the stage quickly wears herself out, and then where are you? Sweaty on a freezing-cold stage, because for some reason she's never been able to figure out, they keep the place freezing, while the girls are, of course, naked, or nearly so. And you can't leave the stage until your relief comes, no matter how cold you are or how bad you have to pee. You're stuck there, the little windows going up and down as customers in tiny booths stick money in the slots. The only thing you can leave the stage for before your time is if you have to puke.

Right now it's "Love Shack" on the jukebox—one of the most frequently programmed songs. She's sick of it, every girl in the place is. It almost never leaves the rotation. Management likes it, they feel it epitomizes the spirit of the place. Naked girls gyrating on stage, naked girls on the videos, a naked girl in the booth, all enticing men to part with cash. Love shack bay-beee!

Naoko liked the B-52s too, and Shauna had to put her foot down. "Augh, Naoko, don't play that, please! I'm so tired of it!"

Naoko had looked at her with surprise. "B-52s are great," she protested.

"Not to me, they play them all the time at the theater. Please, don't make me listen."

Naoko had pursed her lips and rolled her eyes. They were in the bedroom where Naoko had a summer sublet. There was a gym bag full of CDs she's brought from Japan.

"Play something Japanese," Shauna urged.

"Japanese rock music is pretty bad."

"It can't be worse than French rock music."

"Oh, so you had a French girlfriend, too?"

"Yes."

"Another summer pianist?"

"No, no."

"You get a new one every summer?"

"This is the first year I've been at the conservatory. I didn't even know about your program last summer."

"So who was she?"

"She was a friend of my brother's, if you want to know. Somebody he kayaked with."

"What's that?"

"It's a little boat. Never mind, just put on some bad Japanese rock."

"I haven't brought any."

"Really? What do you have?"

"Nirvana. Garbage. Madonna. Nick Cave. Carpenters."

"The Carpenters?!"

"Many Japanese people like Carpenters. They like a sad story, beautiful girl."

"Oh, God. All right, put on the Carpenters." And they made out to sad, beautiful Karen.

Later that summer, the Castro Theater sneaked an unadvertised showing of Todd Haynes's *Superstar*—the Karen Carpenter biopic he made with Barbie dolls when he was twenty-five, the film that had a permanent injunction against its screening because Haynes had not bothered to get Richard Carpenter's permission to use their songs— onto a midnight showing. After eight hours of word-of-mouth about the rare opportunity, there was a line stretching all the way down the block an hour before the show. Shauna and Naoko made it in and sat among screaming queens as the "Karen" Barbie doll deteriorated more and more from anorexia.

After the showing, Shauna was exuberant. "That was so great!" she said, throwing her arm around Naoko as they left the theater. "That was so hilarious. What did you think?"

Naoko had only a puzzled look on her face. "I thought, it's a sad story. So why is everyone laughing?"

"Naoko! Didn't you get it? It's a joke! The director is using artifacts of popular culture, these Barbie dolls, to show how hollow and false the whole romantic world of love songs is. And he's satirizing the way pop music was produced on TV in the 1970s, with those colored lights—didn't you hear everyone laughing at the lighting?"

"The lighting? They were laughing at Karen getting sick. It's not funny, it's a sickness."

"It's more like he's making fun of the whole world she was caught up in. It's satire."

Naoko shrugged. "I guess it's hard for Japanese to understand another culture, so even harder to understand satire."

"Oh, you didn't get it," Shauna groaned. "Oh, God. You can't understand American culture without understanding satire. Practically everything in popular culture today consists of satire. Like this place here." They were passing a hamburger joint that faithfully reproduced a 1950s diner, with red vinyl booths, miniskirted waitresses, and pale green milkshake mixers behind Formica counters. "This place is a joke. It's about the look of the place as much as about the food. You go there to participate in the joke."

Naoko gave it a brief glance. "I'm not stupid."

"I didn't say that! Don't get offended."

"Maybe if I take you to Tokyo, you won't understand some things."

"Of course. I'm sorry, sweetie."

It was hard for Shauna to get Naoko back in a cheerful mood that night. Even after apologizing as sincerely and sweetly as she could, Shauna couldn't pierce the barrier of anger Naoko had put up. It turned out that Naoko really, really liked The Carpenters and had been expecting a sort of

TV-movie version of Karen's story. She was completely taken aback by the Barbie dolls and by the audience's response. And she really didn't get the satire. After several attempts to explain, Shauna came to the conclusion that Japanese people, or at least Naoko, just don't understand irony.

Finally one of the guys who works there comes to clean the glass. She hasn't had any customers in the last twenty minutes anyway.

The guy is a fairly new employee, a typical punk in his early twenties. He goes about cleaning the window and the floor with an unpleasant air, as if he's on detention.

Shauna turns on the microphones and says, "Hey, thanks for doing that."

"No problem."

"What's your name again?"

"Rick."

"Mine's Shauna. My real name."

"How ya doin'." He doesn't look very interested, and she isn't either, to tell the truth. But it doesn't hurt to make friends with the staff.

"You're kinda new here, right?"

"Wouldn't be cleaning up come if I wasn't." That's true enough. The guys lowest in seniority have to clean up the come, while the more senior ones confine themselves to refilling the change machine and manning the front desk.

"You from around here?"

"Michigan."

"Oh man," she says sympathetically.

"Most fucked-up place imaginable."

"Must be."

He departs. She opens the curtain to the hallway and watches his almost nonexistent butt recede into the dimness as he carries the cleaning implements back to their closet. Then she turns her eyes back to the Prokofiev score.

About the fourth time they had sex, Shauna stripped for Naoko. She sat Naoko up in bed, put on an old Billie Holiday record, and did a slow striptease in her bedroom. Naoko was entranced and clapped at the end.

"You didn't tell me you're a dancer," she said.

As the record continued, Shauna crept onto the bed and removed Naoko's clothes as seductively as she could. The Japanese girl melted like butter on a hot griddle. By the time the record ended, Naoko was on her knees and Shauna was fucking her with three fingers, very slowly in and out, making Naoko howl. It wasn't the high-pitched grunting she usually emitted, but a deep wail that came all the way from her cunt. That was one of the sexiest scenes Shauna had ever been able to produce. It made her feel the power of her own sexuality in a way she never did at work.

When they finished, Shauna told Naoko about her part-time job. "I sit in a glass booth," Shauna had said, "and give private sex shows for ten dollars."

Naoko's eyes had gotten wide. "Ehh?" she said in an astonished tone.

"I know it sounds sort of gross, but it's all right…. It's not like it's fun, really. It's just something I do for money."

Naoko said, "Ehhh?" again.

Shauna felt uncomfortable. "There's no customer contact, of course. I'm on the other side of a piece of glass. I never touch the customers. They just get to look at me."

Naoko repeated "Ehhhh?" a third time. Shauna had been with her long enough to know this basically meant "Huh?" The more the tone rose at the end, the more surprised Naoko was. It was getting really high by now.

"Yeah, well, that's my job." They both seemed embarrassed and Shauna dropped it. She had thought that Naoko might be surprised, but in an interested way, not embarrassed. Another lover might have asked questions, seeing the link between the show Shauna had just put on and her job, and understanding that she had just gotten the best of Shauna's stripper soul. But Naoko never asked questions, and Shauna never brought it up again. Shauna concluded that the whole idea of stripping for money must seem so déclassé that Naoko, coming from a rich family, just couldn't handle it. From then on Shauna simply referred to her job as "work."

Down the hallway, wearing a hooded sweatshirt that covers as much as possible, comes a young woman. She waves briefly at Shauna and disappears around the corner: one of the dancers about to start her shift. The dancers have to walk through the customer area to the nondescript, locked door that leads backstage. Since the whole attraction of this club—for the dancers—is that there's no customer contact, they power-walk the whole way through, never meeting anyone's eyes except those of the girl in the booth as they pass by.

The later it gets, the more men come through the place. The guy in jeans and dark jacket is still wandering around an hour after Shauna spotted him. She knows he's cruising the other customers. It may seem odd for a queer guy to cruise a het strip joint, but some gay guys like the idea that they're blowing a straight guy. They have to walk a very fine line at this joint, though, because first of all they don't want to proposition some homophobe, and secondly because only one person is permitted, officially, in the video and peep show booths. ("Couples" can come into the Live Nude Girl booth, but that's supposed to be a male–female couple. Two guys never come in—a straight guy doesn't want a girl to watch while he's getting blown by a queer. It would have to be two gay guys—two kind-of-twisted gay guys who were entertained by having a girl watch them fuck.)

A dyke couple did come in once. They were celebrating one's birthday, and the birthday girl's lover put eighty bucks into the slot and finger-fucked her girlfriend while Shauna masturbated wildly. It was the high point of her career as a Live Nude Girl, and one that the other dancers listened to with envy. It wasn't so much that some dykes had come in, which happened once in a blue moon, but that she'd had some customers who both spent some dough and were actually fun to watch.

In fact, they were both pretty unattractive, but Shauna left that part out. Leaving something to the imagination makes it more fun for people.

A big, muscular guy with an attitude comes in. He hauls out his dick, saying, "Hey bitch. Whatchoo think about this?"

"I think I'd like to have that in my pussy."

"Fuck you, bitch, you ain't getting it in your pussy. You're getting fucked in the ass."

"Ooh, I don't know if I can take it."

"You're gonna take it and squeal for more, bitch." This guy drops forty bucks.

An older Chinese guy comes in. He has a delighted smile, not much English. When Shauna starts stroking her pussy, he says, "You put in finger?"

"Putting in a finger is extra," Shauna purrs.

"How much?"

"One finger ten dollars extra, two fingers twenty."

"Okay, one finger." He puts another ten in the slot while she spreads lube on her pussy. Inserting a finger, she puts on some excitement. Maybe she can work some more fingers out of him. But he comes after thirty seconds, smiles and waves, doesn't clean up his mess.

A middle-aged white guy comes in. This guy doesn't know what he wants. In fact he leaves after the time runs out on the first ten bucks without saying much or touching himself.

If she's learned one thing in the booth, it's that a broad spectrum of male sexuality exists that she never knew existed. Some guys, like the last guy, seem so fazed by the whole situation that, despite all the elements that are part of a fantasy—a sexy girl *wants* to watch you jack off—is a real situation. There really is a girl there; you do have to communicate to some extent.

This makes the ten-dollar bill the most basic form of communication. Even a language barrier is no barrier to an encounter as long as the guy has ten dollars. The Chinese guy who could only say, "Put in finger" communicated better than the white guy who didn't know what he wanted. The guy who just got down with the fantasy about fucking her in the ass was the best of all; he had a fantasy and got her to participate in it. It didn't matter how pretend-abusive the rap was; he saved her the trouble of having to coax it out of him, and he dropped forty bucks.

The middle-aged guy comes back after ten minutes and puts in another ten. She can see he has somewhat of a hard-on now.

"Hi, I'm glad to see you back."

"Thanks."

"You gonna tell me your name this time?" said flirtatiously.

"Kevin."

"Hi, Kevin, I'm Trixie."

"So...."

"So are you kind of horny today?"

"Kind of."

Mister Tentative, she thinks. "Why don't you show me how horny you are?"

He undoes his pants slowly.

"I'm kind of horny today too."

"Oh really?"

"Yeah—sure. I like sex. I wouldn't work here if I didn't like sex."

"Um," he says. He's got his cock out now. Decent size, cut.

"You gonna show me how you play with that?"

"I guess so."

"I'd like to see it."

"Oh really?" he repeats. He does show a little skepticism, at least.

"Yeah. Is there something you'd like me to do?"

"Maybe…touch yourself too."

"I can do that," she says, struggling to keep a straight face. She starts to rub her pussy very gently. She has to do it gently to preserve it over the three hours shift. She could use lube to reduce the friction, but that means wiping it off after each customer, and wiping it off repeatedly ends up making her cunt more raw, not less. So she usually doesn't use lube unless she's doing a finger or dildo show for extra money.

But the gentle touch reminds her of Naoko, too, and how softly Naoko used to touch her there. If she closes her eyes, she can almost imagine Naoko doing it; but customers don't like it if she closes her eyes. To them, it means she's ignoring them. Which she would be.

Silence from the other side of the glass. She glances down; he is pulling on his cock fairly energetically. She decides to try to draw this guy out. He's already spent ten dollars twice; maybe he's got a lot more.

"It feels kind of good to me," she says. "Does that feel good to you, too?"

"Sure," he said shortly.

"But you know, I'd kind of like to use some lube. It feels better that way."

"Oh really?"

"Would you like me to use some lube?" she presses.

"Sure."

"But it might take a little longer…. Can you afford to stay a little longer?'

He shrugs, stops jacking off for a minute, and pulls a few twenties out of his shirt pocket. Putting two of them into the slot, one after the other, he says, "Okay, knock yourself out."

"All right," she says enthusiastically. She watches the counter click up to 48 as she picks up the lube and dabs it on her pussy. "I do a dildo show too, for twenty more."

"Let's just go with the fingers for a while."

"All right, fine…." She was going to say his name again but she's forgotten it already. She's going to have to do that mnemonic thing for people's names.

She starts jacking off in what she thinks of as the wet-pussy way, imitating the way women masturbate in porn movies so that the viewer can see as much of the pussy as possible while at the same time making it look like she's really laying into it. That's what some guys really want—a porn movie. They don't want to interact with a real girl. The hallway is lined with video booths that are a hell of a lot cheaper, but if he thinks he wants to be in here, fine.

"That's starting to feel really good to me," she says after a few moments.

"Me too," he says. He's jacking off faster now.

"Ooo," she says in a vague way. He can take this either as delight in his motions or in hers. She wishes he would give her some kind of sign as to which it is, so she can go one way or the other, but he's like a cop with his closed face. Maybe he actually *is* a cop—not that what they're doing is against any kind of law in San Francisco. No, he's too much of a wimp. He's probably a lawyer.

Having sex with Naoko was usually mysterious. She was noisy, so it wasn't difficult to tell that she was aroused. It was the degree of arousal that was the problem. Except for the time Shauna had stripped for her, Naoko's high-pitched sing-song never varied from the moment Shauna slid her fingers in through orgasm to the end. Fortunately Shauna could feel the spasms in Naoko's vagina when she came; otherwise she'd never know what was happening.

Shauna wanted to break through Naoko's aloofness. It was one thing to finger-fuck her and make her come, but Shauna wanted more. She wanted Naoko to get interested in her, to fall in love, to want to stay when the summer was over. Even in the middle of July, she started counting the weeks and days until Naoko would go home. So it was annoying when Naoko started teasing her by singing some lousy pop song that had the phrase "my summer love" in it. The rest of the song was in Japanese; Naoko would sing it, blah blah blah, then suddenly the phrase "my summer love" would pop out in English.

"What's that fucking song?" Shauna asked.

"A Japanese rock song."

"I can tell that, but what's it about? What's all this 'summer love' shit?"

Naoko shrugged. "It's about 'my summer love,'" and she sang it again.

Shauna tried everything to penetrate Naoko's reserve. She was aggressive; she was passive. She wined and dined her and took her to meet a friend who was a rehearsal pianist at the opera. She made love to her every way she could think of. Once Shauna approached Naoko wearing a strap-on and Naoko literally jumped off the bed to get away. At first Shauna laughed, but Naoko was so freaked out by the fact that the dildo resembled a penis that Shauna got a little offended, even though it was attached to her only temporarily. It made her understand why some men in the booth were reluctant to haul it out, and why they reacted so positively when she told them their cocks were beautiful. Women had laughed at those guys at some time in the past. She felt compassion for them now. To a point.

"Your cock looks so good hard like that," Shauna says to the now-nameless guy. "I love looking at hard cocks. You've got a really nice one."

"Thanks," he says, cracking a smile. He pushed his hips closer to the glass.

"Mmm," she says. "That's right, let me see it. Oh, it's a nice one. You've got a beautiful cock."

"You think so?" he says, his voice still arch.

"Yes. I wish I could suck on it."

"Oh yeah?"

"Yeah—I'd like to pretend that I am."

"Sure, baby," he says, nodding and smiling slightly. He jacks himself off in such a way that she can see his prick better. Now they are both really showing off to one another. Shauna feels a sense of accomplishment when she gets an awkward customer to this point. It's like a little bit of therapy for them.

The counter is down to 23. Plenty of time left; may as well give him his money's worth. "Oh, it feels so good in my mouth," she says.

"You like having cocks in your mouth?"

"You bet." *Not,* she adds to herself.

"What are the chances of you meeting me later?"

"Oh, we're not allowed to meet customers."

"Right, but, how much would it be?"

"No, seriously, we aren't. Let me just watch you do it now."

"Come on—I'm not a cop."

"No, really. It's not possible. That's not what we do here."

He hadn't stopped jacking off.

"So you won't be my little whore, then?"

She starts moving her hand again. "I'll be your little whore in here," she says. "I'm your little whore right now."

"Oh yeah," he replies. His hand clicks into a sudden, fast, regular rhythm. She's found his turn-on.

"Yes, I'll be your dirty little whore right here," she encourages him. "Come on, you've paid your money, now come on my face. I'm just a little whore, you can do anything to me. Come on."

"Ohh...." His hand gets faster.

"I'm your dirty little whore, come on, you can come on me, you can, I'll take it. I'll take it on my face."

He starts coming. His eyes snap shut as the first squirt of come leaps out of his dick. She keeps her hand moving even though he isn't watching anymore. It is starting to feel a little good to her, just from friction.

"Oh yes, come on me, I want your come dripping down my face. Come on your whore, come on your dirty, fucking whore."

He finishes coming and lets out a deep whoosh of breath. "Whoo—damn."

"You like that?"

"Yeah." He's smiling now.

"I liked it too."

"So really—how about later?" he asks as he plucks tissues from the dispenser and cleans himself up.

"So really—no. I'm sorry," she says, then kicks herself mentally.

"You mean you'd like to, but you can't."

No sense encouraging him now. "I mean I can't, and I don't want to. I don't work here to find dates. That's not what this place is for. If you want contact you need to go someplace else."

"Where?"

"Well, a lap dance place, for example."

"How about a hundred bucks? Two hundred," he adds, realizing a hundred sounds ridiculously low.

"No, really. That's not what we do here. No."

The guy is putting his pants back together now. He seems resigned, even surprised. At least he isn't pissed off. "Do you think girls at the lap dance place would do it? See me on the side?"

"I can't say. I gotta go now."

"Is my time up?"

"Well, no, not actually." She looks balefully at the timer, which is on 6.

"How much do I have left?"

"About a minute."

He sits there for a moment, then takes another twenty out of his pocket and puts it into the slot. She watches in dismay as the timer clicks up to 25.

"So would you like me to do something else?" she asks.

He laughs. "You're like that doctor on *Star Trek:* 'Please state the nature of the medical emergency!' Yeah, blow me," he says. Now there is anger in his voice.

"Look, you seem like a nice guy. Please don't take it personally. It's got nothing to do with you or with me. There's not a single dancer in this place who would date a customer."

"You're telling me it's never happened?"

"If it happens, she gets fired."

He snorts, in disbelief, or maybe just to say, Who cares? "So this is it."

"Well, yeah," she says, struggling to keep sarcasm out of her tone. "It wasn't so bad, was it? Look, we've got a few minutes—why don't you tell me a little about yourself." Just to turn the conversation to something else.

"Why should I tell you anything?"

"Because that's what I'm here for," she says in her sweetest voice.

"You're here to get to know the customers?"

"Partly. I mean, from the customer's perspective."

"From my perspective you're here to get naked and act like a whore," he says.

"That's right. And so I've gotten to know you a little," she says. "At least I know what turns you on. You want a girl to be your little whore."

He stands up. "That's right. I pay you, and you take it. You do whatever I want."

"Sure. In here."

"What if it's my fantasy that you go out with me? I take you home and fuck you all night long."

"You can tell me about that."

"Fuck you. I get to say what I want as long as it stays in here? What kind of sex is that? It's like I'm performing as much as you are."

She stifles a smile. It's the first insightful thing he's said since he came in. "It's kind of a two-way thing, yeah."

"Except that I pay."

She finally has to smile. She doesn't want him to think she's laughing at him, though. "That's the way it is," she says, as directly as she can.

He looks at her. Probably he's thinking about punching the glass, which doesn't concern her, since it's supposed to be unbreakable. But it's unpleasant. She doesn't like the idea that some guy might be waiting for her when she gets off her shift in...fifty-seven minutes.

But then he slumps, runs his hand through his hair, and shakes his head. "Sorry," he says. "I'm just having a bad week."

She gazes out at him. *I am not going to say I'm sorry about that,* she thinks. "Yeah, well..." she finally says.

"Well. See ya," he says, and leaves.

She closes the curtain automatically and sinks back on the cushions. The counter's at 12. She sits there for a second, then starts wiping the lube off her crotch. A little has dripped onto a cushion and she tries to wipe it up. Then she straightens up and puts her costume back on.

A couple of weeks ago, Naoko and Shauna had spent the whole weekend together at Shauna's place. They'd watched movies and made out and slept and woke and fucked again. Shauna had even induced Naoko to fist her. By late Saturday night they hadn't been more than ten feet apart for more than a day; Shauna felt herself getting drunk on Naoko's smell. She got almost frantic to have Naoko's hand inside her.

"Naoko, I love you."

Naoko snorted and raised her cupped hand. "You love *this.*"

"Yes, I do. But I love *you.* I love being with you."

"Tomorrow makes two more weeks."

"Ohh," Shauna groaned, "don't say that."

"Are we going to Las Vegas?"

"Ha. I know I said we could go to Las Vegas, but...."

"Shauna, come on. I want to see Circus Circus. And New York New York. And Paris Paris."

"I just want to stay here with you." Shauna buried her face between Naoko's breasts. "Don't talk about leaving."

Naoko stroked her hair. "I want to see Blue Man Group."

They went to Las Vegas at the end of August when Naoko's summer term had ended. They saw Blue Man Group at the Luxor, went on the Star Trek Experience at the Hilton, and saw Siegfried and Roy at the Mirage. Naoko wouldn't believe Shauna's assertion that Siegfried and Roy were gay lovers, probably because she had tried to tell Naoko that Captain Kirk and Mr. Spock were gay lovers and a Star Trek Experience employee had contradicted this.

In between shows they hung out in their hotel room, with its view of the collection of satellite dishes on the roof of the casino, and watched cable. With the TV sound down low on reruns of *Cheers* and *Happy Days,* Shauna swallowed up Naoko's fist over and over again. Between fistings she would go down on Naoko. She got Sudafed from the hotel gift shop and they took the little red pills and stayed up for twenty-four hours straight, kissing and fucking. But when Shauna tried to tell Naoko how much she loved her and that she wanted her to stay, Naoko pushed her away.

"Shauna," Naoko said, "this is only a summer love."

When Naoko went to the bathroom, Shauna lay naked on the bed and wondered why she was going through this drama. She didn't actually expect Naoko to stay. The girl was too conventional; she probably wasn't even a dyke, really. This was her big anonymous American fling; Naoko would go back to Japan and get married in a few years and forget Shauna and the feeling of having her whole hand inside another girl's cunt. But instead of discouraging Shauna, the certainty of the outcome only made her express her affection more recklessly. On the way to the airport, when they stopped off at the Bellagio's art gallery to see the Impressionist paintings, Shauna kissed Naoko hard in front of a whole Japanese tour group. Naoko let her; she even pushed back, pushed her tongue deep in Shauna's mouth, and when the kiss broke Naoko said, "Your mouth is like your cunt."

Shauna turned crimson. "You should talk to me like that all the time."

Naoko sniffed. "Learn Japanese."

Shauna paid for the whole trip with her Live Nude Girl money.

After they landed back in San Francisco, in the cab on the way from the airport, Shauna said, "Let's have dinner."

"No, I'm exhausted."

"You have to eat."

Naoko shrugged. "I'll have ramen."

"I'll come over with some sushi."

"Shauna," Naoko said. "You already spent all your money. And I haven't slept in two days—neither have you."

"So when are we going to see each other again?"

"I don't know. It's difficult."

"What is?"

"That's the Japanese way of saying no."

"What are you saying? Aren't you going to see me again?"

"Shauna, you know I'm not staying in San Francisco. I like you but I'm going home now. I just spent four days with you. Now let me go."

"I know you're going back to Japan—that's one thing—but you're going to be here all day tomorrow and Friday and I can't see you? What the fuck?!"

"My host family is taking me to Fisherman's Wharf tomorrow. Friday I have to pack."

"Fisherman's Wharf? That's bullshit. After all the cool places I've taken you in San Francisco, you want to go to Fisherman's Wharf?"

"Shauna. Don't be silly." She leaned forward and told the taxi driver, "Take the Ninth Street exit."

"You're just dropping me off?"

"It's on my way."

Shauna started crying. Naoko sat silently, not comforting her. When the taxi stopped in front of Shauna's building, Naoko wouldn't even get out.

That was yesterday. Shauna slept thirteen hours, dragged herself down to the theater, and now she's in the booth. Listening to "Venus"—another much-played song. The Las Vegas trip had cost her $800 and she's going to be broke when the credit card bill comes. She's going to need some more shifts.

A guy comes in and drops ten dollars, masturbates a little, leaves when his time runs out. Someone else comes in, drops ten dollars, but just sits there uncertainly. Still more than forty minutes to go. She understands the urge of the girl who started singing into the microphone. Anything to break the monotony.

She can't pay attention to the score anymore and shuts it with a thump. Why am I doing this anyway, she wonders. Plenty of the dykes who work here work the lap dance places too, and make way more money. Why shouldn't she? Someone comes into the booth; she hasn't even looked up as they come down the hall.

She shuts the hallway curtain, opens the customer's, and nearly chokes on her customary greeting. Naoko's in the booth.

"My God!" Shauna screams. She fumbles to turn on the microphones. "What are you doing here?"

"I went to Fisherman's Wharf," she said. Indeed, Naoko is wearing a hat, T-shirt, jacket all emblazoned with the name of the city in really ugly typefaces, and is carrying a tote bag embroidered with FISHERMAN'S WHARF in big gold letters. "I made my host family stop here."

"Here?! Where are they?"

"Waiting outside in their minivan. Very surprised."

"Oh, my God!" Shauna says again. "Naoko, you're killing me. I can't believe you came to see me." Shauna feels like crying.

"You were right about Fisherman's Wharf. Total bullshit."

Shauna laughs. "I can't believe you made your host family drop you at a strip club!"

"They can't believe it either." Naoko is looking around. "This is not how I imagined it," she says. "I thought it would be prettier."

"It's kind of…functional," Shauna says. "My God! I have to give you a show!" She starts stripping off her underwear, but Naoko holds up her hand.

"Shauna, it's okay," she says. "I just saw you naked for four days."

"Oh sweetie," Shauna moans, pressing her hands up against the glass. "I want to put my arms around you. God, I've never wanted to bust through this glass so bad."

"I thought after four days I'd be tired of seeing you, but I think the opposite happened."

"Naoko, wait just half an hour. I'll be off in half an hour."

"I can't. They're waiting, I have to go. I've already spent ten minutes looking for you in this place."

"No, you can't. Please." Shauna pounds her fists on the glass.

"Be careful!" She stands up. "Shauna, listen. You've been wonderful to me. I had a wonderful summer. I'll always remember." She places her hands against the window, smiling, then leans over and plants her lips on the glass, leaving a big red imprint. "You look beautiful, Shauna. Bye-bye."

"Naoko!" But she leaves.

Shauna presses her cheek against the imprint. "Goddammit," she whispers, striking the glass one more time.

She sits there for a few minutes until she is startled by a knock on the hallway window. She flings the curtain open, but there's just some guy on the other side. "You open?" he asks.

Shauna stares at him. She's still stark naked. Other guys in the hallway—now crowded in the late afternoon—are turning to look.

She looks at the clock—half an hour to go. "Sure," she says. "Come on in." She closes the hallway curtain, hurriedly dabs at her eyes with a tissue, and goes back to work.

Couple

I met them at a café near the Castro. It was easy to tell which ones they were, among the other patrons. As advertised, she had long, straight black hair and pale skin; he had short hair, was smallish and slender, and didn't look quite like her type. But lots of couples in San Francisco look a little mismatched. That's the beauty of the place: You can't tell who anybody is, really.

We introduced each other and drank coffee. That is, I introduced myself, and then he introduced her and she him. That was so cute.

He sounded the way he had on the phone: polite, a little nerdy and a little depraved at the same time. "This is Julie. She came here when she was in college and never went back to Hong Kong. She lived for a while with some rich lawyer she met at a temp job, and then when he got sent to prison, she went to work stripping on Broadway. She looks extremely imposing, but she basically does anything I want her to."

"Huh, you just haven't found my limits yet. This is Larry—" she pronounced it not exactly "Lally," but somewhere between an *R* and an *L*—"and he met me when we were both temps. He has a band. Once in a while I would sneak away from that attorney to hear him play. He likes to push me around and he likes to take it up the ass, and the only time I get mad at him is when he can't decide which he wants."

"So we thought we'd get someone else involved and see if we can't all be happy," he said. "Now, about this party—you've been to them before, right?"

"Yeah," I said, "and I'm surprised I haven't seen you there."

He laughed. "I had a hood on," Julie said, a little embarrassed.

When we get there, things have already started. We missed (on purpose) the invocation to the sun, the moon, the Goddess, and the seven directions, or whatever; now the guests are mostly naked, making out on the couches or the mattresses that cover the floor. We take off our clothes and give them in paper shopping bags to the clothes check people, then go into the large, mattress-covered room.

"I'll leave you in good hands," Larry says, giving Julie a pat on the butt, and going over to a couple of women who are making out heavily.

She follows him with her eyes. "Watch, watch," she says. "Let's see how quickly he gets into their pants."

"They aren't wearing pants," I say unnecessarily.

"Shh."

We kneel on a mattress, her in front of me, facing the room so we can watch her boyfriend. I begin kissing her shoulder and exploring her body with my hands. She's shapely, not at all small; I have to peer over her shoulder to watch her boyfriend.

These parties, open by word of mouth only, are attended mostly by sex industry workers, sex information switchboard volunteers, and pornographers. They aren't the "swinger" parties of the suburbs, where husbands and wives swap partners for a little decorous adultery, and where any sign of male–male interest gets you thrown out. At these parties queerness is assumed, and anything goes. Lube, gloves, condoms, and rolls of paper towels are scattered around the room; the mattresses are covered in plastic, like the "walk-on-me" one at the bedding store on Market Street. No, these parties are the real thing, an honest, go-for-it, take-anything-you-can-negotiate orgy.

Julie is wearing a harness, a collar, and black leather boots. Her hair, which falls heavily past her shoulder blades, is loose. She guides my hands over her shoulders, her breasts, her stomach, her sides; she gently prods me with her ass. Larry is making out with one of the girls he interrupted, while her companion goes down on her. The girl Larry is kissing is reaching between his legs, taking his cock, and I can see him getting hard.

The sight of his cock turns me on, even while I have his lover in my arms. I want to go over there and suck it; perhaps it's just as well that he left me with his girlfriend.

"Look at his cock," she says in a low voice. "Isn't it gorgeous? Every time I see it, I cream. Here, feel between my legs."

"You're wet."

"You would be too if you knew what his cock can do."

"Tell me. Tell me while I touch you." Standing behind her, I reach down and begin stroking her cunt.

"Partly it's the way he fucks me. He almost never does it softly or slowly. He crashes into me and starts fucking like a maniac right from the start. It always takes my breath away; I never seem to be able to catch up, and after a while I stop trying, and just lie back and take it."

My fingers are swirling in her wetness. I find her clit and massage it slowly back and forth. "Tell me more."

"When he puts his cock into my mouth, it's the opposite, he remains almost completely still and I have to do everything, and I use both hands as well as my mouth, with one hand I tickle his balls, and jack him off with the other. My fingers are everywhere my mouth isn't. In my mouth, his cock is so warm and smooth, and so alive.... Oh, that feels good."

"Never mind me, just keep talking."

"Well, look, look at the way he's kneeling up now and holding his cock up for her to suck. Look at his hand on her head, holding himself deep in her—he's trying to see how far he can go before she gags—there, that's as deep as she goes. Now he'll just sit back and take it. Look at him, the selfish thing, lying back while that dyke sucks his cock. Mmm, keep touching me.... Now look at his face. See the pleasure he's getting? It makes me want to do it to you."

She turns around, bends down, and picks up a condom from the basket next to where we were standing—condoms for blowjobs and fucks are a party rule. Kneeling, she puts the rubber on my dick. "While I'm sucking you, keep watching, and tell me what's happening. If you tell me exactly what's happening, I'll make you come at the exact moment he does." She begins stroking my balls, and takes my cock into her mouth so suddenly my knees go weak.

"He's smiling," I say. "His head is thrown back and his eyes are closed. He looks exactly like someone who's getting their cock sucked. He's getting pleasure.... She's going down on him pretty fast, her head's moving up and down and her hair is swaying back and forth.... Oh man."

"Keep talking."

"Her girlfriend's got her mouth between her legs, and it's too bad I can't see her face. He's touching his own nipples now. He's moving his torso back and forth a little, he's sort of rocking. Now his head is swaying from side to side."

Her mouth is working on me. It feels like a warm whirlpool has captured my cock and is trying to pull it down into the depths. Her hands expertly touch my balls and asshole, and I find myself getting ready to come. It's soon, it's hard for me to come this way, but she's tremendous at this. I'm excited by this new lover and her boyfriend.

"I'm feeling really good...I think I'm getting ready to come...he's clenching his teeth, now he's panting, now it seems like he's growling, sort of...." Julie's mouth closes down on me, trapping me. The only person who ever made me feel like this was an older faggot who was a total expert at blowjobs and who could blow my head off every time. A woman has never done it this well, not to me.

"Now I think he's starting.... I—he's scratching his own nipples, the girl who's sucking him is pulling him close to her, she's got her arms around his butt, oh...."

I close my eyes. The sensation of my orgasm starts in my balls and the whole area around them, a rushing feeling that lasts for a second, then spreads into the rest of my body. I feel my skin flush with blood, and the come rockets up from my balls into the rubber. Julie pulls on my cock and wraps her other hand around my balls now, squeezing out another, stronger spasm. Feeling the come spilling out of my cock makes my prick feel like it's shattering.

I grunt, my throat tense along with the rest of my muscles, and now in the middle of my orgasm I open my eyes to see Larry looking back at me, across the room and also coming, also shooting come into some woman's mouth. His eyes and mouth are gaping wide with the sensation, like he's been shot.

Julie sucks harder now on my prick, determined to drain every last drop from me. Her lips go up and down, sucking. I look down and see her ass, turned away from me toward Larry. When I finally stop coming, she stops sucking and mumbles, "Just a second." She stands and takes a few steps toward Larry, then squats in front of him and masturbates for a few moments. Larry's eyes grow big again as he stares at her pussy, and he seems to come even harder. He starts bucking into the woman's mouth and moaning loudly.

I'm kneeling with my prick in my hand; it's pulsing, still hard. The orgasm was so good I forgot I had a rubber on.

Finally Larry sinks backwards like a tree falling, and so does the woman who was sucking him. Her partner, who's been going down on her the whole time, checks for signs of life and then goes back to her pussy.

Julie comes back and lies down in front of me, spreading her legs. "Sorry," she said. "I just wanted to give him a little thrill." She raises her knees and skootches down close to me so her cunt is in position to get fucked.

"I think you did," I say.

"Don't fuck me," she says, "just because I'm dripping wet and right next to your cock. Just because I've got your come dripping down my chin and your cock, which is still hard, is right here"—she reaches down and puts her hand around it, then takes off the rubber. "Just because you could, right this instant, don't fuck me."

Of course, since I have a condom on, she doesn't have come dripping down her chin—she's just saying that to be nice. "Okay," I say.

"With this cock of yours, that would feel so good in me, just because it would feel so good, don't fuck me."

"Did you want me to do something else?"

"I want nothing else, I want exactly to get fucked by you, but don't."

I'm starting to get the idea. I reach over and get another condom. But by the time I open it and start putting it on, I'm getting soft finally. "Oops, sorry."

Larry is sitting down next to me. "That was a nice little show you put on," he says.

"Same to you."

"Now you guys are both soft, what am I going to do?" Julie asks.

"You pick," Larry says to me.

"Okay," I say. "I'll lie down. Julie, you squat over my face and I'll lick you while you suck his cock. Then when he's hard, we can switch, he can fuck you from behind, and I'll still be underneath, I'll lick your pussy while his cock fucks you."

"Hmm, that's nice," she says. "But you have to use a barrier here."

"Oh yeah," I say. "Hmm, I guess we could try it."

"Great." She pushes me down on the mattress, tears a piece of plastic wrap from a roll in the basket, and positions her pussy over my mouth. "Get to work." I hear her tear off another piece. "I guess I have to use this for you too, until you get hard enough for a rubber."

Her pussy is a marvel of pushed-out labia, pink tissue turning almost dark in places, and wet. Reluctantly, I press the plastic over it and gently push it around so it conforms to her nooks and crannies as much as possible. She shifts her weight to bring her pussy lower. I press my lips and tongue to the plastic and try to feel for her clit. If you've never had to do this—and consider yourself fortunate if you haven't—imagine kissing someone through a piece of plastic wrap. I can smell her pussy, so close, but I can't touch it. As she sucks Larry's cock, she keeps moving around, and I can't do anything but try to follow her. I hope it's more fun for her than it is for me.

After a little while, she shifts away from me. Larry's cock is erect. They look down at me. "How you doing?" he asks.

"Not bad," I say gallantly.

"It can't be that great," Julie says. "Let's just take turns. Larry can fuck me first. Then you."

She kneels down on the mattress and he positions himself behind her, putting on a condom. "Let me help," I say. I put my mouth around his cock for a few moments, getting it wet, then steer it with my hand into her pussy. "Oo, that's nice," she says, so I squat next to them and keep my hand there to feel him start to slide in and out of her. "Can you feel his hand?"

"Yeah," he smiles.

"I'm touching his cock while he fucks you. It feels so nasty. It's like what I always imaged virtual-reality porn would feel like: You get to touch everything that's happening."

She sinks down on her elbows as he starts putting it to her hard. I have to take my hand out as it starts to get in the way. I reach behind him and tickle his balls while he fucks. "Oh ho ho," he laughs. "Oh man, that's great. Do that."

"What's he doing?"

"He's touching my balls."

"I can't wait to see you two boys fuck."

I touch his balls for a while until it seems to get old, and then there's really not much I can do except watch. Of course by now I'm just one of several people, mostly unattached like me, who are watching them fuck. I lie down on the mattress next to her, leaning on one elbow, and look up at Larry's face. He's grinning as he concentrates on her reactions, on the feel of her pussy, on how close he gets to coming. He's already come once in the other girl's mouth, and between that and the rubber, it's probably easy for him to control his orgasm.

"Oh yeah, do it, fuck me," she says. "Fuck me hard, boy. That's it…." Larry speeds up his thrusts as fast as he can go and still keep a steady rhythm, *pum-pum-pum-pum*. Finally one of them shifts and it falls apart.

She rolls over onto her back and he jumps back on top of her and fucks her hard again. "Oh shit," she says, her eyes squeezed shut.

"Yes," he says.

Julie is reaching down and doing her clit while he fucks her. "Oh yes, right there, do it," she spits out, and arches her back and clenches. She moans and then says loudly, "That's it." Her head rolls from side to side and she says, "Nnnn, nnnn, nnnn" and comes. She looks beautiful coming—I think everyone does.

He keeps up his pounding until she's done.

He stops and stays inside her while she comes back to the room. I look up and see three or four people watching and smiling and turning away, back to their own partners. A lone guy is standing there fingering his cock in that way unattached men do at sex parties, trying to keep themselves at least half-erect. "Want to watch?" I say to Larry and Julie as I roll to my knees and say to the onlooker, "Let me suck your cock."

He's just some white guy—I don't get much of a look at him. I watch him put a rubber on his cock—the rules again—and then I take him and start sucking. Larry and Julie sit back and watch.

It's odd, sucking a guy who's wearing a condom. I've done plenty of blowjobs with and without, and of course it's much more fun for both people without a condom, unless the person doing the sucking is a latex freak or really scared of diseases. But in some cases it's not an option, like at this party. They're strict about the rules at events like this, not only because they don't want people to spread disease, or even to keep from being liable, but because it's politically correct. If you're in the business of eroticizing safer sex, your sex party becomes a big demo lab for all the different ways to do it. So naturally people have to use condoms for blowjobs because that's safe.

Actually I kind of like the fact that I don't have to worry about what this guy may or may not be infected with. The other thing is that, because of the loss of sensitivity, there's no point in being subtle. You just have to go for it, adopting the full-on blowjob motions seen in millions of het porn loops. And the fact that it looks like a porn movie actually makes it more exciting for some people who want their sex life to look like that. Definitely more pornographic for Julie and Larry.

Just suck suck suck. I do, of course, touch the guy otherwise—tickle his balls and his butt. In fact, he takes one of my hands as it explores his ass cheek and pushes it against his ass. But you need a glove to touch somebody's asshole at this party, so I take my hand away.

I hear Julie and Larry stirring so I look over at them, as much as I can. I don't want them to get bored and go away. But it's just Larry going off to the toilet. Julie comes over and gently takes my cock in her hand and starts whispering in my ear.

"You look nice sucking a cock," she says. "You need to suck my boyfriend's cock sometime."

"Mm-hmm," I agree, still sucking the guy.

"But I'd rather talk about fucking you—isn't that what we were talking about before he came back over? I want to have this in my pussy." She's stroking my penis up and down in her soft hand, not seriously but in a way calculated to make me hard. She puts her other hand on my butt. "This is nice too…. I want to watch you having homo sex with Larry. You two fuck each other and I'll lie back and watch."

"Mm-hmm."

"I'll masturbate and watch this ass of yours going up and down while you're fucking my boyfriend's anus…. What you can't see, while your mouth is full of dick, is that my cunt is still wet, still really wet where you licked it, and I still need to get fucked. I got fucked once but I want you to fuck me again. I want this…."

I'm getting pretty excited, with a mouth full of cock and her whispering to me like that. About this time, the guy I'm sucking either gets miffed because he's not the center of attention, or he wants to save his orgasm for later. He backs away, says thanks, and walks off, peeling the rubber off his cock.

I turn and look at Julie. She's smiling back at me. We kiss, pushing our tongues into each other's mouths. I give her a little shove down on her back and straddle her, my dick safely rubbing on her belly. She touches both my nipples and gets them hard. Looking into my eyes, she says, "So listen. I want to tell you something while Larry's still in the bathroom."

"Uh-huh?"

"I'm not supposed to fuck other people. Even at parties. But I want to fuck you."

"Oh yeah?"

"I'm going to call you in a day or two."

"Okay."

Larry comes back and squats down facing me, behind her head. "What are you doing with my girlfriend?" he says playfully.

"Plotting behind your back," I say in the same playful tone.

"We're running off together," she says.

"Okay, whatever," he says, going along with the joke.

"Can we fuck?" I ask, as if we hadn't had our private little conversation, because it's natural I would ask, and we haven't officially negotiated it yet.

"No, we only fuck each other," Julie says. "Sorry."

"I meant him," I say as a joke. "I want to fuck *him*."

"Oh, sure, go ahead."

He doesn't look like he wants to, and I really was just kidding. "Actually I'm going to go exploring," I say. "I'll see you guys later."

I spend the next hour or so watching people screw around in various ways. There's a place in the basement to tie people up. A big, Amazon-type white girl with her blond hair in corn rows is attached there, getting flogged by a Unix hacker type with long hair and a beard. There's also a short guy standing close to the girl getting whipped, trying to excite her with his fingers and talking urgently to her, but she seems to be paying much more attention to the whipping. The guy whipping her knows what he's doing; he gets her going up to a point and then, judging by the noises she's making, backs off, starts in again, and takes her a little higher, then backs off. The girl is really getting into it, her voice completely under his control; his methodical pace lulls her into his rhythm and lets him take her higher and higher. During one of the periodic pauses in the whipping, she says something and the little guy walks off. For a few minutes I watch the whipping continue. After a few minutes the little guy comes back and stands next to me and watches.

He glances at me and mutters, "Some date."

"You mean you came to the party with her?"

He nods. The expression of lust and frustration on his face is priceless.

In another room in the basement, two guys are doing a piercing scene with a bunch of hooks and fishing line. They have a big sheet spread out and have actually hung up a little sign that says CAUTION! BLOOD PLAY! They have a charming, casual air and I'd like to hang out and watch and flirt with them while they dig fish hooks into each other. But there's something so intimate about the scene that I feel I would be intruding.

After a long time I go back upstairs. The energy is less intense than before; a lot of people are just lying together and chatting like at any party, only horizontal and mostly naked. There are still a bunch of guys standing around with desperate expressions trying to keep their cocks hard, looking more and more conspicuous. Larry and Julie are lying down, her head on his shoulder, not doing much. I stop by and chat a little, then thank them for the fun and get my clothes and leave.

Standing on Divisadero in the cold wind, I wait for the number 24 bus and get a little depressed over the evening. It was fun playing with Larry and Julie but I was kind of hoping for a little more action from somebody else, just to prop up my ego with the phenomenon of being desired by a stranger. I envied the ability of Larry to just plunge into the scene between those women; I've never been so socially confident. To make myself feel better, I remember how excited Julie made me when she was playing with my cock and whispering to me about wanting to fuck me. When I get home and into bed, that's what I think about as I jack off before going to sleep.

Still, I'm surprised when she does call me two days later. "Hey," she says. "What are you doing?"

"Reading the Sunday paper. There's an op-ed by some right-winger about how consumer choice is going to make China more free."

"Oh, yeah, that'll work. 'Bite the wax tadpole.'"

"How's that?"

"That's how they first translated 'Coca-Cola' into Chinese. They used characters that can be pronounced *Ke-kou-ke-la* but actually those sounds mean 'Bite the wax tadpole.'"

"I'm so glad you told me that. That makes my day."

"Want to go for a walk?"

"Sure."

"I'll come over there," she says. I give her the address.

I take a shower and put on my Shonen Knife T-shirt and some sunscreen. She comes over after half an hour, her long black hair like a flag in the wind blowing across my stoop.

"Where do you want to go?" I ask.

"Nowhere," she says, barging through the door and pushing me against the wall in the hallway. She shoves the door closed and takes the hat away from me and throws it on the floor. "What, did you think we were going *hiking?*"

"Yeah."

"I told you," she says. "I said I'd call you. Why do you think I called you?"

"Aren't you being monogamous?"

"Watch me."

She kisses me, pushing her hands up under my T-shirt. She presses her tongue against my tongue, grabs at my flesh with her hands, rubs her palms on my skin.

"Whoa," I say when the kiss was over.

"Come on," she says. "Where's the bedroom?"

"Down there."

"Good, let's do it on the couch in here." She sits down in the front room and starts taking off her boots. I go to get a towel and rubbers and lube, and by the time I come back, she's naked on the couch, her arms behind her head.

I take my clothes off, smiling at her. "You look amazing," I say. "Enticing. Scrumptious."

"You going to fuck me now?"

"Yeah."

"Good," she says as I approach her naked. "You still have to use a condom, though."

We fuck on the couch—me on top at first. After a while she flings her legs over my shoulders and I fuck her deeper, hard, the way she said she likes it. Then she turns around and I fuck her from behind while she holds onto the armrest. We change again and she stands on the floor and braces herself on the couch while I enter her from behind. Finally she turns and sinks back against the couch and I enter her frontwise again. She tells me to come and I do. It's glorious.

I stay inside her for a few minutes, with her thrusting at me from time to time as my cock softens. Finally I have to take it out, and she protests playfully.

"I hate it when they have to take it out! Get hard again! I want it again."

"I've got a strap-on if it comes to that."

"Oh, don't worry. We have ways of making you hard."

She takes a deep breath, staring out into the room for a moment. Then she scrambles up on her knees, facing me with one knee between my legs, and starts kissing me again. We do that for quite a while.

"Kissing is great," I say when we break off.

"Sure it is."

"So…." I'm really wondering why she is here, doing this, but I don't know how to ask.

She kisses me again. Then she says, "Can you go down on me again?"

"You bet."

"No plastic this time."

"That's good."

"I've got until five o'clock," she goes on.

"That's enough time."

"Then I have to go."

"Okay, I'll eat your pussy until five."

She laughs. "I wish!"

We mess around for the rest of the afternoon. When she is ready to leave and we are kissing at the door, I say, "So how about next Sunday?"

"Yeah, maybe," she says in a blasé tone, as if I'd asked her if she was going to watch TV later on that evening.

"'Yeah, maybe?'" I echo. "Come on."

"I'm being noncommittal," she says. "I am in a relationship, you know."

"Right. A monogamous relationship."

"Yeah, so I can't just go and fuck people," she laughs sheepishly.

"I see."

She kisses me again. "This was fun," she says. "Don't call me, though. Here's my e-mail, if you want." She hands me a card. "See ya."

A few minutes later I go out and do some errands. I go to the video store and get some takeout sushi at a counter in the supermarket. Walking along 24th Street in the early evening and looking in the windows of the shops, I recall all of the day's high points, from the moment she phoned me to the way she kissed me in the shower when we were done. I try to take snapshots of the day, inscribe the sounds and sights and feelings in my memory. It makes me so happy to be desired by someone, to play all day with them, to part fondly, even if I don't know when it might happen again.

I don't get home until after seven. As I'm eating my California rolls and watching the ball game on TV, the phone rings.

Could it be her calling back so soon? I go get the phone and bring it back into the living room, because the Giants have a man on first and the game is tied. "Hello?"

I almost drop my chopsticks when I hear the voice of Larry, Julie's boyfriend.

"Hey, that was fun the other night," he says. "I was kind of sorry you went off so soon."

"Yeah, well, you know...." I say vaguely, keeping my eye on the TV. Barry Bonds is batting while Marvin Benard, the Giants' pint-sized center fielder, takes a lead off first base.

"So listen," he says. "You know, me and Julie are supposed to be monogamous."

"Yeah," I say, dreading the confrontation.

"But I was wondering if—you know—you wanted to get together, you and me," he says.

Benard takes off running. "There he goes!" exclaims the baseball announcer. "Swing and a miss...the throw is on line...and he's safe! Benard steals second."

"You and me," I echo. "Yeah. You mean to mess around?"

"Yeah, if you want to."

The catcher goes out to the mound. Now they'll probably walk Barry, with first base open.

"Sure...when?"

"Julie's out tonight," he says. "We can meet someplace and then, I dunno, go back to your place?"

"So this is kind of a monogamous-not-monogamous thing?"

"Yeah, kind of."

The catcher walks back to the plate. Hmm, they're going to pitch to him.

"Do you tell her?"

"Mmm…not really."

"So…what do you want to do?" I ask.

"What do *you* think?" he says.

Bonds swings and misses at a slider, low and away.

"No, you have to tell me on the phone," I tease. Now that I understand what's going on, I feel in control. "What do you want to do when you come over here?"

"I want to suck your cock."

"Oh yeah?"

"Yeah."

"Tell me about it."

"I want to feel your dick in my mouth. I want to grab your butt and pull you close to me and make you feel good. Ever since I saw your cock at the party, I've been wanting to do it."

"So why didn't you do it at the party?"

"I don't like using rubbers."

"Oh, so you want me to come in your mouth?"

"I totally do. So how about it? Are you busy?"

The pitcher checks the runner at second, then hurls the ball to the plate. Bonds's eyes get big as he sees the curve ball float toward him, failing to dip, staying up, and then all at once he swings and hits it a mile.

"There it goes!" the announcer screams.

"Yeah, come on over," I say.

Kill Me with Your Kiss

Joey showed me his gun for the first time one afternoon after we fucked. He had come over early that day, while I was working on a song, remixing the tracks for a dance tune to complete a record that was four months overdue. He rang the bell just as I was wrapping up a vocal track, the second lead vocal that said, "Kill me with your kiss."

I looked out the window to see him bouncing up and down on the front step, charged as usual with energy. But when he came in I saw he was more bouncy than usual. He came into my room and grabbed me by the shirt front and pulled me down to his mouth. I was holding in one hand a pen that I had been using to make notes; in the other hand was an empty coffee cup. I thought we would go down to the kitchen and make coffee and chat, like we always do before we start fooling around, but he had burst into my room before I could even get to the doorway.

After a minute I dropped the pen on the floor. After another minute I dropped the cup. It broke. We never made it downstairs.

"What? What?" I asked, laughing, as he dragged me down on the floor next to the bed. I've got a thing for doing it on the floor, so that meant he was happy to see me. You never know with Joey. Sometimes he's all torn up over some chick he's seeing, or, more often, not seeing. Women drive him crazy. I, on the other hand, make a lot of sense. That's me, the logical one.

He dragged me down to the floor and started pulling my T-shirt as if he wanted to rip it apart. He wasn't getting anywhere with ripping it, but it seemed as if he might strangle me. After a minute I knocked him away and took off the shirt real quick before he could do any damage to it. He bounced back and hugged me close, dragging his nails down my back. That gets me every time. I arched in response, my cock stiffening, my throat opening with a groan.

Then his hands were on my pants, grabbing. He was so hyped up I thought he might be on something, but I didn't really care, as long as he didn't introduce any sharp objects and cut me too deeply by accident. My legs have a weird collection of scars from one such day. We had taken ecstasy and in the middle of our trip, after we had fucked and slapped and whipped each other crazy, he picked up an X-acto knife I had lying around and said, "I always wanted to try this." Before I knew it, he had made a long mark down his arm that dribbled blood. Then he brought his arm to his mouth and sucked it and swooned. "It's fantastic, try it," he said. A half hour later we were both carved up like high school desks. We had just barely enough sense not to get blood all over each other, not that it mattered.

I was kneeling, and my cock sprang out as he opened my pants. "Joey, what's going on, man?" He shoved me on my back and swallowed my dick. I gave up asking him to what I owed the honor, and just lay back and closed my eyes. His mouth was all over me; his hands were slapping my thighs and my belly, anything they could reach. He was out of his mind. I didn't even ask before I shot off into his mouth, shouting.

Then he was turning me over, yanking my pants down to my knees, jabbing at my butt with his prick. My naked cock, still dribbling come and sensitive as hell, scraped against the floorboards, making me yell. He swatted my ass with his hands, and for some reason paused to put a rubber on. "Oh God oh God oh God," he was saying. I was secretly squeezing my ass muscles, desperately trying to get enough control to relax them before he shoved his cock in me selfishly. "Men don't care," an old girlfriend used to say to me as she eased into my butt with her fingers, "they don't go slow, they aren't gentle, they only want your hole. They go hard and fast and they don't stop. They're men."

His spit dripped down my ass. I hoped the rubber was lubricated. Then I felt his prickhead jabbing against me. I clamped down tight one last time, then relaxed as he found the spot. Instantly I was fucked. He was starting to yell, the same words over and over, "Oh God oh God oh God oh God." My eyes teared up—he was hurting me, I was choking—then I was yelling too, the adrenaline making me heedless of my cock as it scraped over the rough wood. I got stiff again. I tried digging into the floor with my fingernails, then I pounded it with my fists. A cramp starts, so intense I think I'm going to throw up; then my body surrenders. He shouts with triumph, "You fucking slut! You fucking slut!" His hands claw at my back, slap me, and the only reason I'm safe from his teeth is that he likes coming in low and feeling his balls rub the bed, or floor. "Fuck you, fuck you, fuck you, fuck you," he chants, then comes, screaming, pounding me. I've never been fucked so beautifully, I wish he had the knife in his hand now and was stabbing me, cutting me, dissolving me into liquid the same way his prick is dissolving inside me, his mouth drooling, his nails digging into the scars we made together, and his voice screaming to God to fuck off and die.

When he finishes he collapses on me, still shouting—he's really groaning but he's so hyped up that he's shouting as loudly as he can. I imagine people on the street pausing outside in alarm, then rushing to their homes to call 911. I roll him off me and find his mouth with my prick. He's breathing too hard to suck me, but his hot breath feels good.

Rocking his hips from side to side, his hands held between his legs like a girl, he finally calms down. I consider flipping him over and fucking him, but he's so clearly in his own world it wouldn't make a difference. The only thing that matters more to me than fucking him is having him pay attention to me when I do, so I hold off, stroking myself. The rosette light fixture on the ceiling hovers above us, and the afternoon sun comes out.

After ten minutes he finally opens his eyes. "Hi," he says.

"What the fuck got into you?"

He laughs, sits up. His face is coated with drying sweat, and the corners of his mouth are wet.

"Whatever it is, give me some so I can get as high as you," I say, more to the point.

He laughs again. "It's not that," he says huskily. I love his voice after he's just come, so relaxed and full, so sexy. I wish he were like this all the time instead of always so wired. Sometimes he practically squeaks. I call him Lucy then, like Lucy Ricardo. Ricky and Lucy, that's us.

He notices me touching myself. "Do you want me to…?"

"Later."

He struggles to his knees, goes out into the hallway of my apartment, picks up the jacket that he peeled off on his way into the room. "Look."

He reaches into the pocket and takes out a gun. It's the first gun I've ever seen. It's a pistol—no, a revolver, black and shiny; it looks brand new. He holds it casually.

"Fuck," I say.

"Don't worry, it isn't loaded."

"Fuck," I say again, drawing the word out.

"Look at it. Isn't it beautiful? It's a .38 special. It's a little smaller than other .38s."

"Where did you get it?" My cock has gone totally limp.

"San Francisco Gun Exchange on Second Street. I paid for it two weeks ago and just picked it up today."

"Fuck," I repeat.

"And look at this."

He goes back into the hall and gets his bag. He takes out a complicated brown leather strap thing, puts it over his head—it's a holster! He sticks the gun in it, kneels down on the floor again. I look up at him, leaning on my elbow. I have to admit, he looks indescribably delicious, shirt off, cock hair wet, sweaty, dangerous, mean. I want to go over and lick him, suck him off, submit to him. I want him to rape me again, slap my face until my mouth is bloody, beat me up like Frank Silvera got clobbered in Stanley Kubrick's *Killer's Kiss*. I'm a slender girl who wants to be crushed against him, slammed against the wall, enslaved on a dance floor, made to say anything. My cock is getting hard again and, against all expectations, he lowers his head and, still wearing his gun, sucks my prick.

An explosion; for a brief instant, sunlight on the ceiling.

↶

A sunny Saturday. We drive through the city, over Portola, past the zoo, out Skyline Boulevard. In Colma we peel off the highway and drive past cemeteries and housing tracts, shitty garages and motels. We stop at red lights, stare straight ahead, listen to *All Things Considered*. The wind is heavy in the eucalyptus trees.

We pull into a driveway between two cinderblock buildings, park next to Buicks and Broncos, get the small hard plastic case out of the truck, pay at a beaten wooden counter. It's like a bowling alley for bullets. We put on ear protectors, go to a tiny enclosure, take out the weapon from the plastic case and two boxes of bullets from my bag.

There's a target of a man wearing a mask, like the Beagle Boys in *Uncle Scrooge*. The gun spurts again and again, the cubicle is filled with explosions and flashes. He teaches me to breathe, to pull the trigger and squeeze, and the only time we touch is when he stands behind me and helps me shoot. We nod at each other's scores and are careful not to touch again, or to smile at anything. My prick fills in my pants. The Beagle Boy is dead, over and over.

Outside the wind is stronger than ever, and my ears are ringing. The world sparkles as if I'm on acid. We drive back up El Camino. I point at a motel. He parks, goes inside, pays. I follow him dumbly to a room, where we close the door, fall to the floor, do nasty things. The carpet stinks of cleaning fluids, and the polyester burns my knees and elbows.

Finished, we lie together until the neon sign outside blinks on. He wants me to piss right here on the floor. His voice is low, urgent, his teeth bite my back and shoulder. When I do it, he groans, his voice becomes high, and I turn, direct the stream between his legs, call him names. My fingers inside his mouth, he doesn't have a chance to answer.

We do this—go to the shooting range, then to the sleazy motel—every few days for a month.

༄

The dance record is finished and sent to the "producer"—really, a friend of mine who releases my compositions to the world. He decides to cut some single CDs. If they catch on we could make some money; if what usually happens happens, the song will be bought by a bunch of Germans, for some reason the only people who've taken a liking to my work. Naturally the song he picks for the single is the one I was working on when Joey did me. I can't listen to it without thinking of him.

He has disappeared. His voice mail records me faithfully, but he never calls me back. I don't even know where he lives.

I see my girlfriend, Carry, and tell her about Joey's gun. She sucks me, dragging her nails down my legs, then makes me suck her, hard silicone latex in my mouth, saying, "Put your mouth around it, that's right, faggot, let me shoot into your throat, take me. Now tell me who I am. Who's doing this to you?" She doesn't give me a chance to answer.

I happen to go to my doctor. He looks at me, shakes his head over the scars on my legs and back, and looks at me with an alarmed expression when I ask him to look at my ears. A referral to an audiologist confirms a slight hearing loss. That's from the shooting.

After the appointment with the audiologist I go outside into the wind. I'm sleepy from staying up half the night to work on a new song, a recording that includes the gunshots I recorded at the range one day. The song has the words, "I want to put a bullet in you, a missile of love that goes right through you"—typical shitty rock song words. It's not me speaking.

I take the streetcar to the beach and stumble along the sand in my inappropriate shoes, listening to the wind roar in my ears. I realize how stupid, how banal, it is for a musician to have hearing loss, but to me it's just another scar, a product of my love for that boy, a way he marked me. A souvenir.

It's cold. I want to lie down, but instead I keep walking, south, south, south, past the zoo and toward Devil's Slide. A hang glider lands a hundred yards in front of me and I realize I've gone all the way to Fort Funston. I help the guy carry his rig up the dunes to the parking lot as it gets dark, go with him for a beer, wonder if this is a seduction. It's not. He lets me off in front of my house after telling me about Jesus Christ. I assure him my boyfriend prays to God all the time.

ॐ

When he reappears, Joey has too much money and needs to lay low. It's night and the streetlight throws the ceiling rosette into stark relief. He falls asleep with my tongue in his mouth before we do anything, and I cover him and go to bed in the spare room. It takes me two hours to finally get to sleep.

He sleeps for thirteen hours. Downstairs it's morning and I'm weeding the tomatoes when he sticks his head out of the spare room's window. I squint up at him against the sun. "Want some breakfast?"

He tells me, between bites of eggs and pancakes, about San Diego, lying on the beach, turning tricks at a bar full of Marines, getting beaten up, having his connection recruit him into the business. For two months they sold crank to Marines and truck drivers;

then they got jumped by some fucked-up street gang kids. Somehow Joey ended up with the money and beat it up here. He hasn't checked his voice mail all this time, but I know what's on it: "Hi, it's Mark, where are you, Joey, did you forget my number?" and my fucking number and maybe even my address all over the voice mail, I can't remember.

I explode at him, telling him he's a stupid fuck-up, cursing him for getting me mixed up in it, telling him to take a shower while I pack. I push clothing and the hard disk into a duffel bag, then load all my equipment, the mixers and keyboards and thousands of dollars worth of electronic shit, into the back of the car and drive two blocks away to leave it with my girlfriend. Back at the house, I burn my address book, burn the folder that has receipts for my storage space and voice mail, consider burning the whole house down. Joey is cheerful, friendly. He thinks it's all a joke, so I humor him, ask him to humor me by shutting all the windows and turning off the electricity in the basement, and would you please get in the car now.

We stop at my bank just long enough to empty my account. Then it's east on the freeway, we flee toward Nevada. Paranoically I pay for gas and meals with cash, as if some drug gang from Tijuana has the pull to check my Chevron bill. I don't care, I'm the logical one. Just get me out of here.

In Salt Lake City we abandon the car at the airport, take a shuttle to the bus station, and head east again. By the time we reach St. Louis I figure we're safe. On the phone, Carry tells me that, as far as she can tell, my house is untouched. Good, let it stay that way for a few years.

I take Joey to a college-town Holiday Inn on a bluff overlooking the river valley. We stay for a week, coming down from the road, finally getting relaxed enough to have sex. We score some acid from a college drug pusher and have a celebratory weekend, one last fling before getting a shitty flat in St. Louis and living out the decade.

High, I love him again, remember how much I missed him. "If you had just come back earlier," I say, over and over again, "we wouldn't be here." I'm lucky: He wants me. While we're high, we fuck on and on. The huge sign comes on and explodes against the sunset, the Holiday Inn star beckoning us into the stratosphere. After we've done everything we can think of, I pull the gun out of his holster. It's dirty and scratched now, I suppose from all the paranoid drug runs it's been on. He's on his knees before me as I stand over him, telling him I own him, telling him to do everything for me. I take out the bullets without him seeing. "Open," I say, and push the barrel into his waiting mouth.

"Suck. You're mine now, you bitch. You'll suck me forever. Suck me like you want it. Suck my hard thing, faggot. Tell me you want it. No, don't talk. Just show me. That's right."

It's hot. Outside in the parking lot a car goes by. From its stereo, my song is booming, and before I come, I know he'll fuck me again, just like on that first day, coming and screaming and hitting me, like he really does care about me, like it really does matter.

Quizzle

The night began with an invitation from my brother Gel.

"I want you to come with me to this new club called Quizzle."

"Quizzle?" I said into the phone. "What's that mean, they ask you trivia questions at the door?"

"No, you idiot, it's for 'Queer Sizzle.' Come on, it's going to be hot. Get it? Lots of cute young boys. Sizzle. Hot."

"I get it. But darn, I think I have to do the laundry. It's getting out of hand," I said, looking across the room at the piles of freshly folded T-shirts and jeans on the bed. "Also, Daylight Savings Time ends this weekend and I can't stand losing an hour's sleep. I turn into Morey Amsterdam."

"You never want to go out, how can you complain you never meet anybody?" he said. "Are you going to sit in your apartment for the rest of your life?"

"Till menopause."

"Johnny, who do you think you are, the French Lieutenant's Woman? So you're a widow already. If you don't get out and meet somebody, your face is going to get bedsores. And besides, you don't lose an hour's sleep, you gain it. I'm picking you up at ten."

"All right," I said. "But no drugs, can you promise that?"

Gel had hung up.

I dressed simply, in familiar clothes, while playing familiar music. I got sleepier and sleepier and considered canceling once Gel arrived. It was getting more and more difficult to get out of the house, it was so comfortable and quiet. But I didn't want to disappoint him.

I had just resigned myself to going and had put on my favorite jacket when the doorbell rang.

"Ooo, nice Brady Bunch T-shirt, but the jacket has to go," Gel said as soon as he reached the top of the stairs.

"The jacket?" I asked, shocked.

"It's sweet, but more like for a funeral. Try this," he said, slipping off his jacket made of blue ostrich feathers.

I didn't move. "Gel, I always wear this jacket."

"I know, that's why it has to go."

"It's Michael's jacket," I said, drawing myself into it protectively.

"I know, Johnny. That's the other reason it has to go."

"Gel, don't start lecturing me now. We're not kids anymore, you can't push me around."

He was already shoving me up against the wall, using one of his Queer Safety Patrol techniques. "You got two choices, mister. Give up the jacket or go to jail."

"Okay, okay," I grunted, face flat against the molding. "Take it. Just hang it up, okay?"

He slipped the jacket off my back and held it on the end of one finger. "I'd say burn it but I'm a sentimental guy at heart. You can keep it to wear while you jack off looking at your boyfriend's picture, just don't wear it out of the house anymore, okay?" He let the jacket drop to the floor.

"Look, Gel," I said in a normal voice, "let's not go too far with this."

"That's just where I'm taking you, Johnny," he said, propelling me toward the stairs and throwing the blue feather jacket after me. "I'm taking you too far."

Gel, née Jerry, was younger, but had always been the boss. From about the time he was five and I was seven, he could beat me up through sheer ruthlessness: He was the first person ever to kick me in the balls. When I hit puberty and started to grow faster than he did, he took judo to maintain his advantage. He came out before me and wouldn't let me rest until I had, too. He told me about safe sex and why I had to do it. He steered me away from a relationship with a closeted married man who was afraid to be seen with me in public. He took me to queer rights demonstrations, dragged me with him to the front lines, then protected me when the cops went bananas.

I always expected people to find him insufferable. Instead, the older we got, the more people loved him. At some point he figured out how to be charming yet modest, and he's had men, women, children, employers, shop clerks, bartenders, and total strangers lining up for his attention ever since. I've always thought he developed his drag Alice-in-Wonderland persona in self-defense, so all those people wouldn't overwhelm him.

A taxi was waiting downstairs. Gel walked up to it and struck a pose by the back door. Obviously the driver wasn't going to open it, so I did. Gel ducked his head and climbed in.

I got in after him and saw another man sitting on the other side of Gel. He was dressed in Elton John drag similar to Gel's, with giant sunglasses he had to take off when he wanted to see anything. Presently he had them pushed up onto his forehead so he could see to unwrap a little square of aluminum foil. "Here we are," the man said, giggling.

Gel took something tiny from the foil and popped it into his mouth, chasing it with a swig from an Evian bottle he pulled from his purse.

"I thought we weren't doing drugs," I protested, feeling excluded.

"That's what you said," he yawned. "Change your mind? Want any?"

"No, and I'm not babysitting you, either," I snapped.

"Try and be a little less hostile, Johnny. I'm taking you out, remember? You don't really think I invited you out so I could get you to take care of me while I'm high, do you?"

"I did the E, what did you do?" asked the other guy.

"I'm doing acid, it's better for dancing," Gel replied. "I don't feel like loving everybody in the world, it's too hard to dish their outfits."

This made me snicker despite myself. Gel said, "See, I knew you weren't really mad at me. I'm glad. We'll find you a special someone tonight as long as you have a good attitude."

"I'm Ginger," the other guy said, replacing his eyegear.

"Gingivitis," Gel put in.

"Gin gin gin goes the trolley," Ginger said as the taxi passed a motorized cable car full of tourists.

"This is Johnny. Johnny, is Ginger your type?"

"I'm sure he is," I said with optimism, wondering what I was missing on television.

"Well, someday he'll come along, the man you love," Gel concluded.

Ginger instantly started singing, but immediately ran out of lyrics. "What comes next, Johnny?"

"Penetration," Gel suggested.

Ginger squawked like a chicken and changed his tune. "I want a brave man, I want a caveman, Johnny show me that you care, really care, for me."

"Honey, stick to lip-synch," Gel said.

The taxi hurtled through the Tenderloin and then turned south toward Market Street. I looked up at City Hall when we passed. Other nights I had stood on the steps with Michael at candlelight memorials, or with Gel at chaotic protests. Now it was quiet and dark, but inside you could see wooden joists, installed to prop the place up after the earthquake a few years ago. Gel and Ginger were chattering about fabulous events that had taken place recently, friends' bon mots and faux pas, and the Halloween costumes they were preparing. Their energy was impressive; I reminded myself that they got up in late afternoon and this was midday to them.

We pulled up to the club and stood in line to get carded. Gel insisted on paying my four dollars. "It's a benefit for the police brutality focus group," the doorman announced.

"Do they give lessons?" Ginger asked loudly. The music was already really loud.

"Cool jacket," the doorman said, giving me back my driver's license. I looked him in the eye, cruising for practice, and of course he was gorgeous in a beefy way, but after giving me a friendly smile, he turned to the next person in line.

"The jacket is a hit!" I shouted, turning back to Gel and Ginger, but they had vanished in the crowd. I went unconcernedly up to the rectangular bar that dominated the center of one room and ordered a beer while I dug in my pocket for my earplugs. Staring into space, I drank the beer and listened to muffled booming. Standing there became boring after exactly one minute, so I eased away from the bar and struck out in one direction. I knew from experience that making one's way slowly through such a crowd generally provided enough distractions so I wouldn't have to think about missing *Star Trek*. This time, I was the distraction.

"Johnny, new look, huh?"

"Hey, Big Bird!"

"Ostrich plucker!"

I turned to see who had said this, and found myself looking at a slender...well, at first I thought it was a dyke, and on second glance I was still confused, but the figure finally resolved itself into a slender, olive-skinned boy wearing a ribbed white tank top, which is what fooled me because all the dykes were wearing ribbed white tank tops that year because of that actress in *Bound*. "Oh my God," I said. "It's Gina Gershon. Hi, Gina!"

"'Oh Caesar,'" he pouted. "No wait, that's the other bitch. 'Oh Mr. DiGiacomo. I'll fix your plumbing.'"

Gina, or whatever his name was, laughed and sipped his beer. We turned away from each other for the requisite five seconds, then found ourselves looking back at each other.

Suddenly we were too close to do anything but kiss. But you didn't do that in the open in this bar; making out in front of everybody was thought to smack of a slightly older generation of Castro clones. I took his elbow and steered him to a darker back corner and we made out next to a tower of beer cases. I liked the feel of his waist under my hands, and I liked the fact that his face was smooth and not scratchy. Maybe he really was a dyke. Maybe I was getting a contact high from all the drugs that everybody was on.

After making out for a few minutes, we simply stopped, smiled at each other, and parted. I had half a hard-on and a slight feeling of disorientation. It was like eight or nine years ago, around the time I met Michael (as if I don't remember the exact date), when I went to clubs a lot. They were even playing a song from that time. I felt dreamy, partly because of the earplugs, which gave me a detached feeling, like wearing sunglasses at night. I headed upstairs.

There was a narrow, dark stairway with people standing along it, talking, and people going both down and up. You could hear voices more clearly because the music wasn't as deafening and the walls were close together, so I heard loud voices without understanding them, and as soon as I managed to squeeze past one person, another loomed up behind him coming downstairs. It was like a murky dream of a video game, in which figures would pop up in your way and you'd have to maneuver around them; or like driving on Mission Street.

When I finally made my way to the top and into the upstairs bar, I ordered another drink and looked around. There were mostly couches up there, filled with people dressed more like Gel than Gina. Lots of Elton John knock-offs and refugees from *Priscilla: Queen of the Desert.* Come to think of it, in my blue feather jacket I was hardly in a position to judge.

My beer arrived at the same time that someone came up behind me and just stood there. Holding the glass of beer, I turned, sipping, and saw a short person with a buzz cut and a lot of makeup. He, or she, wore a pink sweater and a leather mini-skirt and thigh-high boots. The head was round and the whole package reminded me of Charlie Brown in drag. I honestly could not determine the gender of this person, and I smiled, bemused.

"I have something for you," said the person.

"First you must tell me your name," I shouted. The music was still loud upstairs.

"Akula," was the answer. That was no help.

I shrugged and smiled. But Akula turned and walked off.

I blinked after Akula, then raised my glass. Glancing down, I saw floating in it, exactly in the center, a tiny scrap of paper with little perforations on two sides and the printed design of a smiley face.

It was LSD. I don't know how the person got it in there without me noticing, but at least he or she had the decency to tell me.

I looked at it floating there. All thoughts went out of my head. Sipping, I transferred the scrap of paper to a position under my tongue. Then I put the beer on the bar and walked away. I can't really claim to have made a decision, because I didn't really think about it. But I knew it would still be my responsibility.

I went over to the side of the room that faces the street. There were windows there, but they were painted over. While I waited to come on, I reflected on how both the Akula person and Charlie Brown were essentially sexless. Sexless bald people, like monks—sexless like I had been, living in the years since Michael died. But I wasn't bald.

I felt the small wave of anxiety that precedes a high, something entirely emotional: Have I done the right thing, will I be okay, so forth. I quieted myself and stood at the edge of the room.

I knew it was starting when I felt like I had to take a dump. Acid always opens up my ass. I made my way to the bathroom— fortunately there was one on the upstairs level. It was occupied, though, and while I waited I meditated on the sensations of my intestines relaxing and the vibrations coming through the floor from the bass speakers. I said to myself, "Oh, I'm just more aware of the vibrations now because I'm coming on," and for the next few minutes

I dismissed everything with the thought, "Oh, it just seems that way because I'm coming on."

I emerged from the bathroom with an empty ass and a shining face; I ordered a mineral water, and turned to survey the room, monitoring my expression in the bar mirror from time to time. One of my tactics, while high in public, is not to show that I am. I kept my face composed and friendly without seeming too unreasonably cheerful. Still, it grew increasingly difficult not to find amusing practically everything I saw.

Here's a confession: I never hallucinate, and I never forget that what I see is influenced by the drug. Instead of seeing things that aren't there, I have the impression that everything has been set up for the entertainment of someone on acid—as if someone arranged for me to encounter just the kind of too-ironic silliness that is perfect for the drugged mentality.

Being in the club helped. Consider the drag queen who now approached me. I couldn't tell if she, in her four-inch heels, bright red tube top, and skirt made of plastic drinking straws, was high too, but since I was, I felt on the same wavelength and appreciated her all the more. She stopped in front of me, did a runway turn, and planted a kiss on my cheek. I laughed and thanked her.

"It's the least I could do for a great big bird like you," she said.

I looked down at the blue feather jacket—I had forgotten about it—and broke up laughing. But I was careful not to get carried away; composing myself, I asked, "What's your name?"

"Margarita deVille."

"Well, you look great."

"So do you, honey, so do you." She leaned close to me and whispered, "Come and see me in the room later."

I nodded, uncomprehending, and she tottered off. Did she say "the room?" What room? Must be something known by the initiated. I pushed off the bar the way a cosmonaut pushes off against the wall of the space station, and floated across the room. But I could see from my reflection, caught in a big piece of plastic that was part of a neon sculpture on the wall, that it looked as if I was walking across the room just fine.

I reached one of the couches that had a momentarily empty spot and sat down next to a dyke who was wearing a white shirt and a black vest, as if she had just come from being best man at a wedding. She did a double-take at the blue feather jacket—how she had avoided seeing it up to now is explained by the fact that there were many other outfits vying for attention—and burst out laughing. "Oh my God!" she cried. "That is too great."

We started talking, and she mentioned that she was a Muni bus driver. After a few minutes, I asked, "Say, is there another room to this place?"

"Another room?"

"Yeah, somebody said to me a few minutes ago, 'See you in the room later.' Any idea what that means?"

"Well, there's downstairs," she shrugged.

"Hmm," I nodded. That sounded good. By going downstairs I would keep the upstairs in my mind as a haven to retreat to if necessary. I pushed off the couch and drifted across the room again, vastly amused by my fellow clubgoers.

The nice thing about being on acid, I thought as I eased down into the cavern of noise that was the main floor of Quizzle, was that you don't have to be quite as cool. Ordinarily in San Francisco you don't *notice* anything. Drag queens are as common as pigeons; teenaged hoodlums walking around wearing their jackets backwards are part of the landscape; internationally known pop stars stand in front of you at Cala FoodMart. No matter how cool somebody looks—or especially if they look extraordinarily cool—you pretend not to even notice. You just give them a little extra…space.

On acid, however, the rules don't matter quite as much: You can smile widely at someone. That's as far as it goes—you don't want to slobber all over them. I always keep myself from seeming whacked-out. But you realize that a smile never cost you anything, people can take it any way they wish, and, as babies quickly learn, others find it charming.

The volume on the main floor was quite extraordinary, but my earplugs were handling it. Conversation was out of the question, however. I floated to the edge of the dance floor and let everything wash over me, the amplified sound, the smell of sweat and metabolized chemicals, the flashing lights. I laughed to myself about the fact that they still have flashing lights in discos, and began to gyrate, now feeling the full blast of the high, happy for the first time in many months.

I don't know how long I whirled, but after a while I became conscious of thirst and quickly went to the bar and got a bottle of plain water. That's the kind of careful person I am around drugs. I keep myself hydrated. Drinking the water, in the relative darkness of the bar area, I realized I was drenched in sweat. It felt great. I wondered for a moment if my being covered in sweat was disgusting anyone, but I noted there were several other people who seemed to be in the same state and who possessed a loopy, shiny look that went beyond being sweaty.

One of them was a beefy, middle-aged guy in a white tank top that showed off his considerable muscles; on his head he wore one of those leather Civil War caps that marked him as a leather aficionado. He seemed to be panting slightly. He noticed me looking at him and came right up to me and grabbed me around the neck. I guess it was his way of saying hello.

"Want to go to the 'other room'?" I asked, as he was shaking me.

"Where is it?" he asked.

"I was hoping you'd tell me."

We went instead to the hallway by the cigarette machine and the bathrooms. Getting into the men's room was impossible; some of the people standing there seemed to be in line for the toilet; others were just hanging out. I looked around to see if anyone was having open sex, and they weren't, and I didn't see any secret passageways either.

But—and maybe it had something to do with the two of us starting to kiss and causing some kind of critical mass—people started right then. Guys were making out, getting on their knees, dropping their pants. The leather guy's face was scratchy and his tongue was aggressive. He was feeling me between the legs, and my cock, which I realized had been slightly erect for quite a while, got hard in my pants.

We broke off the kiss for a minute and I looked around. Nobody was doing anything special. Shit, I was hallucinating. That never happens.

He replied by kissing me again, roughly feeling my prick through my jeans with one hand and clamping onto my neck with the other. I kissed back but after a while I felt a little faint. I don't know if it was because I couldn't breathe or because he was shutting off my carotid, but I suddenly began to collapse. He responded by slamming me up against the wall and going after me again. As I started to pass out, I tapped him on the wrist and he understood and let up on the stranglehold.

I swallowed, seeking a distraction. "Wish there was someplace we could go," I said, seeing spots, and not from the acid.

He shrugged and led me to the end of the hallway and opened an unmarked door that looked like it led to a closet. Beyond was total darkness. He put his hand on my neck again and we went through; I felt as if I had to submit to his force to go with him into whatever beyond he was taking me. After a few steps I saw a light farther ahead, down what looked like a long passageway. As we got closer I saw it was just a naked bulb on the far side of a room that was filled with men.

In here, the music was just as loud, so when I said, "I guess this is the 'other room,'" he merely smiled and drew me inside.

It was the size of a living room, but there must have been fifty guys in there. Most of them were butt naked except for their shoes. My companion led me to another hallway where there was a clothes check. I surrendered the blue feather jacket and the rest of my clothes, put back on the hiking boots I'd worn, and, protected from moss and slippery rocks, went into the fray.

The guy who had led me in there got down on his knees and started sucking my cock. I don't know how some of these leather guys do it, but his mouth was wet and insistent, the sensations everywhere. Instantly I was not only rock hard but felt I was going to come in about ten seconds. I pulled away slightly and we switched places.

It had been a long time since I'd had sex, and even longer, I realized, since I'd sucked a stranger's cock. His dick was big, and I had to remember how to suck one pretty quickly or risk being suffocated by all that meat. He was pulling my head into him, and only my hand at the base of his prick kept me from being impaled. But I gave myself up completely to him; if my ass was opened up by the acid, so was my throat.

He didn't come, but once he pulled away and drifted into the crowd, I saw there were more people who had gathered around us to watch my mouth get drilled. I turned to one of them. He had another long penis, but narrower, and I adjusted to its girth. I played with his hairy balls and sucked and licked in such a dedicated way that the guy came. Come rocketed into my mouth and my throat; then the guy pulled out and shot a little on my face, just to let everyone else know I was a come whore and would take it.

I don't know how easy it was, in that dim light, to see that, but from then on I had a pretty long line of people wanting to fuck my mouth. Every cock was wonderfully different and I devoted myself to each. Because I was completely high and had no sense of time anymore, each act of cocksucking took on a life of its own. It wasn't that one was short and another was long, it was as if each one were a novel I was reading, or a lifetime I lived. But it couldn't have taken as long as it seemed, because each guy came. Their come, too, was different; this one's jizz was copious and loose, that one's was metallic, another's had a faint taste of asparagus. After each I turned to another. Come was dripping out of my mouth and down my chin, and if anyone saw it, I had to assume it was okay with them, because I didn't care. I was loving it.

But after about the sixth guy, I began wishing I had something to kneel on, and rather than ruin my knees, I stood up. There was come all over my face, but I felt amazingly energized, like a warrior emerging from battle streaked in blood. I found a bathroom where I could wash up. This was about the only refuge from the sound system, and it felt cool, quiet. After a few moments, though, out I went again.

When I entered the room again, it seemed even more crowded, and was permeated by a smell, to which I contributed, of sweat and chemicals. On one side of the room I saw a couch. Perched on the back of it was Margarita deVille. She had gotten rid of the plastic straw skirt but kept the patent leather red heels and the tube top. With her long legs exposed, she looked about seven feet tall. At the moment she was kissing someone and feeling for his dick, and because there was an opening in front of her and between her legs, I sank to my knees and put my mouth against her balls. I heard her coo and reached my hand upward and stroked her cock gently. It was just about as big as the leather guy's, but before putting it in my mouth, I wanted to lick her balls to indicate how I might lick her cunt if she had one. I was convinced that between my high and hers we might just convince ourselves she really did have one. But after a minute, she shifted slightly and touched my chin and said, in a voice that was less than a shout, "Suck my cock, baby."

I raised myself, and as I lowered my mouth on her prick, shuddered as another wave of the drug hit me. There was no way to know what time it was, and I had lost all sense of it; I only knew I had dropped at about eleven o'clock. As the new high kicked in, I had to remind myself that the cock in my mouth was not part of me so as not to totally lose myself in the sensations of my own mouth. Forcing myself to make long, slow strokes up and down, I tickled her balls with one hand and steadied myself with the other on her flat belly.

"Oh, baby," she said, stroking my head.

I raised my head. "It's okay if you come," I said, "but I kind of want you to fuck me." In all the cocksucking I had never forgotten my gaping ass and how much I wanted to be fucked.

"Oh!" she laughed. "Well, what a choice. Got a rubber?"

I had snagged a few from the bowl at the clothes check on my way back into the room. She opened the rubber and had it on her cock in a flash. I stood up and bent over the back of the couch—the guy she had been kissing had disappeared—and she got behind me. Looking back, I laughed at how tall she was on those heels.

Then I felt her cock against my butthole. "Yes yes yes do it," I yelled above the music, pushing back at her. My head was floating, and I was so happy.

Her prick went in my ass easily, and instantly I began to feel the intense and perfect sensation of being fucked. My fingernails digging into the dirty, rough fabric of the couch, the *boom-boom-boom* of the disco music fading in my consciousness, I concentrated on how every single nerve ending in my ass was being tickled and stroked with a penis, on the sensation of fullness and delightful union with the person whose hands were on my shoulders, on getting plowed by the perfect long cock of a drag queen. I tossed my head and smiled. I didn't want to overdo my happy reaction but at the same time wanted to communicate that she could certainly do that as long as she ever wanted.

"Yes yes," I called.

"Hmm, baby, who's the queen here?" she teased.

I shouted "Do it!" again. There were people gathering around to watch and I looked in their eyes. They seemed mightily entertained and only some of them wanted to meet my eyes but I was beyond self-consciousness or even exhibitionism. I was perfectly content to be watched and it wouldn't have mattered if the lights were bright or if we were doing it on the mound at Candlestick between games of a double-header—I was so happy and fulfilled on acid getting my ass fucked by a drag queen.

Someone sat down on the couch and turned and kissed my mouth, another man with a scratchy face, and I took his tongue into my mouth for as long as he wanted to put it there. Then he stood up on the couch and put his cock in my mouth; now I was getting fucked on both ends. I reached out blindly and was even able to snare someone else's dick in one of my hands. I felt sacred and perfect and utterly happy absorbing the endless pricks in that club.

Margarita said, "Baby, I'm coming." She pushed hard and deep in me, but my ass felt like Superboy's, invulnerable.

After she was finished fucking, rather than get plowed by someone else, I turned and flopped over the back of the couch onto the cushions. I still had enough sense left to realize I shouldn't get my ass fucked by an infinite number of people. People realized the show was over and turned away.

Sitting on the couch, I was surrounded by slowly circulating men; it wasn't possible to see anything besides asses and backs and pricks and knees. But someone was coming toward me and I realized it was Gel. He had a gentle, amused expression on his face as he sat down next to me.

"Having a good time?" he asked.

"Didn't you see?"

He looked at me more closely. "Oh," he said. "Are you high?"

I grinned.

"How are you doing?"

"Did you see me or not?"

He licked his lips. "Yeah, I did."

I looked down at his prick. It was half-hard, stirring slightly. Somehow it held my attention; despite all the cocks I had exercised that night, none of them had been like this: None of them had been my brother's. I felt very warm and affectionate toward his cock, and found myself developing a notion to do something about it. But rather than address the matter head on, I asked, "Have you been dancing?"

"For a while, then I came in here. I watched Margarita fucking you."

"She's great," I exulted, then swallowed, realizing I sounded drug-addled. "What time is it?"

"About four."

I idly scratched my knees. They seemed none the worse for wear. I realized I couldn't bring myself to tell Gel I wanted him to fuck me. I sat looking down at my lap, only I was really looking at his prick and wanting it in my ass. Finally I said, "Want to go dancing somewhere?"

"I'm kind of coming down," he said. "I think I wore off the drugs dancing."

"Mmm. Do you want to go home?"

"What about you?"

"I'm still really high," I said. "But maybe this is a good time to go."

We made our way to the cloakroom and put our clothes on. There was a different exit, one I hadn't known about. When we got out onto the sidewalk I realized the club was closed and the backroom sex club was actually in another building off an alley. I was mightily disoriented.

The night was foggy and still; the cars from the elevated freeway were the only noise. Cabs were lined up to take people away. I had a druggy thought of how there was an alternative universe where I was still inside the club fucking my brains out, and I felt very loving towards the self that was doing that. My ass was spasming a little and I wanted to get to a bathroom. The cab zoomed across town, the driver not paying much attention to the flashing stoplights, whether yellow or red. I hoped *he* wasn't high.

We stopped in front of my apartment and Gel came inside. Michael's jacket lay at the top of the stairs where he'd dropped it; I stepped over it.

In my bedroom I kicked off my boots and my pants and lay there in my T-shirt and underpants. Gel flopped down in a chair. After a while I said, "I guess you're the one that's more tired and should be in the bed." So he came and lay down next to me.

We were silent for a long time. Then I said quietly, "If I can say this...I feel like saying this. You don't have to do anything; I'm just saying it: I still feel like I want to get fucked."

Silence. I turned my head. He had his arm flung across his eyes: asleep, or pretending to be. I was disappointed I'd never be able to see the look on his face when I said I wanted him to fuck me, because I doubted I would ever say it like that in front of him again.

I eased myself onto the floor on my side of the bed and got the cloth bag that contained the sex toys from under the bedside table. I pulled a pillow down off the bed and put it under my belly, and reached inside the bag and got out the lube and the dildo, the one that was exactly the size of Michael's prick. Putting lube on the dildo and on my asshole, I eased it into me. It went in super easy, I was still really high. I turned over on my back and flung my legs onto the bed so that I was in astronaut position, and holding the dildo with the fingertips of my right hand, I fucked myself while my brother lay near me on my bed.

Because of the drug, one moment I was completely lost in how good it felt to fuck, and the next moment I was looking at myself there, masturbating on the floor while my brother lay on the bed near me. I never forgot he was there, but I wasn't thinking about him. I thought for a minute about Michael and realized that, for the moment at least, the thoughts and memories that I'd been cherishing were all used up, as empty and deflated as the jacket lying limp in the hallway. And just like that, I moved on. I felt incredibly grateful that Gel was still alive, still around and hanging with me and getting me into situations like tonight. From time to time I even laughed at myself, there on the floor, and when the waves of pleasure diminished I got up and showered and took three ibuprofens. Just as light started coming through the windows, remembering that we had an extra hour in which time did not matter, I lay down with my arm around Gel and waited for sleep.

Lizza

I. Lizza

When I was in high school I found out I could fuck a lot and nothing
bad would happen to me. Everything they said, that I'd turn into a
whore, that people would think worse of me, that I'd get pregnant:
none of it happened. Instead I found out I had power. Great hulks of
linemen would freeze with fear when they were alone with me,
because they'd heard about me and how good I fuck. They found out it
was true, that I could be fucked, but they also found out what it was
like to be led into a strange jungle with a guide who turns on you and
devours you. Every one of those boys emerged shaken and changed,
speaking in strange, disconnected phrases to his fellows waiting
outside, yet they all returned again and again. I was the fucking queen
of that place.

When I went away to college I found out about men instead of boys and though I never lost myself, I found out that men could take me and lead me down paths of their own, and sometimes those paths were long and dark, and it took a long time to emerge. I was even partners with some of those men.

But I miss boys. I miss their downy chests, their long smooth fingers, their muscled legs. Most of all I miss their cocks. You can say, "Penguin at the zoo" or "Chevrolet" in a certain voice and their cocks shoot out like railroad semaphores. That's part of the power, to speak casually about some bullshit, and then simply to look into the eyes of some boy and say, "Onomatopoeia" and watch them lose control. And then to make them so glad they lost control.

I miss that. It's Christmas vacation after Christmas, and my parents have gone off until school starts. I'm alone in the house with my brother Bill, who has just found out about sex. I can tell by the way he looks furtive, disappears into his room, clears his throat. I know he's jacking off in there, he's touching his cock lightly and almost coming; he's afraid to touch half the parts of his body because he doesn't know what's dirty and what's clean. He has in mind the bodies of hundreds of women he's seen only in photographs and one little twit from across town. He doesn't even know whether his cock is big or small.

I go by his bedroom in the middle of the day, stop and listen. He's in there with the door closed. If I listen closely, I can hear his breathing because the record he put on to drown out his sounds has already played through and he can't get up to change it because he's busy touching himself. I stand by the door, imagining his body and those of the boys I fucked, his classmates' older brothers, trying to think of one whose body might be like Bill's. As my breathing synchro-nizes with his, I hear it: a small wet sound, perhaps his saliva, squeaking between his cock and his hand. My little brother's jacking off, he's going faster, he even lets out a little moan, only a hum—he doesn't even know that that's okay. There—there—a grunt, impossible to suppress, a slowing of the wet sound, a sigh.

I walk away from the door sweating. I go into the bathroom and sit down with my pants around my ankles. My fingers dip into my cunt, trying to see how wet I got listening to my little brother masturbate. Then I'm doing it, two fingers inside, then rub my clit, two inside then rub my clit. Slowly. His hands on his prick, his balls swelling, my cunt getting wet in my pants at the door, my eyes closed, my cuntlips swelling for my little brother. Bill Bill boy, you boy, you new cockmeat, you pink sweet for me to suck. My fingers not in my cunt but in his asshole, drumming, showing him. Ugh. Ugh. Ugh.

My head clears. I wipe off my fingers and piss and flush. I hear his door, and when I go into my room I hear him go into the bathroom, the toilet still running. The shower starts.

I sneak into his room, see the bed mussed. One sticky Kleenex in the garbage, one that missed. I pick it up and pull apart the edges, breathing in the musky smell. Strong boy come, fresh. His hands soaping up where they'd been stroking.... I kneel over his bed, feel the warmth, and there, yes, the smell. I bury my face in the spot, the Kleenex in my hand.

I wait until evening. He's reading in bed with the door cracked open. I go in and sit down; it's not unusual for us to visit each other. We talk for a minute and then I say, "I know a girl who might like you."

He gives a small, cautious smile, oh Bill, still free of irony, bless you. "Who's that?"

"She's the sister of a girl in my dorm. She lives over in that new subdivision. She's about the same age as you, I think." What else. "She's on the track team or something. They're new in town, they just moved here this fall."

"What's her name?"

"Lizza. Elizabeth like me, only Lizza. I saw her picture, she's really cute. You like girls now, hmm? Not just baseball?"

"Sure, I guess so." He's never been afraid of me, sweet boy. I'll have you like a kitten has cream. "I've gone out a few times."

"No one special? I bet she'll like you. Here, look." I pull out a letter, not sealed, addressed to "Lizza Thompson" at some fictional number. "I wrote her a letter."

He's very startled. "Huh?"

"I told her how nice you were, what you did, and I told her, well, here, read it."

"You wrote her a letter?" He's pulling it from the envelope; he can't believe it. I'm sitting on the bed, but I swing my legs up and bump against him to read over his shoulder, my body pressed against his warmth. I wonder what he has on besides this T-shirt.

"Go ahead, read it. Silly, I wrote it, I know what it says, don't try to hide it. I just want to read over your shoulder." My hand is on his leg, innocently, for balance.

He reads silently; I read along, listening again to his breathing. *Dear Lizza, Your sister Maggie has told me what a cool girl you are, and I'd love to meet you. Maybe you should come over sometime, I think you're on the track team, and so was I, and we could talk about it. You could meet my brother Bill, too, he's really cute, and I think he goes to your school.*

He lowers his arms. "You can't send this, it's awful." Does he already have a hard-on? He raises one knee—that's what boys do to hide it.

"Shut up, just read it."

He goes on, at first appalled, then fascinated. I rope my arm over his shoulder, slide it up again so my hand is on his neck, his hairs. *Bill is really cute, only he doesn't know it. Isn't that the best kind of boy, the one who doesn't even know how cute he is? His legs are long and muscular, and he's strong. His butt is really hard, he works out. He has the softest, curly black hair….* I lightly run my fingers through his hair; Bill is becoming my victim. *He's just discovered girls but he's still a virgin. You probably are, too, so you don't know how good it feels when a guy puts his prick in your mouth or squeezes your nipple or your earlobe really hard; when he pushes you down and strips your pants off so he can see your ass, which is as hard as his is.*

"Uh, is this how girls really talk to each other?" he asks in a quiet voice, trying to make light of it. His crotch has started to glow red through the covers; now he has both goddamn knees up to his chest.

"Sometimes," I say, my breath in his ear. "Go on, read it, you'll learn something."

Maybe if you're really lucky, Bill will ask you out. He'll take you somewhere and charm the pants off you. You know what it feels like when you get turned on by a guy: Your nipples get hard and your cunt gets red and wet and swollen. The come starts to leak out and get your panties wet. You get weak in the knees and all you want is to see his long prick. My hand is full of Bill's black hair, my breathing in time with his. He can't read fast enough. *If you're lucky he'll start touching you and kissing you and making you all mushy and ready to come, you'll really want him bad. He doesn't know it but I saw his beautiful prick. He didn't know I was watching him jack off but I did and it turned me on. My brother was jacking off his fantastic long prick and I got to watch him spill his come all over his fingers, and my pants got wet and I wanted him.*

Bill's reached the end of the page and is too scared to turn it over. I do it for him, and put my hand closer to his sex. *If you're really lucky, Lizza, he'll stick his beautiful prick in you. It's perfect, no one's ever touched it but him. Except one time, well, a lot of times, when he was a baby, I used to wash him, and imagine he was mine. Even then his cock was beautiful and I used to wish I had one instead of my slit. That was before I knew how good it felt to get fucked.*

I'll make sure Bill calls you up soon so you can go out. Love, Liz.

Bill has finished the letter but is too scared to lower it. I take it out of his hand and put it on the floor. He won't look at me, but whispers, "You're going to send that?"

I kneel up on the bed facing him. "No, Billy, I'm not going to send it."

"Oh…." He tries to laugh, but still has no idea.

"Not if you don't want me to." He looks at me. God, boys are lost so easily. He has no idea. I can't fucking wait any longer. I hike myself closer to him until I'm straddling his legs. Bill, my little brother, I've got you. Turned on by your sister, sweet one?

"Don't you think I should send it?" I reach out with both hands to touch his nipples, which get hard instantly. His eyes widen as I start to gently rock my crotch against one of his knees. Now he knows. Now he knows. God, I'm wet, even his fucking leg is doing me. "Don't you think it's true?"

"Uh…I don't know…" and it's almost the last thing he says. I pinch one of his tits suddenly, hard. He starts, and before he can move another inch, my face is right in front of his. "Don't you think it's true?" I repeat. "About your cock? Your *penis?*" His mouth quivers. "Well, I'll tell you, half of it's a lie." I let him think about that for a minute, ride his leg, trace his jaw with my finger. "I didn't see you *mas-tur-bat-ing.*" It's the clinical words that get him, I notice with amusement—they're the only words he's had the courage to use himself. "I never saw your *pe-nis*, never saw the come spurt from it." My hand on his hair tightens.

"But I want to." My other hand goes into my pants, comes out with wet fingers, which I smear across his face, almost slapping him. "You think that's a lie? That's no lie."

"Jesus Christ, Liz," he whispers.

"Don't call me Liz," I tell him. "Call me Lizza." And then my tongue is on his lips. I've got you, little brother, you don't even resist, you are lost, you are lost. My tongue under his lips, gradually penetrating him. "Do it," I hiss. "Do it. Call me Lizza."

"Lizza," he says in a tiny voice. I back away for a moment.

"Am I your sister?" I ask, smiling wickedly. He's utterly lost. "Am I your sister, Bill? Tell me that."

"Yes."

"Yes, I am, what?"

"Yes…Lizza."

Then his mouth, then the covers off, nothing at all underneath. His cock like a stick of dynamite. "I was right…it's beautiful." My head goes down slowly—let him wait—and he starts quivering. Still afraid to touch me himself. The moment my mouth touches his cockhead he starts coming. I suck it. He's almost afraid to thrust, but then he loses it, cries out, "Oh God no," and shoves it suddenly in my mouth. I fuck him with my mouth, my small mouth. All his come squirts out. "No no no," he whimpers. Boy, you are finished.

He collapses against the pillows, but his prick remains hard; he whimpers when I suck it, I know it's supersensitive because he has just come, but I'm doing this for my pleasure now. And he won't stop me. I suck on his meat. It's been such a long time, all those men I did. Now a boy. It isn't the same. I need this. My ass is rocking back and forth; I need to come. His eyes are blinking open and shut.

"Bill, baby, I tricked you," I smile. "Do you know that? I know you've been jacking off a lot in here and I just got turned on. I wanted you. I wanted my little brother's cock." My ass is rocking; he's watching it, hypnotized. "You think that's wrong?"

"Huh?" is all he can say.

"You think it's wrong to *fuck* me?" I say clearly. "That's what I want. I want you to *fuck* me."

He can't stand it any more. "I—I can't!"

"Oh, but you did, Billy. You already did. You fucked my mouth and came in it." Now he's getting just a little soft. "You understand? You got turned on by your *sister* and *fucked* her in the *mouth*. And she wants you. Still. Your sister got a mouthful of your jizz. And I liked it. You understand?"

"Jesus Christ, Liz," he says, completely at sea. No one told him the world was like this. I decide to test him. I suddenly get up and go to the door. "You call me Lizza. Understand? You call me Lizza when we're like this or you won't get it. Lizza." I stand with my hands on my hips.

He looks at me for about two minutes. Come on, Bill, it's not that difficult.

Finally he mumbles, "Lizza."

"Lizza what? What do you want?"

"Come back...Lizza." I do.

"You've got to tell me now, Billy." I stroke my cunt lightly through my pants; it seems as if I'll never get to take them off.

"Liz...Lizza...just...talk to me for a second."

"Okay, Bill." I sit on the bed.

"What are we doing?"

I pat him on the leg, the lower leg—I'll be reassuring. "We're having fun, Billy."

"Fun?"

"That's all. Just fun. And it's okay."

"It is?"

"Sure it is. People do it. They touch each other. It's easy, you'll do it a lot. And I want to do it with you because I love you."

"Oh." He seems calmer, smiles. "You sure it's okay?"

"Well…" I smile. "Don't tell Mom."

He breaks into laughter.

"Now you tell me," I say. "Have you ever seen a girl with no clothes on? It's nice. I've got a nice body, Bill, you're lucky. I've got long legs and a big ass." I'm standing now, taking off my clothes. "Tits, not tremendous, but who gives a fuck. Pretty nipples. Touch 'em? Ever done that? Touch 'em, they won't break. Squeeze 'em a little, like this. I can take it. Yeah…now the other. Yeah. See, that's how you turn a girl on. Every girl isn't this horny, even if she wants you; you have to play with them a little. They have to get aroused."

"I know," he says brightly. "I read about it—foreplay!"

"Good boy. Now practice. Do it, I don't have to tell you. Hmm, yeah. Touch my nipples, squeeze them, yes, oh, yeah. Do them, baby. That's how. Now, with your fingers like I'm doing you. Oh yes!"

He's getting hard again.

"Now I'm going to touch myself, it's okay to do it when you're making love. I'm touching my cunt, Bill. Oh, don't stop touching my nipples, yeah, just do it. Oh." I'm silent for a moment. I close my eyes. How long before I finally get his dick? But he has to take me. "Baby. Yes. Oh. Billy, I saw your prick. Your prick. Oh, don't stop that. Just, yeah. Say it, say it to me. Say, 'I did it to you.'"

"I did it to you."

"Whisper it."

"I did it to you."

"Yes. Uh…. Say, 'my prick.'"

"My prick."

"Say 'cock.'"

"Cock."

"Say any fucking thing, please, just turn me on, just say it. Dirty words, you get it? Say it."

"My prick. My cock. My cock. My cock…uh, coming in your mouth."

"Yes, baby!"

"My cock in your mouth, prick, red, cock, I came in your mouth, you sucked me."

"Yes!"

"You sucked my cock, you sucked my cock, you sucked my cock…."

He keeps squeezing my tits, keeps whispering, my hand on my cunt, finally I come in a shower of sparks. "God fucking bitch come gee fucking dick your fucking goddamn dirty prick, ugh, Jesus!" I blabber. When I open my eyes his cock is rock hard again, but he's staring at me like I've gone bananas.

"Bill, dear, people talk like that. I came. You know what that means. You did it in my mouth. I did it on my hand. And you said, 'No no no.' You know how much that turned me on? That's why I wanted to hear you talk dirty to me."

"Lizza."

"Yes, baby, my little brother." I nuzzle his cock.

"What are we doing?"

"Having fun. Let me lie down." I turn on my stomach. "Now you take me."

"I don't know exactly what to do."

"I'll help you. But I don't want to make it too easy for you, so I'll make you fuck me from behind. In the cunt, but from behind the way dogs do it. You've seen pictures? Or at least you've seen dogs or something? Like that. I'll help you. The first thing you have to remember is that no matter what you do, you'll make me feel good, okay? You can't possibly go wrong. Okay? Say it."

"I can't go wrong."

"That's right, love. Now look at my cunt. It's not weird or scary; it's beautiful. You can see my ass—part my fanny and see my asshole. Did you know that people like to be touched there, too?" He touches me there, tentatively; my fire catches. "Oh, yeah, that's right, baby. My bold brother. You can't go wrong, remember."

"Okay."

"Now look lower. There's a spot between my asshole and my cunt where I love to be touched. Oh yeah. Gently, that's right. Like a feather. Mmmm. Now see my cunt? No, keep touching me. See my cunt? It looks complicated but isn't. I'm going to get on my knees. I'll spread it open for you. See now? The lips on the outside love to be touched. Then the cunt. See where it goes in. Hmmm. You can put a finger in. Oh yeah. See how wet I am for you? I want you, Bill. Oh yeah with your finger. I want you, brother. This is what I wanted, for my brother to take me. Oh yeah. Yeah. You can use two fingers. Fuck! That's good. Oh, and there, my asshole, you fuck. (Don't take it personally.) You. Oh and do it. Just like that. Just like that. It's what I wanted. Just do me with your fucking, sweet, fingers, that did, your, prick. Oh fucking God, yeah. Oh you're going to be good. Mmm your fingers." He fucks me with his fingers in and out patiently, absorbed. I can't even see him. "Talk to me. Who am I?"

"Lizza. My sister."

"What are you doing to me?"

"I'm…."

"Say it!"

"I'm fucking you…."

"Lizza."

"Lizza. I'm fucking you. My fingers are fucking you…."

"Oh God yeah. Oh do it." I rock into it.

"Sister. I'm fucking you, Lizza."

"You are! And you're good, Bill."

"You, I'm fucking your cunt. I'm your brother and I'm fucking your cunt with my fingers."

"Yes, God. Now. Take 'em out. Slow. God. Now. Get on your knees. I want your prick now, Bill. You're going to fuck me. Just get it there and I'll help. You have to give it to me. Drive it in me and kill me with it. Tell me you'll fuck me. Please. There it is."

"I'll fuck you." He's hypnotized.

"Tell me." I have his cockhead against my cunt lips like a spoon. All I have to do is back into it, but I want to stretch the moment out. My brother's cherry. Fuck I'm turned on. Fucking my little brother.

"I'll fuck you, Lizza."

"What are you going to put in me?" in my scared voice.

"My cock."

"Now do it." I back against him slowly. "You don't have to talk now, for a minute. Just tell me you'll fuck me." The cockhead. God I'm wet.

"I'll fuck you, Lizza. I'll fuck you, sister, Liz."

"Oh!" My real name turns me on. "Now just feel it. Your first fuck, little brother. That's not some high school girl cunt, that's your sister's cunt. She's offering it and you're taking it. Oh, yeah. Oh your prick. In, put it in. God, Bill, how long is it?"

"Long," he says unexpectedly, though he sounds strangled, transfixed.

"Baby!" I yell, suddenly moved. "Now just do it. Do whatever you want. Feel it, it's yours. It's your fuck, your first fuck."

He starts to move cautiously, a little bit, back and forth. His cock is incredibly good. I sucked him but I never knew this. My brother. I love his fucking dick.

"Yes baby. Just take it, it's yours. I love it, you're pleasing me. You can't do wrong, just do what you feel. Yes. Yes. Oh your goddamn motherfucking prick. Oh your goddamn fucking cock in me. Fuck me with it. Oh."

What a lover, he's actually holding off! He's fucking me sweetly, but well. And now he starts to build up. Now he's going to do it. He stops thinking.

"Do it," I say, and then shut up. I want to feel it when he comes in me. He has his hands on my hips, I don't even know when he put them there. And he's fucking me. A boy fuck, irresistible, what I wanted. His long cock. "Uh uh uh uh. Oh. Oh. I'm...." He's fucking me, he's going to jizz me.

"Please do it, please do it in me, Bill Bill Bill my lover, please. I want it. I want it."

"Uh. Huh. Nooooo." He's starting. His wet sex pounds me now, no longer gentle, just out of control. "Oh...."

"Yes."

There, he pushes, his hand rises a moment from my hip, he

groans deeply, and I feel for one instant the stuff. Groaning loudly. A treasure inside me.

His hand back on my hip squeezing the flesh, hard. That's okay, I want him to forget, I want him to lose himself, to orgasm and lose it, lose everything. He comes, one, two, three, ten thrusts. His breath ragged. Pinching my hips. Slowly he stops. He's somewhere else now.

"Bill. I love you." I reach back to cover his hand on my hip; he squeezes my hand, it almost makes me cry.

We fall down. We cup each other's genitals with our hands, our tongues fall together, slowly kissing, telling each other over and over again, "Thank you. I love you." Fall asleep that way.

II. Nothing Like This Has Ever Happened Before

When I wake up in the morning she isn't there and I think: It couldn't have really happened. Then I realize her panties are clenched in my hand; she left them there as a sign. She did do it. Liz fucked me, my sister. Lizza. I like it, somehow it's better, it makes more sense. Lizza came in here and did that. My sister, also. I did it too. She made me. She made me come in her mouth and put my fingers inside her and then fuck her. But I feel it went by so fast, I hardly even know what she looks like, feels like. I want to have a lot of time just to look at her, to touch her like an explorer. If she'll let me.

I slide silently out of bed and search the house. It's cold and cloudy, the last day of the year. Naked, I pad around corners, down the stairs. She's not anywhere. Suddenly I need her touch more than I needed anything ever. I need to feel her skin next to me, hear her telling me it really happened, that I belong to her, that I'm beautiful.

I never could have used that word for myself before but she called me beautiful and now I believe it and need it, I need to be beautiful for her. I stand perplexed in the middle of the living room, goosebumps rising; all I can think of is that something's wrong, she's not next to me and it's wrong.

Then I hear the car and she comes in, sees me, and all she can say is "Ohhh...." She comes over to me and buries her face in my neck, when did I get to be taller than she is? "Bill, you're still here, I'm so glad."

"I didn't know where you were." Her hands are cold from the steering wheel, she's lightly touching my arms. "I missed you."

"I just wanted to be out for a minute." She looks at me. "Tell me what you want."

"Just to be next to you. Can't you come upstairs?"

"Sure," she smiles, and puts her hand in mine. I lead her up, I realize she wants me to. We go up to my room. It's warm and it smells.

"I want to be next to you," I tell her.

"Undress me," she whispers. "Tell me what to do. Do things to me, Bill."

She stands still in front of the bed. I take off her jacket, press up against her warm sweater, and under it her breasts are free. I want to be warm, naked, right next to her in bed, but I also realize that this undressing—something I've wanted to do to a girl for so long—is now in front of me, that it's an endless slide on her long body that I can do again and again forever.

I unbutton and unsnap her, and every time something gives way, she gives a little sigh and her breathing goes a little faster. My cock starts to get hard. "Did you ever see me naked, Billy?" she whispers. Her sweater comes off over her head.

"Before last night? Uh-huh," I smile. "Last summer. We were at the lake and you met someone at night, when you thought everyone was asleep? He brought you back, you were whispering. You were kissing him, and he wanted to...to feel you or something. Then you stood away from him. I didn't really understand why, but then you started to take off your clothes. He watched you. It only took a second because it was warm and you didn't have much on, only shorts and a T-shirt. You stood naked. I was watching you from my window. You stood there while he looked at you and then you picked up your clothes and came inside, and after a while the guy went away."

By now we're in my bed, the covers over us. I'm lying on top of her, fitting inside her legs. Her hands are warmer now, stroking my back, pressing hard in places I didn't know were there.

"Yeah, that guy. He wanted to fuck but I didn't feel like it. I said I'd strip for him if he went away. Funny, he was kind of a cute guy. I don't know why I didn't want to do it."

"Have you done it a lot?"

"Yeah, a lot." She smiles at me unconcernedly. "I won't lie, I don't have to, I'm not ashamed. I love to fuck, Billy. I love sex. It's not dirty or weird or anything they say. It's a fucking gas. Including this. This is the proof, as far as I'm concerned. I don't feel bad doing this, do you?"

No, I don't. I just want her. Her body is like a dream to me, warm and mine. I can't believe it, it seems like nothing bad can ever happen to me now. I press my face against her neck. "I want you, Lizza."

"Please," is all she says. "Do anything to me, Billy."

I go exploring. Her breasts are big to me, I don't care what she says. I nudge them with my face, I try the nipples, go lower. She's moaning, and suddenly I smell something I never smelled before. It's weird to encounter things I've heard about. It must be her cunt. It smells hot and sour and heavy, and despite the fact that everything about the smell seems strange, I have to go there.

Her cunt hair is short, curly, somewhere between soft and wiry. I realize I don't know what color it is, it's dark under the covers. I bury my nose in her skin, the smell calls me to itself. Slowly I go down, kissing. Now. Her legs are moving, suddenly I'm surrounded by Lizza. I reach forward blindly with my lips, and I meet lips. The smell strong like a drug. Her fingers are clenched in my hair, she's moaning and saying something about her brother sucking her but I can't really hear. Slowly I go down on her cunt. It's like it's all around me, and everything is moist, my mouth and face are wet. My tongue shoots out blindly, licks anywhere. A stiff little spot, she cries out and pushes her crotch against me, it must be the "clitoris." Her hips are working now, I try to suck and lick and drink everything at once. The smell, the taste of come. Like mine, and totally different. Her cunt against my mouth, up, down. Suddenly she stops, I can hear her clearly because she's yelling as loud as she can: "Sweet motherfucking Jesus boy fuck! Damn I'm coming! Fuck you motherfucking cock, you fucker, you goddamn prick you made me come! God! Oh!" And her cunt is contracting around my mouth, squeezing and pushing, I feel as if she's wiping me against her like a rag. Nothing like this has ever happened to anybody before.

I slowly come out of the burning hot covers; she's lying with a hand between her breasts, her head to one side, then turning slowly to the other side. I look at her in wonder. Finally she opens her eyes, and Lizza looks at me. "Now put it in," she says in a voice I never heard before. "Fuck your sister with your beautiful goddamn cock."

It's already close to her cunt. I rub it against her, she reaches down and helps me in, her eyes riveted on mine. "Do it, please, if you never do anything else, Bill, fuck me now yes." It goes in little by little, she throws her head back. I move slowly. God it feels good. Her sticky come on my lips, I can still taste it. Her cunt surrounds me, it's different than last night, this way it's like diving into a pool and yet the dive never stops, just goes down and down and in and in. This is too good, it's not really happening—the world could not hold this pleasure, but it does, it's happening to me.

Her eyes open. "You saw me naked, Billy."

"Yes."

"You wanted me."

"Yes," though it was too soon even last summer for me to be sure what I'd seen. "I saw your breasts and your cunt and I remembered. And when I'd jack off I'd think about you." That much is true. How easy it is to confess, here between her legs.

She reaches up to my nipples, and it's as if someone pulled the plug and everything starts rushing.

"Oh…" I say, my eyes wide.

"That's going to make you come, Billy," she says.

"Yes—" is all I have time to say and then I'm shooting in her violently, my cockhead burning, pounding her. I hope I'm not hurting her but her head's thrown back, she's meeting my thrusts, and now to my amazement, she does what she did last night, squeezes her eyes tight, grits her teeth. Her cunt is squeezing my prick, and she's like an animal, grunting. "Fuck your come, your dirty come, fuck your prick, goddamn." Suddenly she shakes me by both shoulders like a stuffed toy, my head flops around. "Aaaarrrghhh," she shouts.

I realize I love it when Lizza comes. I love to see her go inside and tense up, to flail her head and body not knowing what she's doing, to hear her talk dirt. Nobody has ever been as dirtymouthed as Lizza.

Fuck it turns me on. I want to make her do that. I want to give her that, to make her go…wherever it is she goes. I have to see and hear it. It's like being present at the creation of the world. That's what it feels like.

I read once that some women have trouble coming and some men have trouble getting hard. I don't see how that could be possible.

III. The Mud Queen

He's still sprawled on top of me, his legs just outside mine, his cock still parked inside my cunt. The flash of my last orgasm dies out and all I can feel is the male on top of me, inside me. He's heavy and insensate; I need the flash again.

I go back inside my body. My shoulders, my mouth, I lick each with a finger. My right hand presses across my hip sticking out. I love that spot, smooth and buttery, though it's so exposed. I always start there, rubbing the palm of my hand back and forth like sandpaper, then over to the cunt hair. I fantasize I have long beautiful dripping black cunt hair, my hair is like the fur of a jaguar. My cunt hair is the only thing that doesn't fit on my body, my short sparse cunt hair, now it's long. I can run my hands through it, comb it, braid and bead it. It deserves to be dressed like the cunt of a queen, a mud queen whose cunt is the mud that her tribe sprang from. Everybody can see it.

Bill's watching me now, he moves to give me room to touch myself, the sweet boy. I'm so glad I touched myself the first time with him, so he'll know I do it when I want to, that there's nothing wrong with him. His cunt hair's even longer than mine. I mean his crotch hair. Fuck it, it's cunt hair even on a guy. Especially sweet Bill. With his boy body he could be a girl for me sometimes. I wonder.

His cunt hair's so soft. (How come he got it and I didn't?) It leads down to a cunt anyway, my cunt. His cock's still half-hard and it's stuffed inside me like a sausage; at the bottom of my cunt lies his sperm. I clear away my cunt lips from his cock, it makes him press in deeper, as much as he can. Uhn. My slimy cunt lips wrapped around my brother's cock, uhn, where they belong, uhn. My flesh, flesh of my flesh. I go off the pill and have his child, uhn, and raise that child to fuck me, uhn, so I can be fucked totally by my own flesh. Me, a middle-aged woman being fucked hard from behind by my own child. Even as a little child s/he could fistfuck me, uhn, put in a bony little hand and whale away, uhhn.

I'm creaming, my hips are moving just a little. There's my ass, too, he's hardly touched my ass. He'd do it if I showed him. One two fingers up my asshole, then his dick, uhn. Jerry fucking me in the ass all that summer when I didn't have any birth control, his dad who's gay told him how, and we fucked ourselves silly. So dirty to assfuck. Like shitting and shitting and never stopping, shitting out your whole insides. But then having it stuffed back inside you. It isn't even that specific, it's just motherfucking intense. It takes a long time to know what's happening to you, it takes a patient lover. Then finally you can feel the difference between your asshole and his cock and you want to be rammed. You've got to feel him spill it in you, just to know that his sperm will get all shitty before it drips out your ass. To feel so dirty, commy, wet, the mud queen.

My finger's on my clit, Bill's cock curled inside my cunt, I have to squeeze it out before it gets hard again. I steady my breath, the sensations start to spread from my clit to my insides to my tits. He's rubbing my body with one hand, now on my nipple oh God now my face. I don't dare speak, he's like an executioner who shit up my cunt and will kill me before I get away. No. His cock curls there hidden like the baby I'll take from him. My finger drumming. I don't know if I can keep it up. My cunt makes wet sounds, squeezing his cock, I have to squeeze it out of me. Harder, his nipple, his finger. With my free hand I grasp his throat. "Do this to me," I whisper.

He puts his hand around my neck tentatively. "Yes, it's okay, harder even," I hiss. My eyes are squeezed shut, I don't want to open up to him, I just want to expel him but he's threatening me, the killer is going to strangle me, he's killed me with his dick. I have to squeeze out his cock or die.

My finger more and more. Suddenly it's there, his hand on my neck, his cock oozing out covered with jizz, and just as it finally slides out I come. My finger moving at the speed of light, his hand around my neck harder.

I sprawl. Bill, baby, I didn't mean to expel you, where are you? I push him over on the bed, gather his limpness in my mouth, suck on it. When it's soft I can take the whole thing in my mouth, a little baby-ness. I tickle his balls with my nails, he moans. I raise my head to say, "Little brother, I'm going to teach you to talk dirty. I'm going to suck your cock and I want you to talk. Make it as dirty as you can. You can't possibly offend me or say anything wrong, you can only turn me on. Just say anything. Say everything." I start sucking him again.

"Your mouth on my cock," he starts dreamily. It takes a while to let it loose. People don't realize they have to spill out their fantasies. I'm licking our come off his prick, soon he'll lick our come out of my steaming cunt. I haven't been this turned on in a long time, not since those two guys took turns doing it to me that night in Tahoe. First one and then the other and then the other, I got lost in a fantasy of never-ending cockfuck.

"Your cunt goes deep, there's no bottom, when I'm inside you I feel like I'm falling…." Oh you are, Billy, you are. You don't have any idea how far you've fallen, how completely your body is mine to play with, always here, my toy, mine. Now your cock's getting hard again, especially when I tickle your balls there. You moan, you like it. I spit in my hand and jack you off so I can lick that spot with my tongue. When my hand goes down to the base of your cock I feel the soft hair.

"Oh Lizza yeah your tongue fuck on my balls oh…oh yeah…."

"Don't stop, Billy, you don't have to describe me or what's happening. Talk about the dirtiest thing you can imagine." I lick him. He wants to lie back and enjoy, but we don't have time, if I want him to be my lover he's going to have to learn to talk dirty.

"Dirty, huh? Well, here goes. There's a guy at school who's on the track team, he's tall and good-looking, all the girls like him, he fucks everybody—"

"Will he fuck me?" Suck him.

"Huh? Uh, yeah, I'm sure. He fucks anybody he wants to. And there's this girl I like, Susie, she got fucked by him, and I want to watch him fuck her, I want to watch her get it because she's so fucking stuck up, I want to watch him throw her down and strip off her panties before she has a chance to stop him and stick his finger in her and his tongue down her throat and make her suck his finger and his cock hard and slap her and she can't get away and, uhn, he makes her suck his cock until it's wet and then he shoves it in her, uhn, and fucks her…."

Wow, Bill's taking off, it must really be his fantasy. I'm getting turned on, my cunt's swelling.

"…she can't get away, uhn, and then she starts to like it, she starts to get excited, she wants it, but he won't stop fucking her, he fucks her harder and harder, uhn, and slaps her face and tits—"

I stop sucking Bill before he comes, I'm flushed, I want it from him. "Do it to me, Billy. Just like you said."

"Like *that?*" His eyes are glazed but he's still holding.

"Just like that. Only harder. Only worse."

He reaches out for me. I draw back, playing Susie. He grabs my arm and tries to push me down, I fight back. "Do it! Really do it," I shout. "Fuck me if you can!"

"Bitch!" he slaps me.

"Uhhhn!" I cry. He stops, unsure. "Yes," I tell him, looking straight at him. "I want it." He seizes my wrist again, we struggle, I pull his hair. He slaps me again. It feels good. "Bitch, you cunt!" Now he's free, flying. He pushes me down, I flail at him, he catches my wrists, that's right, Bill. Make me.

His hand on my throat for a minute, he inserts his cock, it slides in, this is already the third or fourth time my brother's fucked me, it's so good, he's giving it to me hard, he's bigger older stronger more powerful, his cock is all. He's clawing at my breasts. "No," I whimper.

"Fuck you, bitch! Take it!" My brother the rapist. Did he learn this or dream it up, or is it true what they say, that there's a rapist inside every man?

"You can't do this to Susie," I say, "she's too good for you."

"Fuck that!" he screams. "I'll fuck that bitch sideways until she can't see!" He fucks me harder and harder. "She's just a little cunt! She gets screwed in the mud of the fucking park and then pretends she's too good for everybody. But she fucks. She does it."

"No!"

"Shut up! Take it!" He turns into a mad fucking machine, a crazy engine bent on blowing itself up. This blur. The rhythm makes me come. "Oh goddamn yes you fuck you burning cock you horse, uff, augghh, you shit." He comes with a long wail. His come burns into my cunt right through me into my rectum into the bed burning a hole straight through the floor. He pounds and pounds, deprived of speech. Finally he collapses.

IV. The New Year

We go out of the house grinning, out to eat breakfast at noon. He's silent, smiling, calm. Keeps smiling and laughing silently at unknown things. "Things look different today," he finally says.

"I'll bet they do."

"I feel so strange. Powerful. I feel as if I've got a secret nobody can take away. Like in those kid stories where a kid found out he could fly or something."

"Yeah, a secret's powerful. But you know where the real power comes from? Look around."

We're sitting at Denny's. All around us are ordinary families. "See all these people? You're different from them. We're different. What we did, and what we're going to do every chance we get, is completely against all this. Not just the families and the complacency. This table, the vinyl seats, the pancakes. We're against all of it."

"Maybe not the pancakes," he says. "But I know what you mean. It's all so stupid."

"That everybody's crazy except us. But what if it's the other way around? That we're the weird ones, the sick ones? That's what society says. And that's what anybody will say if they find out what we are."

He's silent for a minute. "Nope," he finally says, "I'm not the crazy one here. Neither are you. They are."

"That's right, Billy."

"Lizza, were you ever Lizza before?"

That makes me smile. "I think I've been becoming Lizza ever since I was your age—fucking, swearing, taking drugs, but those aren't the important things, not even fucking. The important thing is to be against. Against all this shit, an opposite charge. A free electron." He's laughing. "Don't laugh, you feel it."

"Um-hmm."

"But no, I've never been Lizza until now. You made me Lizza."

"That's nice." He takes my hand. "I'm really glad. I love Lizza. I love you."

"I love you, Billy."

"'Billy'? Can't I have a cool name too?"

"Oh, you've just started, honey. Wait for it, it'll come."

He looks out the window. "I want to do it with you again."

"We will, whenever you want. Take me right now in the car in the parking lot. Or draw it out until we get home. Or be next to me all day long until you can't stand it anymore. I'm ready."

That night, New Year's Eve, we decide to drive the two hundred miles to the city where I go to college. We go to a party, my friends are surprised and pleased to see me. I whisper in the ear of a woman, a friend of mine who's as free as I am. She seduces Bill, dancing with him, feeling his leg, knowing I'm watching him, filling his mouth with her tongue at midnight. When everybody else has laughed and stopped kissing, they're still kissing, her hands on him. They go into another room, I slink along to watch. I've never watched Annie fuck before. Her gorgeous fat cunt gets filled up with him; she comes when he pulls her hair. I go out and come back with a guy I hardly know, Eddie. I tell him it's my little brother underneath Annie, we watch her fuck him. Then to his astonishment I go over to the bed and get on top of Bill and fuck him, looking at Eddie. Annie sucks him off; he looks into my eyes like someone drugged. Then Annie brings his come in her mouth to me, she kisses me and I swallow it. Eddie disappears, and Bill and I tie Annie to the bed face down and start to beat her, Bill does whatever I tell him to, sometimes he doesn't even need to be told. He puts his fingers in her while I beat her ass, and she comes. Then she helps him get his cock in my asshole and he fucks me in the ass while she kneels behind him and talks dirty to him to make him come. He shoots his come in my ass. We tie Annie to the bed again and beat her.

In the morning when I wake up Bill and Annie are on the floor doing it. The smell of her come fills the room. As I watch them, I can't decide whether it turns me on more to watch her or him. She turns me on because she's coming, but she's coming because Bill's doing it to her.

I quit school and Bill and I move in together. We start holding up 7-Elevens for money, they're so easy. We dress Bill up as a girl sometimes, me as a man. The police have no idea who we are. In the car with the money on the floor we pull off to a deserted road and fuck, I pull apart his bra and lacy underwear and get at his soft cunt hair. We live in a big old house out of town and go in on weekends to hear bands and steal. I shoplift clothes and weapons, Bill steals money out of cash registers. We live on nothing but Coke and potato chips and each other's come. His hair gets long and he starts to go out during the day dressed as a girl. He starts hanging around transvestite bars and sucks the guys off or lets them fuck him for a hundred dollars a shot. The out-of-town guys, he steals their wallets.

With one of the credit cards we take a plane to New York where we live as lovers. He gets a job as a bike messenger during the day; at night we mug people. I'll sidle up to a tourist and then act horrified when Bill shoves him and steals his wallet, though I'm actually hanging on to the mark's arm "in terror." We dress like the opposite sex; we live on cheap Chinese food; the police have no idea who we are.

He fucks me puts a dildo in my ass sticks his cock in my mouth makes me suck the shitty dildo. He picks up guys and brings them home, we fuck them and do whatever they want. He makes me squat in my own piss and beg to lick it up. I tie him to the radiator and it burns him. I beat his ass until it blisters. We don't go out of the apartment now, marks come to us. The whole place is just a sea of come. A guy comes up, he's fucking me bent over the window, Bill comes up and strangles the guy, at first he thinks it's part of the scene, then he dies, his cock gets hard enough to split me open. We dump his body behind the building and move to another apartment. Bill plays with a knife, we cut each other, there are drops of blood on the apartment floor. He fucks me with a knife at my throat, one touch of the blade makes me come. He begs me to fuck him in the ass, I refuse. He starts to cut himself, I stick the dildo in his ass, he gets hard and comes, the sperm mix with the blood on the floor, we both scramble to lick it up.

Bill is now Bet, sometimes Beth. We argue about which of us can go farther. Beth makes me take her shit when it comes tumbling out. I make her lick my cunt and asshole, I make her suck my blood. We're both faint a lot of the time. He hits me over and over.

I'm going crazy I want to dissolve and die for him I want to kill him and wear his skin I want her cunt hair a knife up his asshole her cunt bloody. When the sun rises there's nothing left in the apartment, I'm alone only blood and piss and shit everywhere. I roll in it, Bet is nowhere, it's like he's melted totally into these liquids. If I hurry I can melt, too. Lizza, Bet, Lizza, Beth, Lizza, Bet. My finger, my ass slapping the sticky floor. When I come, I open my eyes. Bet is standing over me, says, "I want you again."

Penetration

I'm lying on my stomach in the sun, my ass warm and glowing with heat. It's a small bedroom with a window that looks out on the roofs of buildings just a little lower than this one. I don't look out the window to see the elevated train tracks off to the south, or the main boulevard half a block away. I lie there because I'm waiting. The sun shines off my body and fills the room.

Beneath me I feel the texture of the tatami mat, both rough and smooth. I gently rub my fingertips over its straw ridges and grooves.

He kneels down next to me and parts my legs to look at me, the sun warm on my balls and thighs and butt. His hands divide my legs, then I feel his tongue on my balls wet hot. The sensations inside me: I'm afraid, I can't be touched like this, I need it, I won't please him. I have to be pleasured.

His tongue makes wet circles on my balls. Then I feel his face between my legs as he burrows deeper and sucks my balls into his mouth. His hands stroke my legs, make me vibrate. I want him to open my ass, his tongue goes to the place between my balls and ass, then his hands pry my buttcheeks apart.

I'm moving, I need it, my head is bent down and moving slowly back and forth. Now his tongue moves in slow circles around my hole, the steely lips; I murmur. He says he's going to fuck me, tells me to relax my ass, it'll be easier for me. He gets it all wet, inserts his wet finger. This is how I like to be fucked, slowly by a long, thick finger. A nasty pleasure. Now two: It's more intense. His other hand holds my head down, his teeth nip my shoulder and neck. He's stronger than I am.

His other hand goes to his cock. He makes pleasure sounds, I hear a sticky back-and-forth sound. Slowly he takes his fingers out of my ass, I miss them, I need fucking. His cockhead on my asshole, he pulls my head back by the hair and pushes inside me, his cock impossible, doesn't even hurt just big as hell. I'm limp, a thing being fucked, totally flat on the floor, as if I'm being steamrollered. My asshole filled up, he's still entering me. Saliva drools out of my mouth, I'm so helpless I'm so flat, the only three-dimensional part of my body is my asshole getting fucked. Slowly I relax and get into it, I move again, tell him I want him, tell him to fuck me. He slaps my face, yells, pushes harder.

He is moaning, or yelling, wordlessly, and calling me *bitch*. Like the separate thrusts that become one motion, like the separate bodies that become one body, his words become a single song he is singing to me. I tell him to give it to me, to give up everything he ever had, to pour everything into my asshole. So that there will be nothing left after he comes. He continues to howl, an uncivilized sound. Then he orgasms, shaking me by the shoulders, stretching my ass in several directions, uncaring. Even when he slows down, he continues to pound my shoulders and back with his fist, and the blows get just a little more gentle until he finally stops.

"What's it like," she asks, "having a cock?"

I look down at her body lying next to me. The hollow between her breasts is sweaty and her breath is slowing down.

"You're asking me?"

She grins at me. "I mean…" she says, speculatively feeling the tissue of my breast, my nipple, brushing the back of her hand against the sparse hairs. "May I be frank? There's something about it coming out of men's bodies—that it's part of you—that doesn't happen on girls. It's one thing to thrust and penetrate with your hand or your tongue, but to do it with this thing sticking out of you…. You know what I mean?"

"Mm-hmm," I nod, closing my eyes. She strokes my chest in a way that's both erotic and affectionate, a comforting sensation.

"Hey, don't go to sleep."

"I'm not, I was just thinking about your question."

"Well? God," she laughs, "don't you love to be the center of attention! A man gets asked for his expert opinion on matters penistic, and milks it for all it's worth. Like you don't think about it all the time."

"Do I?"

"You said you think about me all the time, but you're really just thinking about fucking me."

"Ha. Well, let's see. To use a prick for fucking…. It's about something in the center of your body reaching out and penetrating someone. It's external and yet you control the movement with your abdomen and hips, so it's like dancing. It feels as if you're fucking from your very center."

"Ah, that's more like it."

"But come to think of it, I've never used a strap-on, so I can't be sure it's not about the same."

"It's not even close to being the same."

"I should ask Robert this," I say.

"Yeah, maybe you guys can figure it out. Maybe it's a boy thing."

"Why don't you ask him?"

"That's not what I'd ask him," she says, resting her hand now on my chest. "I'd ask him what you look like when he's putting it to you."

"But you guys were involved for, how long? How come you never asked him?"

"Involved, that's funny. Something you'll learn about him, you're never not *involved* with him."

"You mean you're still doing it?"

"Doing it—God, where do you get these phrases?"

"Ah-me-li-caa," I said, pronouncing it the Japanese way. "Back in the old country, we still speak in the old ways." I turn on my side, so our faces are almost touching. I can feel her breath on my mouth, my chin. "How long have you been here, anyway?"

"Two years and three months."

She reaches down and takes my cock in her hands. It's sticky and hot and not entirely soft yet. She hefts it in her palm like a piece of fruit. "I'd like to try having one of these sometime."

"Be my guest. Let's trade."

She turns my prick every which way, inspecting it. She rubs her finger on the ridge of the cockhead, and on the rough part where the foreskin used to be attached. Then she dangles it between her fingers. "It's funny, when you really look at it."

"Yes. Cocks are comedic. Cunts are not. Because cocks are symbols of male power, and all symbols of power can be satirized."

She takes it in her mouth and bites down, not hurting me but enough for me to feel her teeth. "Here's what I think of your male power."

"Hey lady, if you break it, you have to buy it."

She releases it and lifts it to one side to inspect my balls. I'm getting a little hard again.

"What I like about penetration is that it's so undeniable," I say. "When you fuck someone you're invading their body, you're inside them, running rampant. It doesn't matter whether it's a cock or a dildo or your hand: They can't deny it, they can't get away from it. You've really got them."

"Mister man," she taunts.

"It's aggressive, of course it is."

My prick is getting hard again for sure. I think about holding her down and whamming it inside her; the idea contributes to my arousal. She is still holding me, and now begins to slide my prick back and forth in her hand, welcoming my erection, drawing it out.

"How do you make it get hard? Can you control it?"

"It's something you control and don't control. It's like a day-dream that occurs to you and which you can choose to indulge, or put out of your mind."

"You mean you can choose now to stop getting hard?"

"Probably not."

"Go ahead and try."

"I don't want to. I want you to keep doing that. And in a minute I'm going to stick it inside you again."

"I like the idea of such a visible form of arousal."

"I like the idea of getting wet."

"Okay."

"What's it like to get fucked?" I ask.

"You ought to know."

"In the pussy."

"No, we're not talking about me now."

"You want to hear more about my prick?"

"I want to do more than hear."

I reach my finger between her legs. Her pussy is a swamp. "What's it like to get wet like this?"

"Shut up."

A few days later I cross the Bandai Bridge and walk to my boyfriend's house. He's been here longer than Callie or me, and used to work for the same English school I work for now. When each of us came to town, we ended up in his bed—that is, on his futon. But I'm the only one of his lovers who's found his way to Callie.

We take off our clothes and get on the floor and start kissing. I love this time of sex—when the balance is perfect, when you're kissing each other before one person starts to take and the other give. Who'll come out on top? Our kisses grow harder, he shoves his tongue into my mouth, I pull his hair and dig my fingers into the flesh of his ass, he grabs my wrist. Bigger than me, he forces his way on top, his hard cock jabbing me. Struggling has made us both hard.

In fact, each time, all I want is to be taken, to get and get, but lovers have to be teased. They have to know you want them, that their touches turn you on, that you're capable of taking them—before you give up and lie back and take it.

He straddles me, rubbing my nipples. I have my eyes closed. "Callie wants to know what it's like to have a cock," I report.

"Yeah?"

"I told her I'd trade."

"Dream on."

"Haven't you ever wondered what it would be like to have a cunt?"
He snorts.

"I would spend the maximum amount of time getting fucked," I declare. "I would go right down and start picking up guys."

"Wait a minute, in this fantasy are you a girl, or are you a guy with a cunt?"

"It doesn't matter, I just want one for a while. Maybe a few weeks."

"Just long enough to get your period, then it's, 'Stop, Mister Wizard! I don't want to have a pussy any more!'"

The phone rings—he's been in Japan so long he even has a phone, something you have to spend years on a waiting list for—and he speaks for a minute and then says, "Sure, come over."

"Who was it?"

"Who do you think?"

We lie down, I lick his balls and play with him, then get up to piss. "No," he says, grabbing my wrist, making me kneel down next to him. "You go when I say."

My cock is a big warm sticky roll, tingling with the need to piss. "I need to," I whisper, and put my hands behind my back as if they're tied there. "I need to pee. I need to let my piss come out, please, or I'll do it on myself. Please let me."

"No." He kisses me, fondles me. "When I say."

"No, it's dirty. Please." We go on like that; it turns him on tremendously. I'm the first person he's ever been with who likes piss, and he loves talking about it with me, teasing my fetish out of me. Talking to people about their turn-ons turns him on.

Abandoning my pretense at being tied up, I reach out and start fondling him, running my fingers gently over his prick.

"Put it in my cunt," I say.

"You've got plenty of places for me," he says. "You'll get it, don't worry." He closes his eyes, sitting on his heels, absorbing pleasure. I'm bending down with my fingers on his cock, looking at him as closely as Callie looked at me. I want to take it in my mouth so much, but staring at it and thinking about doing so makes me excited too. I've just about decided to go ahead and start sucking him when there's a knock at the door.

I put on a robe and answer it—it's her, of course, grinning.

When we walk back into the room Robert is still kneeling naked on the floor just as I left him—sitting back on his heels, his half-hard dick lolling between his legs.

"I hear you have penis envy," he says to her.

She sprawls on the floor next to us, laughing. "What the fuck?"

I kneel behind him and fondle him so she can see. "I told him you want to know what it's like to screw somebody."

"Oh, that. You tell your boyfriends all our intimate conversations?"

"No, I tell all *your* boyfriends."

He closes his eyes and smiles like Buddha. I slide my fingers under his ass and cup his balls. He says, "Mmmm" and smiles even more.

She inches closer, reaches out, and takes his prick from my hand. I move my hands to his nipples as she starts sucking him. His cock gets really hard after this and he starts moaning.

I love the sounds people make when they're getting pleasure.

Before she really gets into her rhythm, I get on my hands and knees, showing them my ass. "Come here and fuck me. I want it."

"Which one of us?"

"I don't care."

He laughs. "She's gonna get my come, not you." She disappears his cock with her mouth. I listen to his noises and look at his face. His olive complexion doesn't grow red, but his mouth twists open, the skin pulled tight and his neck muscles swelling. Then he orgasms, grunting. I feel a mixture of humiliation and arousal, I love it when my lover comes, I just want it.

Callie leans off his cock and spits his come on my ass and wipes it into my asshole with her fingers. "There, now you've got it after all," she says. She keeps pushing her fingers around my anus. Unlike my boyfriend, I'm flushed. All the nerve endings in my butt are sending off fireworks as I brace my elbows on the tatami.

Now she slides one in. "Do more than that," I say. She pulls her finger out and puts another one in. "That's not what I meant."

I'm so turned on by what she's doing. Our sex up to now has been kind of vanilla; I didn't know she could be dirty like this.

My lover comes around and lays his sticky cock in my mouth. It's still half-hard. I'm between them, sucking on his cock, taking her fingers.

"I want to do that too," she says. "I want to stick my penis into the mouth of another boy, feel his mouth all over it. I want to feel the mouth I fuck."

He's silent.

"What does it feel like?" she asks.

"So good," he says in a half-whisper.

"He does me like that too."

"You mean he eats your pussy, or he sucks your cock?"

"Both."

His cock gets soft and I let it go and put my head on my arms, concentrating on her fingers working their way in and out of me.

I hear Robert get up and go over to the closet. He slides the door open and rummages around and slides it closed again. Callie says, "Oh my," and I look around to see him holding a dildo and harness.

He unsnaps various straps and fits the harness around her loins, a pink silicone dildo poking through it. My head is spinning with anticipation and the sheer idea of getting fucked by her.

While he puts a rubber over the dildo and then covers it with lube, he is kissing her, and her two fingers are still slowly stroking in and out of my hole. I can hear them kissing, and the pleasure sounds she makes contribute further to my arousal.

Then I feel his fingers putting lube all around my asshole, and when he tells her to pull her fingers out, her fingers are replaced by his, spreading lube into me.

She inches up to me and he is helping her position the dildo at my butthole. "Here it comes," she says. I can hear her mouth smiling around her words.

The dildo gets pointed in various directions until it finds the right one. "There!" I announce, and she shoves it slowly but steadily home.

"Oh God," I sigh.

"How was it you imagined fucking me?" she asks menacingly. "'Running rampant'—was that the phrase you used?"

"Yes, but not yet," I say. "Just do it slow for a minute."

She laughs. "That's not how you do me, you shove it in without regard."

"If I fucked you in the butt I wouldn't," I said.

"But I'm pretending," she said. "I'm pretending this is your cunt."

Suddenly she shoves it in me hard. I cry out, "Aahhh!"

She grunts low, draws it outward, prepares to shove again. "Uh!" she grunts, penetrating me again. "I think I can feel that in my clit."

"Uh-oh!" Robert laughs.

She pulls out and then thrusts hard again, and yet again. "God," she says. "That feels great. It's kind of like riding a horse and pushing your clit down on the saddle."

Robert is laughing his head off. "Go, go, do it," he urges.

She starts fucking me hard. I've been fucked hard by a prick, and gently by a dildo, but never hard with a strap-on like this. If two fingers made skyrockets go off in my head, a hard fucking by this piece of plastic is like a bomb blast every two seconds. I am whining and moaning in a high-pitched voice, and I can hardly hear anything else.

But I do hear her grunting. "Uh, uh, aw, fuck," she says. "Somebody stop me if I start to kill him, okay? Oh shit, this feels good."

I rest my head on my forearm and then bite into it, just to still my whining. Then Robert is in front of me. He cups my chin in his hand to look at my face. "Are you okay? It might help if you breathed a little and stopped singing opera."

That makes me laugh. Callie is still pounding into me. Her voice is getting higher now. "Robert," she says breathlessly, "touch my tits or something."

He drops my head back on my arm and disappears. My ass is now relaxing more, and I'm starting to get into it. "God," I say loudly, "it's starting to feel really good."

She is breathing fast. "Fuck you," she enunciates. "I've got you—I'm fucking you. I don't give a shit about your pleasure."

"Attaway," Robert encourages her.

"Oh yeah, touch my tits like that."

I guess she doesn't need any encouragement from me. I go back to grunting and groaning. My prick is getting hard against the straw mat and the roughness is irritating. Also, I really did have to pee back then. I balance on my elbows and rub my own nipples.

Callie's thrusts break in their rhythm and she starts pushing in and out really fast, not covering much ground, just trying to stimulate her clit as much as possible. Her voice starts vibrating, she's moaning now. The dildo almost stops.

Then she starts to come, and pushes it suddenly really hard all the way to the bottom. We both cry out, and she starts pounding me there, squealing, babbling, pushing her clit against the rough leather on the inside of the harness. Her orgasm is louder than any I've gotten out of her before. In the last few seconds of it, I finally relax all the way and the pleasure from her pushing is as intense as any I've ever felt.

Then she finishes and falls on top of me with a final "Uggh!"

Robert starts whooping and applauding and laughing. I'm not nearly done, meanwhile. I look back at him and say, "Now can I suck your cock?"

We do this stuff for the rest of the afternoon, and in the evening we go out and eat a big dinner and see a kung fu movie. Then we go back to his house and sleep on his futon under a sheet in the hot night.

In the morning I wake up about the same time as Callie. I look at her mouth and we start kissing. Then she jumps up and says, "I have to pee."

I follow her into the bathroom and stand stroking her hair while she pisses. This, too, is intimacy—an intimacy of fluids where nothing is hidden.

Robert wakes up and calls to her, so she goes back into the bedroom and I stand there and look at her piss in the bowl. The dildo is there on the sink, washed last night.

I take the dildo and dip it into her piss in the toilet bowl. Then I ease it into my ass. I can hear them in the bedroom sighing and moaning, and the thing fills my asshole as I kneel on the floor. Who is it that's taking me now? Is it Callie whose urine is inside me, is it Robert who told me that whenever I got penetrated, no matter how it was happening, it was him doing it because my asshole belongs to him? I rest my head on my arm, leaning on the toilet, and forget about my lovers in the other room, gradually becoming only the hole that's being taken, filled and satisfied with the huge prick inside me.

Afterword

Origins of a Sex Writer

When I was growing up, there were all kinds of things I looked forward to becoming or attaining, because I knew that once I had become or acquired these things my life would be all right. A new bicycle, a spot on the Little League team, joining the Boy Scouts, starting high school. My first job, my driver's license, finishing high school, having sex, graduating from college, moving to California. Growing up, getting real jobs, getting a car and a credit card. And so on.

Inevitably, once I had gotten something or attained some status, either it was completely bogus and not at all what it was cracked up to be—like Boy Scouts, or high school—or once the initial thrill faded it became just another thing, like everything else.

Except sex.

The first sex I had, starting about six weeks into my freshman year in college, was good—mostly because of the woman who was my first lover. She was humorous and loving and patient and never made me feel ill at ease. She liked doing just about everything I could think of, and we made up lots of swell ways to make each other come.

And one of the things I remember thinking, at some point during the first few months of sex, was, "This is fucking *great.*" Unlike everything else in life up to that point, sex wasn't a letdown.

It was this experience and the ones that followed, along with the sexual politics that I learned during that time—in the '70s and '80s—that shaped my sexual attitudes. I learned, both in theory and in practice, that sex is fun, that it's about pleasure and not about possession or procreation, that pleasure is liberating, and that there are a hell of a lot of different and interesting ways to get off.

At the same time, I had aspirations of being a writer. And some of my early favorite writers, the Beats, wrote about sex—at least a little. Others, like Henry Miller and Anaïs Nin, did so prodigiously. Since I was picking up all these sex-positive theories that were floating around, and also since I had moved to San Francisco in 1979, it's not surprising that I started writing about sex.

My first sex stories were much more Anaïs than Henry. I considered myself a feminist, and the only people looking at these early stories anyway were lovers (or women whom I wanted to be my lovers), so there was a lot of heavy emoting and vague touching and not much intercourse. One of the first stories I wrote was about two women out picking blueberries for fun, and one of the women had a big crush on the other. So after they went home for the day, the girl who had the crush started masturbating thinking about her berry-picking buddy, and sticking some of the berries in her cunt—for reasons, I think, that had something to do with the way I thought ben-wa balls worked. (Ben-wa balls were a big erotica item in the late '70s and early '80s before everyone found out they more or less don't work.) While she is thus engaged, her buddy knocks on the door, and the first girl just has time to scoop the berries out of her cunt, plop them back into the bowl, and pull down her skirt before answering the door. And then they eat the berries together. Oh, the erotic thrill of the second girl unknowingly sharing in the first girl's pussy juice! That was me trying to write like Anaïs Nin.

To save the world from nicey-nice erotica, along came two groups of pioneering dykes: the Samois Collective, and *On Our Backs* magazine.

The Samois Collective was a group of underground lesbian S/M practitioners in San Francisco in the late 1970s. They published a pioneering anthology of leather dyke–written porn called *Coming to Power*. Pat Califia, who became the best-known member of the group, published a piece on lesbian S/M in *The Advocate* back in 1979. I'm not the only one who did a triple-take when walking by the newsrack that weekend in June, reading a headline that exclaimed humorously, "Lesbians and S/M—They Do THAT??"

Coming to Power was, and still is, one hell of an anthology. It featured not only a number of straightforward S/M pieces, like Califia's "Jessie" (which still turns me on), but stories about piss, scat, bestiality, and other perversions as well. Not all the writing was as good as Califia's, but everything in the book was so fucking *real*. That, as much as the material itself, was what proved such a turn-on for me—the fact that this stuff hadn't been written to formula by some hack but instead had been wrenched out of the hearts and cunts of the people actually doing it.

As for *On Our Backs*, I don't think many people realize what *OOB* meant back in the early '80s. First, the title said it all. At the time there was (and still is) a biweekly lesbian feminist newspaper called *Off Our Backs*, which was a very good newspaper and indispensable reading for the baby dyke and the flannel-shirted, granola-crunching, goddess-worshipping, Birkenstock-wearing lesbian she grew up to be. *Off Our Backs* was also antisex and almost completely humorless, aside from publishing "Dykes to Watch Out For" for the last twenty years. That's why the joke—"Did you hear the one about the feminist who had no sense of humor?" "That's not funny"—*was* funny: because feminists, as typified by the *Off Our Backs* types, were so unrelievedly serious.

So when a bunch of pro-sex San Francisco lezzies came out with, gasp, a lesbian porn magazine and called it *On Our Backs*, it was just too funny. The title alone, and, more importantly, the rollicking approach the magazine took toward practically any kind of dyke sex, was enough to put everybody in stitches—except, I'm pretty sure, the *Off Our Backs* people. They probably still don't think it's funny.

On Our Backs took the kind of sex-positive attitudes that had been rampant in the gay male community and popularized them in the lesbian community. Now, anybody who was around at the time—not including me, since I was still hanging out with hippie contact-improvisers and being just as clueless about what was going on all around me as I was in high school—knows there had always been a certain amount of behind-doors fraternizing between dykes and leather daddies in San Francisco. The public wall between the gay male and the lesbian community that supposedly didn't really come down until the AIDS crisis was never completely solid in the first place. But until *OOB* started talking about it, no one had ever told the dykes through-out the rest of the country that penetration was okay.

It was news to me, too. I had thought that, to be accepted by women, I had to be a Sensitive New Age Guy and write like Anaïs Nin. But here were actual women writing really great, dirty stuff and calling things by their own names: cunt, cock, fuck, shit, bitch. None of this blueberries-under-the-moonlight stuff. I thought to myself that if one day I could write brave, funny, dirty stuff like these women, I would be okay.

Writing with that kind of fearlessness means I had to reach a sort of escape velocity from the Sensitive New Age counterculture in which I came of age. My only problem is that I waited until my late twenties to do it.

I recently had a conversation with a writer friend who told me of her wild youth. Emancipated from parental control at an early age, she vagabonded, did sex work, did drugs, was an artist full time when she was barely out of her teens. Since I had had a sheltered, middle-class suburban upbringing and took the safe choices throughout my adolescence, I listened to her story with a combination of envy and awe. I didn't work up my courage to do drugs, have perverse sex, and otherwise do most of the stuff that I had been afraid to do, until I was 28 or 29. While it's true that waiting to do some of that stuff until I was older and wiser kept me out of trouble I would not have been prepared to deal with, I do regret being afraid all those years. Not only did fear keep me from doing the things I wanted to; it also kept me even from fantasizing about, and writing about, these things. All the while, I was living in San Francisco, where it was all happening right under my nose. I had ten years of vanilla sex before finally growing up enough to get into more complicated stuff.

I can't today say I'm a really serious SM practitioner or that I hold any particular fetish. But my experience and my interests are finally broader than they were when I was in my twenties and hardly daring to let even my fantasies go beyond soft core.

Turning Fantasy into Reality, or Not

Everyone has wild fantasies, whether or not they put a name to these fantasies or do anything about them in real life. Look at the *Ally McBeal* television show, to cite something wildly popular among young straight people. In every episode there are these weird, dreamlike moments when the characters suddenly act out their wild fantasies—they have sex in the middle of the courtroom, or they slug their boss, or something even weirder happens that looks like outtakes of that Jim Carrey movie *The Mask*. Millions and millions of straight frat boys and sorority girls (or ex-) watch this show religiously. And they think the fantasy moments are funny because deep down, even though they may never show it, they feel they are like those characters. They too are dirty, perverted sluts whose desire knows no bounds.

Perhaps if I lived in Pittsburgh or St. Louis or Keokuk, I wouldn't have this conviction that everyone is just as perverted as everybody else. Perhaps if I lived in one of those places, I never would have had a lover who asked me to pull her hair, thus introducing me to SM. I probably never would have gone to a sex party, I never would have published my own sex magazine, and my writing never would have gone beyond the Anaïs Nin stage. I would have been certain that I was the only person who had such urges. Out in San Francisco, not only have I found a place to do these things, I'm just one of thousands.

Being isolated is deadly. To prevent it, I moved the hell away from the Midwest and, like many before me, came to San Francisco. If you are isolated where you are, then you need to either move to someplace cooler or pervert your town from within. I recommend the latter (rents are hell out here).

To pervert your town, the first thing you have to do is find a way to live out your fantasy. Let's take an easy one—sucking cock. In any American city, a guy can go down to a peep show and within fifteen minutes can be sucking a dick. It doesn't matter what you look like or how old you are, and no one asks you for your rainbow sticker or your homosexual identity papers. You will get a chance to live out your fantasy. Of course, you'll be doing it in an environment where you have to kneel on a nasty concrete floor, doing it with a total stranger whose face you won't even see clearly and whose dick you will definitely not see clearly. That environment does not lend itself to guilt-free experimentation, so maybe you'd like to control the environment more. Fine, post an ad. It takes longer and you have to deal with a bunch of social jockeying that the peep show experience skips completely. But you can eventually suck cock in your own bed, if you want.

Blowjobs are easy; other stuff is harder. Let's say you want to do SM. Well, there are clubs for that. In many cities there are classes you can take. And again, you can post an ad. Or let's say you want somebody to piss on you. You can post an ad for that too, or go to a nasty gay bar on a certain night with a golden handkerchief in your right rear pocket. For all this stuff, the only thing that prevents you from trying it is fear. Of course, you also want to avoid getting sexually transmitted diseases; learn how.

Now we get to the hard stuff. There is a lot of stuff that, if you tried to do it, you would be arrested for it. And for most of the stuff, you *should* be arrested. Even if you figure out, at some expense, how to do some of the things and reduce the risk to yourself, it's still not right. Going on a sex tour to Asia so you can fuck a 12-year-old is morally reprehensible. Raping somebody is morally reprehensible. Just because you can conceive of this stuff doesn't mean it's all right to do.

That brings us back to fantasy. I can't have sex with children, and wouldn't want to. But I *can* have sex with a lover and we can, for a few moments, pretend that's what it is. I was once playing around with a woman who was about to go down on me. She got a gleam in her eye and whimpered, "Oh, Daddy…. Your cock is so big…I don't want to." And we launched into this intense, two-minute scene where I was yelling, "Suck Daddy's cock, you little bitch!" and she was crying, "No, Daddy, no, it hurts, it's too big." After the scene, we lay back and she chuckled, "Whew, I'm glad I wasn't really molested, or I couldn't go there."

I don't know why it was so hot to do that. Before that, I didn't have any particular fantasy about making my "daughter" (which I don't have) suck my cock. But when I was in the moment, I fell right into the role, playing it to the hilt. And it was really hot. By which I mean it was fun and exciting and helped me to come.

Pornography is a way for writers and readers to have those kinds of fantasies in a longer, more detailed way. If you're lucky, maybe porn can clue you into something that you never thought of before but, now that you know about it, turns you on tremendously. I had never heard of piss in an erotic context before I picked up Nancy Friday's *My Secret Garden* at age 18. But ever since then, it's been a turn-on for me. Maybe there are a couple of those for you in this book; if so, I'm happy to have played a part in opening up your imagination.

There are still puritans around who think it's wrong even to think about such things. They see a spiritual connection between imagining something and actually doing it. Jesus himself said that if you even think of murdering your brother, that makes you a murderer. Then along came Saint Paul, who set up a connection between pleasure and sin. Two thousand years later, some of us are still working that one out.

Most people find it kind of strange that I, who write all this dirty stuff, am a Christian. I'm not going to go into all the ways I work out this apparent conflict, but suffice to say that I do not think there's something inherently wrong with my being bisexual, having nasty sex with many different people, or even writing stories about incest, rape, and murder. I *do* think there's something wrong with hurting and exploiting people. So the idea is to work out our fantasies in ways that are responsible.

I don't want to make it sound like I write this stuff for therapy. To tell you the truth, I write it for the same reasons I tried to imitate Anaïs Nin: because it turns me on to write about sex, and to express in a different medium the same feelings and desires I express in bed. Writing it down solidifies my desires, commemorates it, makes it live outside me. It also tells the people who are close to me—really close to me—who I am and what's inside me.

But (I can hear my mother saying), you don't have to make it *public*. Why in the world do you have to make a story out of it and publish it? It's bad enough that you even wrote it down in the first place. Why do you have to flaunt it (she would say) to the world?

Well, it's pornography. The whole idea is to turn people on and get them jacking off and coming—which is kind of remarkable, if you think about it. For almost any other kind of writing, the reader's response is indirect; if they ever get around to it, they might send you a letter or an e-mail saying they liked your work, or they might recommend it to friends. (And if you like it, please do.) But not that many writers can say, *I'll bet people are going to get so turned on by this story they'll have to do themselves.* That's kind of fun.

The Stories

A few liner notes about some of the stories in this book.... Most of the stories were published in the first edition of *Too Beautiful* in 1999; for the second edition, we've added three stories I recently completed, and scattered them among the original ones.

I wrote the first draft of *Penetration* in Japan, where I lived for two years in the late '80s. That was the first porn I wrote after giving up the Anaïs Nin approach. Homesick for the cultural and racial diversity of San Francisco, out of desperation I started writing porn about what I missed the most—even though the story is set in Japan. It was my way of bringing into my life there the things I couldn't have. I also drafted *Lizza* while living there. It doesn't have anything to do with San Francisco or what I was missing. I was just really lonely and horny, and wrote most of it longhand in one sitting on a cool, sunny spring morning.

Exploitation, the other story set in Japan, is one of several about various aspects of the sex industry. I like writing about strippers and hookers, or would-be hookers (as in *Amateur*), not only because their exploits are natural subjects for pornography, but also because I'm fascinated with the way they deal with others' desires while trying to hang onto their own integrity and sexuality. Besides, in the San Francisco community of queers and artists, sex workers are ubiquitous. I've known a bunch of them as friends. My late friend Stephanie Kulick gave me all the dope for *Booth Girl* about working in the booth at the Lusty Lady Theater, where many a dyke has taken her clothes off for a bunch of men. Even *Caller Number One* is about a sex industry cul de sac, the phone sex party line. This '80s innovation—now, with Web chat and all, increasingly passé—gives everybody a chance to be a porn star, at least audially.

Daddy's Play Party was written in response to a call for submissions from a couple of dyke friends who were editing an anthology of stories about butchness. Since I can't do, or think about, butchness for long without laughing, I got an idea for a story that would define and comment on butchness while at the same time skewering it. This story disappointed the anthology editors, who didn't accept it because I'm not a girl, as well as another dyke friend, who wants me to rewrite the story so that Leonard really does walk into a hot sex party full of Tom of Finland types. There are almost no butch men in my queer stories, except for the narrator in *Too Beautiful*, and in that story the guy who's bottoming has more self-confidence than the narrator and eventually wears him down until he drops the role. The women in stories where there's a toppy guy, like *Trina*, tend to laugh at him behind his back.

I'm actually talking about two things here—the "leatherman" stereotype of butch homosexuality, and the male of whatever sexual preference who acts out a sadistic role. Until the sexual revolution, these were one and the same: a role that, for all the opportunities it afforded the butch male to get what he supposedly wanted, was actually constricting. It equated to macho: You dominated your sex partner, you were as rough as you wanted to be, and if you were homosexual you never, ever took your partner's dick in the mouth or up the ass. In fact, I've read accounts of gay male tops from the old school who refused even to admit they were gay. They were Real Men, dammit. If you go down this road, whether you're gay or not, it's pretty limiting. You can never admit to weakness or that you might be wrong; you can never have the pleasure of a cock in your mouth or of a woman straddling you from above.

When the sexual revolution came along, people learned that their true selves had less to do with projecting and following a role and more to do with their integrity, the choices they made, and how brave they were. Now you can switch from being a top to a bottom; you don't even have to label yourself a switch, you can just do what you feel like. If somebody comes along and wants to top you, and you're into it, bring it on. If you see somebody you want to shove around and they're into it, go for it.

Only in *Pretend* do we have a toppy guy who keeps the mask on for the whole trick. That story is a very personal one for me; I wrote it to commemorate a love affair that had ended. In that affair, and in most relationships where I'm the top, I tend to be less confident than my partner. No doubt that lack of confidence had a lot to do with that relationship ending, since there's nothing worse than an uncertain top. By contrast, the narrator of the story is supremely confident, always does the right thing, never drops out of role. In fantasy the narrator, the "I," does what I couldn't do in reality.

So even though I'm naturally bossy, my male characters tend to be more like the guys in *Sunset* or *Quizzle* or *Kill Me with Your Kiss:* men who seize pleasure when it's offered, without much thought to how it makes them look. The narrator in *Quizzle* gets fucked by a drag queen; it doesn't mean he's more femme than she is, it means he wanted to get fucked at that moment. This ethos is most fully explained in *Penetration*, a story in which gender and the prerogative of the prick are secondary to sensation and desire. In the original version, the characters exchanged genitals as easily as putting on or taking off hats.

While I removed this fantasy aspect in later drafts, this fluidity of gender is my sexual ideal. *Lizza* ends with a similarly wishful gender reversal. The freedom expressed in *Lizza* is the freedom to love outside of boundaries, unconstrained by social taboo or gender—a vision of freedom to which all my characters, in one way or another, aspire.

Mark Pritchard
San Francisco
September 2001

About the Author

Mark Pritchard is the author of *How I Adore You* (Cleis Press, 2001). He was coeditor and publisher of the early '90s sex-and-politics zine *Frighten the Horses*. He is a former San Francisco Sex Information volunteer and a former member of Queer Nation and the Street Patrol. He lives in Bernal Heights, San Francisco, where he is working on a novel about the Rat Pack. He can be contacted at toobeaut@yahoo.com or www.toobeautiful.org.